Mostly Murder

Till Death

a mystery anthology

Patrice Fitzgerald, *Editor*

Elemental Press
an imprint of
eFitzgerald Publishing, LLC

MOSTLY MURDER: Till Death

MOSTLY MURDER: Till Death is part of the ***Mostly Murder*** series produced by Patrice Fitzgerald.

Produced and edited by Patrice Fitzgerald (eFitzgeraldPublishing@gmail.com)

Cover art by Adam Hall (www.aroundthepages.com)

Formatted by Therin Knite (www.knitedaydesign.com)

The stories herein...

Nice Guys Finish Last (*JC Andrijeski*)
Bobby came back from Asia with the perfect wife. Sexy, well-dressed… a dreamboat in every way. But he realizes something's not right with his perfect-seeming marriage when things start to disappear. No matter how much he loves her, Bobby is determined to find out the truth about who and what his wife really is.

Forsaking All Others (*Chris Patchell*)
A home invasion turns deadly for Mally and Jack Gardiner, whose rocky marriage is built upon a twisted bed of lies.

Starter (*Samuel Peralta*)
A couple visits the perfect starter home. But beneath the veneer of new paint and windows, ghosts of the past await.

Pride (*Eric J. Gates*)
Marriage is a commitment, a strong bond if both partners work at it. Even so, sometimes external forces can wreck the best unions. FBI Senior Special Agent Thompson did not know his obsession with solving a case would bring deadly consequences in the last few weeks of his career.

Two Faces (*H.B. Moore*)
When newlywed Vivian Wood discovers that her husband disappears every few days without explanation, she's faced with the reality that Simon is not the man she thought she married.

Loving Frankie (*Patrice Fitzgerald*)
He could be gentle and he could be rough, her Frankie, but Faith would love him till the bitter end.

In Sickness and in Murder (*B.A. Spangler*)
The first victim was found clutching buttons in his hand. But no one had to know where the buttons came from—and no one cared about the nameless, homeless man. And then a second murder was revealed. How far will a man go to protect the woman he loves?

Nun of Your Business (*Jerilyn Dufresne*)
Sister Mary Jordan has a problem. She has a husband. Not only that, he's in the Mafia. Neither of those things is well-accepted in a convent. How she escapes the situation involves lies, murder, and just a little mayhem.

The Long Haul (*Josh Hayes*)
No one ever said marriage would be easy.

A year after her affair, Mary and her husband have finally put the past behind them and are working on their future. Until she receives a letter that threatens to unravel everything they have worked so hard to fix, and brings her indiscretions full circle.

All Secrets Lead to Lies (*Anne Kelleher*)
One love triangle. Two dead husbands. Three detectives.

A prison full of drugs. And so many secrets.

As Good as a Rest (*Lawrence Block*)
Lawrence Block has been writing and publishing novels and short stories for sixty years. "As Good as a Rest" is one of which he's especially fond.

CONTENTS

Introduction

by Patrice Fitzgerald

Who doesn't love a good mystery?

Elements of suspense and mystery are present in most stories, even those that fall into completely different genres. The need to know—to race through a book to the conclusion when all is finally revealed and every intricate plot point is unsnarled—is part of the joy of reading.

Collected here are eleven mysteries; ten of them brand-new. We are proud to include a classic short by Lawrence Block, New York Times bestselling author and Mystery Writers of America Grand Master, who has spent decades crafting brilliant novels and clever short stories. Also featured in this anthology are two USA Today bestselling authors, another who received an Indie Reader Discovery Award and won the Kindle Scout contest for a publishing contract, and yet another whose books have been picked up by Kindle Press.

Open this collection and plunge into the stories… some grim and bloody, some light and even a little bit funny. You won't know what you're getting until you reach the end of each cunning mystery.

Enjoy!

Patrice Fitzgerald, Editor
Mostly Murder mystery anthologies

Nice Guys Finish Last

by JC Andrijeski

I discovered my wife's true nature in our third year of marriage.

It didn't come upon me all at once.

It happened over a matter of months, with me slowly putting the pieces together, reading the clues she left me, however faint or obscure or harmless-seeming on the surface. Eventually, I began to put together the language she was speaking to me as well, in her own quiet way. Where I am now, I've had a lot of time to think about these things.

Eventually, I grew to understand that despite her sweet, loving and delicate exterior, by the end, my wife wanted nothing more than to annihilate my very soul.

The motives troubled me at first.

They troubled me a lot.

See, I really loved my wife.

My brother and a few of my friends joked that I loved her too much.

We met over in the Philippines when I was stationed there for work, but she was actually Thai, from a village in the northeastern part of the country, and had moved to Bangkok to attend college. She just happened to be in the Philippines visiting friends while I was there. Her being in Manila at all—much less while *I* would be there and following a trail that meant *I* would cross paths with her in such a crowded and chaotic city—seemed like nothing less than sheer magic to me. I thought about that for a long time after we met, the number of things that would have to fall into place for us to be in one another's lives.

She was twenty, educated but had no money of her own, and her English needed some work.

She confessed to me later that another man she met while in school in Bangkok, a businessman who came to Manila to set up a call center for an insurance company, paid for her air ticket. She told me that when she met me, she fell so much in love that she broke things off with him and offered to pay him back the full amount.

I believed her. Men can be stupid that way.

Either way, *we* were in love. I'm sure of it.

I don't think she could have deceived me to that extent.

On the surface, she was the dreamboat girlfriend.

Six months later, she was the perfect wife.

Hot as hell—especially when I first met her. Long, silky, black hair. Full lips. Light brown eyes—so light, they were really stunning, as in double-take kind of stunning, as in can't-look-away kind of stunning.

She was on the small side in terms of her chest area, but I

didn't mind. She had long thin legs and a dazzling smile and she dressed so differently from the women I'd dated back in the States. No business suits or ponytails or clunky shoes or baggy T-shirts for my Kanya; she wore short skirts, low-cut blouses, high heels, full makeup, red lipstick.

I never once saw her hair anything but styled or down, no matter what she was doing. She ate like a bird and didn't drink or smoke. Unlike most of her American friends, she kept her figure long after we got married.

I didn't even mention it to her. She did that all on her own.

Not long after we got married, my job moved us to Albuquerque, New Mexico.

It was a relief to be back in the States. Kanya was excited to be a real American, too.

The lab where I worked promised me it was a real position this time, that I wouldn't be moved again in a few months, either to another part of the country or another part of the world. I began to feel like I would be able to really build something in Albuquerque with my new wife, which was a huge relief after that whole incident in San Francisco.

It felt like a fresh start. The freedom to begin again.

Kanya was a big part of that.

Like most people in those years, I was still suffering the effects of the tech crash. Everyone was hurting back then, especially when the rest of the market crashed a few years later, with the housing bubble popping, jobs evaporating, full-blown recession and everything else. Even those of us who managed to hold onto our jobs suffered, and I was no exception, despite my unique skills. My employers had me over a barrel and they knew it, so I pretty much had to go wherever they told me.

I guess I was a little bitter until I met Kanya.

It struck me as prophetic, almost, that they finally let me return home to do my job, and only a few months after the ink on our marriage certificate dried.

I took it as a sign that things were finally turning around for me.

For us. For the first time in my life, I was part of an "us."

I told Kanya I didn't really want children right away, so she decided she wanted to go to school—first to learn English better, then to obtain a business degree. Or possibly something in the arts or graphic design. I supported her in that, and with a few phone calls and some work over her application and entrance essay, we got her enrolled at the University of New Mexico (or UNM) only a day or two before I started work at the new site.

I was forty-six. She was twenty-one.

I thought I was lucky.

All my friends thought I was lucky, too.

They'd all married American women.

Career-obsessed ballbuster types, my friends' wives had no trouble running down their husbands in public, arguing with anyone and anything who didn't march in time with their self-involved bullshit. Their wives whined if they made less money than their husbands, nagged and lorded it over the poor bastards if they made more. They kept their men on such tight leashes half my friends had to text or call every five minutes just to keep from getting screamed at.

Truthfully, the whole lot of them scared the hell out of

me. I avoided being alone with any of them for more than a few minutes if I could help it.

After most of those work and neighborhood dinners, I came home and counted my blessings, feeling more gratitude than I knew how to express for finding my beautiful Kanya.

The day after one of those dinners, I bought her a new necklace with a diamond-studded bird on it. She squealed and clapped her hands.

After the Christmas work party, I took her shopping for the day and let her buy anything she wanted at the outdoor mall on Uptown Blvd.

She bought clothes of course… but she also bought things for the house. And for me.

That's the kind of wife she was.

Really, in those first two years in Albuquerque, I can't begin to express how lucky I felt.

I came home to food on the table, a spotless house, her smile hovering over her slim body in a form-fitting emerald green dress… or maybe a pale blue one… or a white one or a red one or a indigo one. Kanya never minded listening to me talk about my day. She gave me foot rubs and back rubs while I told her about all of the crazy things going on with my job. She *liked* taking care of things for me. If I had any gripe, it's that her cooking was way too Asian, with too much rice and spice and whatever else, but that wasn't a big deal since we ate out a lot anyway.

She handled all the household and yard issues without bugging me for money all the time, although I did let her hire a gardener and a weekly housecleaner when she went back to school.

All in all, for those first few years of marriage, I was happy.

Ecstatically happy, most of the time.

Kanya was happy, too.

At least, she seemed that way to me.

Then, somewhere around the end of year two, I started noticing things.

* * *

First off, things in the house started to disappear.

They weren't all valuable things. Most weren't even personally valuable things—meaning, things that may not have cost much but that I liked for one reason or another.

Hell, a lot of them weren't even particularly *useful* things.

They were just… things.

Most of it was just totally random stuff, stuff I knew had been there, and now, with no ready explanation, simply wasn't. What bothered me more though, is that whenever I asked Kanya about it, she would just smile at me nervously and go back to whatever she'd been doing, whether it was cleaning the kitchen or cooking or putting away the shopping.

Eventually, I had to confront her for real.

Something about not knowing really nagged at me.

Looking back on it now, I suspect some more animal, survival-oriented part of me was picking up on instinctual cues, sensing that I was in danger. At the time, however, getting the truth out of my wife felt more important than I could explain to myself. It became a quiet obsession of mine, and one night, I'd finally had enough.

I remember that evening well.

I'd just gotten off work. I'm the type who needs a lot of peace and quiet when I first walk in the door, even on a normal day, but that day, I needed it more than usual. I'd been stuck in meetings for most of the afternoon, with a particularly unreasonable and petty supervisor who, like most of my managers over the years, liked nothing better than to waste the time of his more highly educated and technically skilled employees.

So yeah, I guess I was already in a mood.

I really just wanted a beer and some silence, followed by something good to eat and then a peaceful evening with my wife for the rest of the night. I already knew what I wanted to tell her about that same boss over dinner. Maybe we'd order in, since I definitely wasn't in the mood for spicy rice crap right then, no matter how much meat she put in it. I needed comfort food, like Mexican or steak or even pizza. I already found myself thinking there would be a movie after dinner, and a foot rub.

Maybe more than that, if I got my second wind.

It was raining that night.

Not normal rain, like you see on the West or East Coasts, but desert rain, summer monsoon, like you get every year in that part of New Mexico. New Mexico rains never really made anything cooler for long, but they made the air smell really good—fresh and clean and strangely nostalgic, even though I'm not from that part of the world. It's like you're smelling the old world as the sun got beaten out of the mesa and dust and adobe walls by the pelting drops, catching the lingering scent of a simpler, more black-and-white life.

Maybe a life more like what Kanya had, in that village in Thailand.

You got lightning with those storms, too.

Loud. You can't hear much through that, for how loud it can be at times.

People cranked up their televisions. Or, like me, they took their beers outdoors to covered patios that had high ceiling fans running nonstop during the day, at least while people were outside. They'd sit out there in the dark and watch the lightning play havoc over the Sandia Mountains and smell the past through the machine gun pattering of rain.

Hell, you could probably set off a gun, and no one would hear it. Not while one of those storms raged directly overhead.

The next day, it would be just as hot as it had been the day before. The ground would be baked dry before you even got out of bed, and there'd be so little moisture in the air you could physically feel each inhaled breath sucking water out of your lungs and skin.

But that night, the rain was still coming down.

I sat on our porch in the dark, drinking a beer and smoking a cigarette, which I try not to do around Kanya if I can help it. Even as tired as I was, I tried to be a good husband, since I knew Kanya hated when I smoked inside the house.

That's when I noticed the next thing missing.

At that point in our mysterious, silent battle of wills, I'd counted only four things that I knew with absolute certainty had disappeared.

The bird necklace I'd given her in our first year of marriage was the first thing I discovered gone. I asked Kanya why I never saw her wearing it anymore, when it used to be her favorite piece of jewelry, and when she was at school, I looked for it everywhere and couldn't find it.

Next I noticed the blender gone from our kitchen counter, after I asked Kanya to make me a margarita one night.

Then one of the tablets we had between us disappeared.

Then both remote controls to our television vanished, too.

I'd broken down and replaced all but the necklace by then, but the mystery of so many disappearances over only five or six weeks had already started to nag at me. I couldn't figure out why and how these things disappeared when only Kanya and I lived in the house.

At first, when the bird necklace disappeared, I'd wondered if it was our cleaning lady, Manuela, so I fired her and instructed Kanya hire someone else. For a few weeks after that, I only let the new one, Rosaria, come on the weekends when I was there. I also had her turn out her pockets before she left. She never had anything on her, not so much as a piece of lint.

Then the television remotes disappeared.

Then the tablet.

Then the blender… which I highly doubt Rosaria could have gotten out of our house without Kanya or I noticing.

I started to wonder if Kanya was giving things away, to the neighbors maybe, or to new friends she'd made in her English classes. She was a sweet, generous person, and too trusting at times. Was someone coming to the house while I was at work and convincing Kanya to hand over our personal things?

The possibility struck me as odd, given the things that were missing.

That night, when I noticed yet another thing missing—this time, something definitely too big to have been randomly "misplaced"—I reached the end of my straws and my willingness to ignore what was going on.

When I first bought the house, I'd bought Kanya one of those tiered, clay pots filled with different kinds of succulent cactuses. We'd been wandering around Old Town Albuquerque and they had a small plant and pottery shop, and she'd been fascinated by it, since the plants were so different here from any she'd ever seen before. So I bought it for her. I had it delivered and everything, since the thing was heavy—and big. It had been sitting in the same spot just below the adobe pony wall around our porch since it first came to our home.

Now, it wasn't. Sitting there, I mean.

Now, like the other four things, the tiered, red-clay pot filled with succulents that Kanya had so carefully watered over the past few years… was just gone.

I couldn't believe it at first, truthfully. I looked away and back a few times, trying to convince myself it hadn't really disappeared. I knew I was looking in the right place. The ring of dirt and water deposits from watering still stained that part of the blue and white flowered tile. But the thing that created that ring, the giant red clay pot with the little holes all over it for different kinds of cactus, wasn't anywhere in sight.

Full of dirt and dripping with plants, that pot had to weigh eighty pounds, if not more. I was pretty sure Kanya couldn't even lift it by herself.

Heck, I wasn't sure *I* could.

Anyway, I don't know precisely why *that* was the thing I latched onto, but it was.

Once it finally sank in that the pot was really gone, I got off the swing and walked around the porch, looking for the damned thing while thunder and lightning continued crashing overhead. Once I'd finished my cigarette, I left the porch, venturing out to look in our actual yard, thinking maybe Kanya was stronger than I thought.

I walked all over that desert-landscaped yard and all around our swimming pool, even though the rain continued to pelt down on our part of the mesa and I still wore my shirt and tie and slacks from work. I even wore my favorite pair of loafers still, which weren't exactly good in the wet sand and fast-forming puddles on the walk.

I walked around the pool a second time, then around the work shed in the backyard, the one hidden behind an adobe wall near the tall desert palms. I considered using my keys to look inside the shed itself, but I didn't. The shed was mine, and Kanya knew that. I usually had that key on me, so Kanya would've had to move the pot there in the middle of the night, and why would she do that? The very idea was insane. The shed was mine.

She *knew* that.

In the end, I left it alone, focusing on the assorted scattering of cactus and succulents that filled our yard, thinking she must have just moved it somewhere else for some reason.

I think I spent some thirty minutes looking, but I never found it. Eventually I decided I just needed to ask her, so I walked back to the porch and then into the house, leaving my shoes outside the sliding glass door.

Once I'd shut the door behind me, I called out to Kanya.

"Honey?" I put the beer bottle on the coffee table when I didn't see her, wandering through the lower level of our house. It was a big place, with an open floor plan made up of a kitchen, dining room and living room with vaulted, wood-beamed ceilings.

"Kanya!" I stood at the foot of the stairs, one hand on the polished pinewood banister. "Kanya! Where are you? I need you to come down here, sweetie!"

I walked up the stairs, now verging on annoyed, but honestly not sure if it was at her or myself. Usually she answered me right away.

Was she in the garage? Had she run to the store while I was outside rooting around our backyard like a fool, looking for a missing cactus pot?

"Kanya!" I bellowed it that time, from most of the way up the stairs. "Are you home?"

Still nothing.

After checking our bedroom and the bathroom, I wandered into my office. She was there, on the floor, staring down, like she was in a trance or something.

For a moment I just stood there, in the doorway.

Maybe I was in shock.

"Kanya!" Biting my lip, I deliberately calmed my voice when I saw her jump. "What are you doing? Haven't you heard me calling you for the past however-many minutes?"

She turned her head, staring up at me with white-rimmed, terrified eyes like I'd hit her with a cattle prod. Breathing hard, her eyes still as dilated as an alley cat's, she lurched to her feet, and the leather-bound notebook that I now realized she'd been holding in her lap fell to the floor.

I frowned down at it.

It was one of mine from work.

Looking back up at her, I fought to comprehend the expression on her face. She stared at me from a half-crouched position, as if she might bolt from the room at any second.

At a loss, I found my voice coming out in a kind of blank puzzlement.

"What are you doing in here? Why did you take that?"

"No-Nothing… nothing…" She stammered the word, her accent coming out thicker than usual. "I wasn't doing anything, Bobby, I swear… nothing. I'm sorry… I know I'm not supposed to be in here. I was looking for a book… a book I saw…"

I stared between her and the notebook on the carpet for about a minute. I was waiting for her to go on, to give me more detail, more of a real explanation, but it never came. She knew what I wanted, but for once, she wasn't my usual, sweet-natured and agreeable Kanya.

She just stared at me, like I was a malevolent spirit. Like one of those beings with the bulging eyes and the sticking out tongues from one of her Buddhist temples.

I considered addressing the issue of her going through my things, then decided that wasn't the relevant issue right then. After a few more seconds of us both just standing there, I decided to go back to the thing that brought me upstairs in the first place.

"Where's that pot of cactus I got you?" I said. "You know… the big one. From Old Town. What did you do with it?"

Whatever I expected her reaction to be to that question, it wasn't what I got.

Her face went white.

I mean, you read about people's faces going white in books and so on, but I'd never actually seen it happen in real life before. Her normally rosy cheeks went a bloodless, corpse-like white. I saw her eyes shift to the pad of paper on the floor again, then back up to mine.

Finally, I lost my cool.

"What is wrong with you?" I motioned towards her with a sweeping hand. She flinched. "What happened to the cactus pot? Why are you looking at me like that? You're acting like I'm asking you something crazy, Kanya!"

Her face still white as chalk, she plastered on a falsely cheerful smile.

It looked grotesque, like some kind of paper mâché mask.

"Are you hungry?" Her voice still carried too much accent, which I knew meant she was afraid or upset or in the grip of some other intense emotion. "I make lasagna for you," she said, still smiling that terrifying smile. "Just like recipe from your mom. Your favorite. Should be ready now, I just get out of oven—"

"No, Kanya! Not until you tell me what—"

"I get it now," she said, her voice still overly sweet, despite that white face and the big eyes. "I get you whatever you want, darling Bobby. Right now. Okay? *Mai pen rai.*"

I knew the last meant something along the lines of "It's all okay," or "It's no trouble" in Thai. She said that a lot, it was kind of a running joke between us at times.

Before I could figure out what I could possibly say to this, she scurried past me like some kind of rodent with its tail on fire and ran down the stairs.

I honestly don't know why I let her go. I don't know why I didn't chase after her and make her say something that made sense to me… but I didn't.

I just stood there, staring down at the notebook that

lay open on the beige carpet, hearing her footsteps as she clattered down the stairs in her high heels. I listened to the distant sounds of her bustling around the kitchen not long after that, the open and shut of the door of our self-cleaning oven, the clink of glasses and silverware as she set the table. I don't remember what I was thinking at the time, but at some point, I must have come to some kind of conclusion. Something that made me decide to let her off the hook, for now at least.

Not long after that, she called me down for supper.

I didn't bring it up with her again, not until the next thing happened.

I don't know why I didn't.

Maybe my friends are right. Maybe my mother is right.

Maybe I love my wife too much.

* * *

The next thing to disappear was the keys to her car.

We tore that house apart, looking for them. They were the custom kind, the kind that cost a few hundred dollars to replace, and both sets were missing, the spare and her day-to-day ones, which made the whole thing that much weirder. After five days of looking, doing everything but ripping up the carpet and digging in the yard, I gave up and ordered her a new set of keys, which set me back a pretty penny to replace both sets.

I didn't know what to say to her about that, either.

She still wouldn't offer much, certainly nothing approximating an explanation or an apology. She didn't even help me look really; it was more like she followed me around as

I looked, wringing her hands until they were red and white in turn. I honestly don't know if she was worried I wouldn't find them or worried that I would.

I tried to find some pattern in the missing things, but I was at a loss.

I considered locking things up that might disappear, maybe in the shed in the backyard that had only one set of keys, but since I had no idea why the things were disappearing in the first place or what might be next, I couldn't see much point to that, either.

I pleaded with Kanya to tell me what was wrong, why she was doing this.

She never told me though. She never told me anything.

After an hour of my pleading with her, she burst into tears.

The next day, I woke up with my first finger missing.

* * *

It's going to sound insane, but I didn't notice right away.

I did my usual rollover, hit the alarm with my good hand, and my body felt heavy and groggier than usual, so I didn't think to look at myself that closely. Looking back on it now, I'd probably been drugged, given how odd and out of it I felt.

It was only when I planted my hands on either side of me on our double-padded mattress to shove myself up and out of bed, that I let out a startled cry.

When I looked down at my bandaged hand, it was like the potted cactus at first.

I couldn't make myself believe it.

I just sat there, holding my breath as I stared at my hand, trying to make it real.

Then it's like an electric jolt of current went through me.

Stumbling and running for the bathroom, I let out a cry when I stubbed my toe on the low riser in the doorway, skidding and tripping on the tile before I caught my balance on the granite counter that rimmed our his-and-her sinks. I stared at the bandage on my right hand, panting, and again noticed the odd shape it was.

I think by then, I knew.

I'm not a medical doctor or anything, but I'm not an idiot either. So I knew, but I didn't want to know… I couldn't make myself put the pieces together to form a coherent picture, at least not without first-hand proof.

Some morbid part of me *needed* to know.

After a few more seconds of staring, I gritted my teeth and tried to unwrap the bandage, one-handed.

When I couldn't do that, I rummaged through the drawers, looking for something to cut the thing off so I could look at my hand. I don't think I'd spoken a word since that initial cry when I stubbed my toe on the tile. I might have been muttering under my breath, and I'm pretty sure I was panting so hard it was full-blown hyperventilating by then, but I didn't speak.

I also didn't hear a peep from the other room, where I presumed my wife had to be lying in bed, listening to this, or else sleeping peacefully.

I couldn't comprehend that she could be asleep, though.

Not now. Not given what had happened to me.

How could she sleep?

Using the utility scissors in the drawer, I cut the bandage

off carefully. I didn't nick anything that I felt, but by the time I'd finished, red had begun to seep through part of the cloth, and by the time I got it off totally, it hurt like hell, almost like my messing with it had woken up the nerve endings for the first time since I'd gotten up.

I stared at the bloody stump of my pinky finger.

Someone had stitched it up unevenly with thick black thread, almost like wire. It looked like something out of a horror movie. I stared at my hand in front of our bathroom mirror, gasping like I'd been running, sweat soaking through the back of my white T-shirt…

…and then I passed out cold.

* * *

I thought long and hard about whether I should go to the hospital that morning.

When I woke up on the tile floor of our master bathroom, Kanya was crouched over me, shaking my arm, panic in her light brown eyes, panic in her small, delicate fingers. Kanya pleaded with me to go see a doctor, over and over in her broken English. She sobbed when I wouldn't answer her, when I only sat on the floor of our bathroom, grimacing in pain as I stared in the direction of my office that was just visible through the open door of our bedroom.

I remember fighting to think through the pain in my hand and my confusion over how genuinely worried she seemed to be about me. That worry seemed so real, so sincere. The depth of my wife's emotion blanked out my brain. I was so afraid of her and confused I didn't know what to do or even what to say to her.

In the end, I didn't go to the hospital.

I didn't even call my doctor at my worksite.

I called in sick instead, and told them I'd had an accident.

Kanya waited on me hand and foot, bringing me anything I asked and a lot of things I didn't ask for. She rubbed my feet and put pillows under my head and collected all the television remotes for me and ordered in food and tiptoed around the house while I slept on the leather recliner in front of our giant, wall-mounted flat-screen television.

Two days later, when I went back to work, everyone expressed the usual concern and curiosity around what had happened. I made up a story about a lawn-mower, even though we didn't have a lawn. I told them the motor of the thing had been so damned quiet that I hadn't realized it hadn't completely turned off. I'd reached in to check the blade for an obstruction and the damned thing cut my finger clean off before I could get it out.

Kanya never told me anything about what really happened to me.

She cried uncontrollably whenever I asked her about it, so eventually I left her alone. I know there are those who would judge me for that, for not immediately calling the police or trying to get her some kind of help, but I honestly felt paralyzed by it all. I couldn't comprehend that this woman I loved so much could do these things.

Some part of me desperately clung to the thought that there had to be some other explanation.

My brain didn't shut off entirely, of course.

I'd always prided myself on giving Kanya her privacy, but the second she took my car to the store to buy more groceries and more beer, I found myself going into her computer and skimming her social media accounts, looking for anything that might explain a change in her behavior. I read her text messages, looking for clues, but of course much of it was in Thai, not English, so I ended up feeling more frustrated than reassured.

I considered taking screen shots of everything and sending it to a translation service to find out the truth… or at least to unearth some real clues.

Clues that she secretly hated me. Clues that she had a boyfriend on the side, someone younger or more handsome or maybe more Asian—someone she had more in common with. Heck, I even found myself speculating that she might owe someone money. I thought maybe she got in with the wrong people back before I knew her in Thailand. Maybe those people found out she married well and now she was being blackmailed or threatened.

I think I would have accepted any explanation, no matter how outlandish, if it might help me understand why my sweet, lovely girl could do such terrible, frightening things.

I didn't find anything, though.

About a week after that, the next finger disappeared.

* * *

That time, I didn't pass out.

I threw up.

After I'd filled the sink with bright-orange bile and what remained of the beef stroganoff I'd eaten the night before, I swayed where I held onto the bathroom counter, looking at my own ghostly pale face and the dark circles under my bloodshot eyes. I looked like a caricature of myself. I'd lost weight. I wondered if I'd managed to lose more hair, too.

I stared at the skin sagging on my arms and the different hang to my belly and I tried to understand what was happening to me. I looked like I'd aged about fifteen years overnight. My face was dusted unevenly with a scruffy beard, but I didn't kid myself there was anything rugged or sexy about it. It was more the homeless man on the street kind of scruff than anything remotely deliberate-looking.

For the first time, it really hit me that she would kill me if I didn't stop her.

I shoved the thought out of my mind as soon as it struck me, but it lingered somewhere, in the less-bright recesses of my mind. I still couldn't resolve myself to call the police on her, and knowing that they would definitely have some awkward questions for both of us at this point, I didn't go to the hospital that time, either. I went into work, and didn't comment on my bandaged hand at all and no one asked, but I knew eventually I would need to come up with some kind of story there, too, at least until I figured out what to do about Kanya.

I knew if I divorced her, they'd deport her right away.

And the problem was the same problem I'd always had with her.

I didn't want to divorce her. I loved her.

More than anything, I wanted her to love me again, too.

* * *

"Could you come in here a second, Robert?"

I froze, in the act of tossing my car keys on the kitchen

counter. I'd never heard the voice before. It was male, deep, with the faintest trace of a Mexican accent.

A complete stranger was somehow inside my house.

My eyes searched for that stranger.

I found him sitting on the leather couch, his hands clasped neatly together where he hung them over his own thighs. The classic, "trust me, I'm your friend" pose that a lot of therapists and social workers adopted. I remembered that pose well from all of the bullshit critical incident debriefing they put me through in San Francisco, when I left the lab there.

Next to him on that same couch sat my wife, Kanya.

They sat way too close to one another, in my opinion.

She wore a sky blue dress, which somehow managed to make her look more Native American than Thai, and she sat forward with her hands clasped too. I couldn't help noticing that the dress was low cut, and the man sitting next to her on the couch was about fifteen years younger than me, with a full head of thick black hair and handsome.

His serious brown eyes met mine over the kitchen bar, and he motioned me over with a graceful flick of his tanned hand.

"Please, Robert." His voice exuded patience. "It's important that we talk in here."

The thing that came out of my mouth next may not have been polite, but you have to remember, I was pretty surprised to find this strange man in my house.

"Who the hell are you?" I heard hostility make the words ugly. "What are you doing in my house? What are you doing with my wife?"

The man's expression remained serene.

Definitely some kind of quack therapist.

"It's your wife's house too, Mr. Davenport. She invited me here…"

He continued speaking as I walked around the counter. I couldn't help giving Kanya a disbelieving look as I made my way into my own living room, where the two of them had apparently set up camp in order to ambush me.

"…She's worried about you," Robert was saying now. "She didn't feel she could handle the situation alone, so she sought help from a neighbor, who happens to be a friend of mine."

"Worried about me? A neighbor? What neighbor?"

At the man's cocked eyebrow, I let out a derisive snort. I saw the stranger, the handsome man who now sat in my house like he belonged there, look down at my bandaged hand.

Watching him assess the bandage there, I scowled. "Did it occur to you that maybe I have a lot more reasons to be worried about her?"

Again, the man didn't react visibly to my words.

"She's worried for herself too, Mr. Davenport," he said gravely. "Why don't you tell me what happened to your hand?"

I looked at Kanya, again, unable to believe what I was hearing.

Was this really happening? Had Kanya brought in an outside party to somehow make her crazy behavior seem like it was coming from me? I hadn't reported her to the police or even gone to a hospital where her violent acts might be reported by someone else.

I'd stayed loyal to my wife, even though I was now missing all but my index finger and my thumb on that hand. I'd tried to protect her while I figured out how to help her… and this was how she repaid me?

"I think you'd better go." I stared at the man, no longer attempting to be friendly at all. "Right now."

"I'd like to talk first," the man said patiently. "Your wife would like us to talk, as well. Are you willing to tell me what happened to your hand? Or what this is?"

I followed his tapping finger to the top of our coffee table. I'd bought that for Kanya too, a dark wooden frame set with hand-painted Mexican clay tile. On that table, under his tapping finger, was the same notebook I'd seen my wife looking at in my office the night I noticed the cactus pot missing.

"That is a design notebook." I heard a haughtier tone reach my voice, even as I continued standing over him, and over Kanya. "I am an engineer."

"Weren't you fired from your job recently?" the handsome man said.

I blinked at him, then stared at Kanya, that time in open disbelief. "No. Where do you think I just came from?"

"Your wife says you spend all day in the shed out back… that you work out there, designing things. Including this…" Again he tapped the notebook on the top of the table with his fingers. He did it more insistently that time, as if willing my eyes to go to the specific area where his fingers pointed, on the pages he'd displayed within the book. "Have you built this particular design yet, Mr. Davenport?" the man said, his voice holding a firmer edge now. "The mechanical hand? Could you show it to me?"

"It is only a design," I said, feeling my jaw harden. "A

design for a new type of prosthetic hand… a 'smart' hand, they call it."

"But have you *built* it, Mr. Davenport?" The man's dark eyes held a colder light. "Your wife says you have. She says you've threatened her with it."

"Threatened her?" My jaw just about dropped to my chest. "Kanya told you I'd threatened her?"

"Yes, she did." The man's eyes remained that cooler shade of brown. "She said you've been locking her in the house. She said you're restricting her movements and her interactions with others more and more often… that you took her car keys from her and then sold her car. That you took away her phone and her tablet so she couldn't contact friends back home. She said you've been breaking things in fits of rage, often while wearing the mechanical hand you built. She's afraid of you, Mr. Davenport…"

The man's deep brown eyes grew colder still. "Were you aware that she was a minor when you married her, Robert? That her parents in Thailand were not at all pleased when you left the country with her without their permission?"

"What?" I stared at Kanya for real that time. "A minor? That's impossible."

"I assure you, it is not. The issue came up when it turned out you'd falsified her enrollment information at UNM. Your neighbor, my friend Lara, confirmed it. Your wife was sixteen years old when you left with her from Bangkok. That story you told everyone, about meeting her in high-end hotel in Manilla because she had a 'businessman boyfriend'… Kanya told Lara and I that was all a lie. Kanya had never been outside of Bangkok before she met you. She didn't grow up in a village, either. She grew up in a suburb of Bangkok itself."

I couldn't believe what I was hearing. I really couldn't.

I glanced at my wife for the first time since he'd started talking.

She stared up at me, wide-eyed.

The perfect picture of the scared, abused wife. The delicate flower being held against her will in a paunchy, middle-aged man's home. Looking at her and looking at me, I knew this man would see what most close-minded Americans would see. That we didn't belong together. That all that mattered was what was on the outside. That she was young and beautiful and I was not would be enough to convict me in the eyes of most.

I'd known I'd be judged, bringing her back to America with me. I knew jealousy would drive people to say and think all sorts of unkind things.

But never in my wildest dreams had I prepared for a betrayal of this kind.

Not from my sweet Kanya.

Kanya had somehow convinced this man that *I* was the one doing all of these crazy things. It may have started with the woman next door, but now, from the way she huddled against this man, it was obvious that she'd positioned him in the role of her savior.

How? How had she conned both of them so thoroughly?

I could almost believe it of that nosey, stupid, fat neighbor woman from next door, but what about this man, who was obviously educated, and likely trained to spot deceits of this kind? How had Kanya convinced *him* so thoroughly?

Was she sleeping with him?

The longer I looked between the two of them, the more likely it seemed.

Why else would anyone believe her? She was a foreigner, barely spoke any English. I was an upstanding member of our community. I paid taxes, had a good job. And I'd been a good husband to her—a blameless husband. I'd only ever tried to give Kanya everything she wanted. I helped her get into those classes at UNM, even though I worried it might not be good for her, to be surrounded by young Americans who might indoctrinate her in Western culture. She wanted it, so I helped her. I bought her whatever she wanted, brought home gifts for her.

Why would she turn on me like this, unless she was sleeping with him? Why else would she try to convince him I was this terrible monster?

"I want to see this mechanical hand, Mr. Davenport." The man's voice was calm again, but firm. "Right now. I don't want to bring the authorities into this, but if I have to, I will. Either way, Kanya isn't staying here any longer. She's not a minor now, so she can decide for herself what she wants to do, but it's clear she doesn't feel safe with you here."

I considered threatening to call the police myself.

I considered threatening to tell them he'd broken in, that I needed him ejected from my home forcefully. But I could see in his eyes how thoroughly my wife had indoctrinated him into her cause. I could see in his eyes that he thought he was right and I was some kind of horrible abuser of my wife.

Looking between the two of them for a few seconds more, I sighed, as if giving in. My wife avoided my eyes now, staring down at the sand-colored carpet.

"Fine." I nodded as if in defeat, combing my good hand through my thinning blond hair and then patting it down on the top. I knew something about this gesture tended to put people at ease, maybe by reminding them I was a paunchy balding man. Nodding again, I sighed more sadly that time. "Come on. Let's settle this thing, since my wife has obviously convinced you this crazy story of hers is true..."

Ignoring the frown that touched the handsome man's full lips, I watched him glance at Kanya. Pretending not to notice that either, I motioned them towards the back yard.

"It's out in my work shed. Like she no doubt told you. I've been working on a few designs at home lately, which is why I've been here, rather than at the lab. My company wanted me to keep some of these patent filings quiet, so I told them I'd work out the prototypes on my own..."

The man's frown deepened. Again, he glanced at my wife.

She returned his look, wide-eyed, like a baby deer, and the man patted her bare knee under her short dress, letting his frown melt to a reassuring smile. I fought not to scowl when I saw it, although clearly he was trying to pretend the gesture was harmless, possibly even paternal. Now I couldn't decide which of them was the bigger fool, this man or Kanya.

I suspected it was this man.

Men were always stupid when it came to women.

Women knew that. They counted on it.

The man with the perfect black hair and the tanned skin and too-white smile and too-full lips and too-deep brown eyes rose easily to his feet, making the leather sigh as he got up.

Kanya followed reluctantly when he motioned her up too, and the two of them followed me out into the yard in the midday sun, around the sky-blue pool on the blue and white tile, and deeper into our desert landscaped garden. We reached the adobe wall where the shed lived, and I pulled the key out from inside my shirt, again using my good hand.

"You keep that key around your neck?" the man observed, giving another frowning glance back at Kanya.

I saw my wife hiding behind him almost, as if using this strange man as a shield from me.

Unable to believe the extent of her theatrics, I swallowed my annoyance.

"I told you… I'm working on confidential patents." I made my voice peevish that time, so that it jarred my own ears. I'd figured out long ago, even before San Francisco, that acting weak caused others to discount me. "…My company is trusting me a lot, letting me do this at home. I can't let any of my work get into our competitor's hands."

I felt the skepticism wafting off the man behind me, but I ignored that, too.

"I work for defense contractors," I added. That time, I couldn't help but give Kanya a colder glare. I saw her shrink from it, clutching the man's arm, and I looked back at him. "Most of our contracts are military. Even if the applications will be broader at some point, I have to be sensitive to the needs of my employers…"

The man only nodded, his expression neutral, his eyes flat.

I knew he didn't believe me, though.

I'd always been able to tell when people didn't believe me.

I could feel it.

Swinging the shed door inward on its hinges, I stopped short as sunlight filled the small workroom I'd designed.

Kanya had outdone herself.

The potted cactus sat on the floor of the work shed, one side of it broken open and soil spilling over the floor. Most of the succulents inside appeared to be dead or browning. Her broken tablet lay next to it on a low bench, along with the blender, which was also broken, and her two sets of car keys and the old remotes.

In the window hung the bird necklace I'd given her.

The diamond glinted in the sun as it twisted gently from the air rushing into the room as I opened the door. I stared around at the workspace, feeling a deeper grief fill me as the truth slowly sank in.

My wife had set me up.

She wanted me gone. Out of the way.

My wife wasn't anything like I'd thought she was. She wasn't at all the person I'd seen, pretty much from the instant I'd met her and fallen in love at that hotel in Manila.

She was something else. Some kind of spiteful manipulator. Someone who pretended to be the perfect wife only to prey on the men who desperately needed to believe such an elusive creature existed. It had all been a lie. A way to take my life from me. A way to hollow out my heart and head until there was nothing of me left.

And she'd enlisted this man to help her. To be her witness. To convince the world I wasn't the man I pretended to be.

To replace me, maybe.

My worst fear had happened.

I'd discovered my wife didn't really love me.

I'd discovered my wife was trying to destroy me.

I looked back over my shoulder at her witness and accomplice, the handsome young Hispanic man with the puppy dog brown eyes. He wasn't looking at the cactus or the necklace or the blender or the remote controls or the keys, however.

He was staring at my wooden design bench, where a mechanical hand lay on a white cloth, like an insect that had flipped to its back, its legs curled in death.

Watching him look at it, disgust and a faint horror in his eyes, I knew exactly what it was I had to do.

* * *

My therapist asks me every so often if I regret it all now.

I never know how to answer that question.

Regret it all? Regret what?

Which part, exactly?

That I left San Francisco? That I let my company shuttle me off to Asia, out of sight and out of mind, so they didn't have to worry about lawsuits from liars and psychotics? That in Asia I found a new start in life? That I met my gorgeous Kanya? Did I regret that I married her and had two amazing years with her before I discovered the true nature she hid behind that lovely figure and face?

Do I regret that I loved her? That I trusted her with my soul? That I was kind to her, bought her everything she wanted? Do I regret I didn't seek help when all of her erratic behavior started? That I didn't see her for what she was until it was too late?

Which part along that twisted, winding path was I supposed to pinpoint the exact instant where I should harbor regret? Request a do-over?

My therapist would always want to dwell on the irrelevant details though.

Not even with Kanya.

He always wanted to talk about San Francisco, which he would always refer to as "where it started." He'd read me the same fabricated stories that I had to hear at the time, from another woman I'd first thought of as a soul mate and an ally, who turned out to be nothing more than one of those hateful, jealous women who live to manipulate and mess with men's minds. Like everyone at my old job, though, my therapist always sides with her.

He drags me through every detail of that investigation—even though I was totally acquitted of all wrongdoing and didn't have a single conviction on my record at the time. When he points out that I nearly lost my job and that most people at my old work site believed I was guilty, that I'd simply fallen through the cracks of the justice system, I try to explain how that woman had manipulated them all into believing that, but he didn't want to hear it.

"Robert," he would say, his blue eyes holding that fake-patience all shrinks seem to perfect over time. "In light of what you did in New Mexico, you must realize that everyone now believes you were guilty of that initial crime, as well?"

Then he would go on and on about the trial in Albuquerque, all of the lies that got told about me there, too. He'd remind me how my employer testified that I'd been fired from my job for too many missed days of work, along with so-called "erratic behavior"… totally omitting the fact that I missed those days because I'd been drugged and *mutilated* by my wife while I slept.

At the trial, they displayed pictures of the shed and our backyard on the mesa.

The shed that Kanya had staged to make me look so crazy and guilty.

They showed pictures of the knives I supposedly used to cut off my own fingers, and the thread I used to stitch them up. They even put the mechanical hand on a table right in front of the jury, posing it in the most menacing way possible and showing how the grip strength and the bruises on my wife and the overly-helpful handsome shrink friend of the woman next door matched with the appendage.

It was all so misleading and taken out of context… but at that point, I could see that I was lost. Kanya had won. Everyone believed me to be the monster she intended. The judge. The jury. Definitely the District Attorney and the cops.

They looked at Kanya and saw what I'd seen in those early days.

A delicate flower. A slip of a woman, nearly a girl, who could never harm anyone.

And how could I blame them for that?

It still shocks me, however, when my therapist uses the word "everyone," though.

Does he really mean *everyone*? Could *everyone* really believe these lies and distortions about me? Do all of the people who've known me over the years, who've seen me and heard me behave as a kind and generous friend, a helpful work colleague, loving husband… do they *all* really believe I could do these things?

All of them? Every one?

And true, none of them have visited me in here, or really since my initial arrest prior to the trial and all the publicity. But that could be for lots of different reasons, not simply because "everyone" believes these awful stories from those who want only to destroy me.

After all, they have their own jobs and reputations to protect.

Besides, I'm sure their wives believe I'm guilty.

I know everyone believed Carina, that co-worker who cost me my job in San Francisco. That hurt, I admit, especially at the time. Like with Kanya, I'd just been so shocked. Carina was always so nice to me. I'd really liked her—which is the only reason I showed her my side projects in the first place.

The next thing I know, and totally out of nowhere, she's accusing me of sexual assault, of "unethical and grotesque experiments," before launching into fake tears and showing my boss bruises that I had absolutely no memory of giving her. When I tried to explain that the company *paid* me to conduct that research, my boss sided with her of course, since she was a woman and she was crying so I just *had* to be the bad guy.

But here's my question for my therapist, one that he's never given me an adequate response to—at what point does a man have the right to defend himself?

Where is that line?

That's all I ask. I want a line.

I'm a nice guy… I know I am. So tell me where the line is, and I won't cross it, even if they do ever let me out of here. But they never say where that point begins and ends, precisely. Tell me where that point is. Tell me, and I promise, I'll remember it when I see it again.

Back then, in San Francisco, a lot of people told me I loved Carina too much.

Perhaps that is my real fault. Perhaps that is the real line I keep crossing.

I love women too much.

Maybe that's what I will tell my therapist the next time he comes to see me.

Q&A with JC Andrijeski

Man, that story left my head spinning! What a turnaround. How did you come up with this idea? No personal experience in this area, I hope?

In some ways this is based on my personal experience, but not personal, *personal* experience, if that makes sense. I've lived in Bangkok, Thailand, for the past few years, and I'm sorry to say I've come across a few guys like "Bobby" (in a less-extreme form) since I moved here. I don't know if it's common knowledge in the States, but a subset of the Western men who live in Asia tend to have pretty bizarre views of women. They come across as somewhat angry at women in general, truthfully, but also kind of sad in their inability to connect or find someone that fits their view of what a "perfect woman" is.

Though they scare me at times with how angry they can be, I have a lot of empathy for them, too, since they often seem very lonely. I also find them weirdly paradoxical and fascinating, in that they are proud proponents of living in Asia, dating Asian women, etc., but at the same time seem to really hate Asia in a lot of ways, and are often the ones who complain the loudest about differences with the West. They often put Thai (and other Asian) women on a pedestal initially, only then to later come back and accuse them of being duplicitous, manipulative, money-grubbing, having boyfriends on the side, etc. There's also a bit of a stereotype of them only being willing to date Asian women who are quite a bit younger than they are. Often, just due to the nature of sexual economics in Asia, those women come from poorer backgrounds and/or rural areas.

So yes, I got a lot of the complaints about Western women (and Asian food) from hearing those guys talk, since they are really vocal about such subjects, both at bars here in Bangkok and on a lot of the Thai forums. Using that as a starting point, I then created an exaggerated character out of some of the common themes.

I should say that in general they are older men (most of them older than "Bobby" by at least a decade), often divorced, many of them retired.

So, I might be being a bit mean to that "type" of guy, (if there is such a thing), but I was more taking aspects of that mentality and seeing how far I could push it for fictional purposes.

Honestly, the character of Bobby scares me, though, because in some ways he's a lot more "real" than most of the darker characters I create.

What got you into mysteries, and what other genres do you write?

You know, it took me a while to realize that I write mysteries. I've read them my whole life and have always loved them, but I always figured I wasn't smart enough to actually write one. Then I got it into my head to take a craft course on the art of mystery writing, given by Kristine Kathryn Rusch, and it kind of exploded a lot of my internal myths about not only what mystery and crime writing were, but also whether or not I could do it.

Since then I've been much more consciously writing mysteries, but I also noticed a ton of mystery-like quirks in things I'd already written. Even now, I still tend to write in a somewhat cross-genre form, but all along I've written my novels with elements of mystery writing in them, especially in terms of enjoying a good twist to my plots and surprises that build off of clues I've left scattered through the texts of my books.

My newest big series launch is a paranormal mystery, the *Quentin Black Mystery* books. It's still a bit of a genre mash-up in that he's a psychic detective who works with the police and with a forensic psychologist named Miri Fox. The tone is gritty and more hard-boiled, but the series has a strong romantic subplot running through it, in addition to the paranormal. With that series, the mystery theme is getting more and more prominent in my work.

As far as other work/genres, I also have a more "epic" series that's urban fantasy mixed with urban science fiction, also with a strong romantic subplot and a ton of mystery and suspense. That one is called *Allie's War* and it's set in a gritty and realistic version of Earth where a second race of beings, called "Seers" are discovered living side by side with human beings. Their presence twists a lot of our regular, "human" history, including world wars, modern politics, technology, race relations, organized crime… even religion. It's been a blast to work on, and in many ways it's probably my most involved work to date, given the complexity of the world, but there's a ton of mystery and suspense worked into those books, as well, and a lot of surprises in terms of the characters and plot twists.

In addition, I have a post-apocalyptic series with aliens called *Alien Apocalypse* (now completed), and I write some non-fiction and even a few children's books. In short form, I've written in a wide range of genres, including: literary fiction, mystery, science fiction, fantasy, paranormal romance, science fiction romance, horror, apocalyptic fiction, and humor.

Tell us what you're working on now.

I've got three projects going right now, all at various stages of completion.

One is called *Red Magic* and is a fantasy romance commissioned as part of a multi-author project set in a post-apocalyptic world. That world, created by the publisher/series organizer, is a lot of fun—filled with deadly creatures called "ravagers" along with witches and warlocks and humans battling it out following a world-wide catastrophe that broke the remaining civilization into districts. My book is centered in District 6, which covers most of what used to be Southeast Asia, so it's fun for me to set another story here in my part of the world.

The next book in my queue (which I can't help working on here and there, since I'm really excited about this series right now), is book six in the *Quentin Black Mystery* series, which has the working title *Black To Dus*t. Book five introduced a whole new slew of twists and turns to the longer series arc, as well as a host of new characters, so in addition to the book's central mystery, I'm having a blast working out some of those more long-running threads.

The third is the final book in the Allie's War series, called *Sun*, a monster project that I don't expect to have completed until 2017.

What else should we know about you, and where can readers find you?

Hmm… well, I hail from Northern California originally but I've been a nomad most of my adult life, so I've lived all over the place, both in the United States and abroad. I lived in

Albuquerque, New Mexico for a few years, which is part of why I set "Nice Guys Finish Last" there—I think I just wanted an excuse to write about the summer desert monsoons, since they're so different from the kind we're having here in Bangkok right now.

Other fun facts? I used to work as a business consultant and a process design project manager, but I've also milked cows, waited tables, mucked stalls, dug trenches, worked as a photo printer and a sound editor and a bartender. I've been a secretary and a teacher of various subjects. I worked as a freelance journalist and sang in a rock band. I love green chili and burritos and sushi in addition to my unflagging fondness for Thai food (as well as sour pickles and ice cream and anchovies and mangos). I love doing martial arts and yoga, sniffing sage, jumping in swimming pools and hugging puppies… as well as taking long, pointless walks in the rain and getting lost in street markets.

I also love talking to my readers, pretty much any time, so if you have any questions about me or my work, feel free to write me directly! I'm even planning to do some video posts to answer some of those questions, so if you ask me one I get fairly often, you might have to deal with me rambling on and on about the topic nonsensically in video format for however-many minutes.

As far as how to contact me, probably the easiest thing to point to is my website, which gives you a bunch of options: www.jcandrijeski.com.

For a few direct links, you can join my newsletter, The Rebel Army. You'll be notified of new releases, have the opportunity to join in some exclusive giveaways of free books, and receive updates and odd pictures and stories about my life here in Asia: http://hyperurl.co/JCA-Newsletter. You can also find me on Facebook here: https://www.facebook.com/JCAndrijeski/, and Twitter here: http://twitter.com/jcandrijeski.

Forsaking All Others

by Chris Patchell

"Mally!"

Someone is calling me, but I can barely make it out. My head swims, as if I'm under three feet of water. Groggy, I open my eyes. Light shimmers and dances around my field of vision, creating a kaleidoscopic mishmash of colors and shapes that I can't make sense of. I squint to pull the scene into focus and cringe as a throbbing pain, like the boom of a bass drum, fills my head.

"Mally."

Again.

Clearer this time, and I know it's Jack. Way off in the distance he calls to me. I try to answer, but the words catch in my throat. My mouth is as dry as sand.

I force my eyes open again, and it's like peering through a lens of broken glass.

"Where are we?" I ask, too woozy for the panic to set in.

"You mean you don't know?" Jack says.

I blink away the fuzziness, and my vision finally clears. I see the islands of boxes, and skis, and other piles of accumulated junk all around us.

"What are we doing here?"

This makes no sense to me. I avoid basements at all costs. They are dark, closed spaces, prisons, places of punishment, or purgatory, depending on your crime. Although this place looks nothing like the dank and dirty cellar in the house where I grew up, I come down here as rarely as possible. A fact that Jack knows well. So why we're both down here together is beyond weird, and I struggle to square it with logic.

Stiff and sore, I try to shift my position and can't. Only then do I realize that I'm bound to a chair. A spike of fear stabs through me as I foolishly try to rise. Move. Escape. Hard restraints bite into the spare flesh of my wrists and pin me in place.

"Jack," I cry, panic invading my voice. "What's going on?"

"Shh…" he cuts me off, and I fall silent.

Up above I hear a crash, like my Grandmother's dishes from the china cabinet hitting the floor and smashing into a thousand pieces. Another crash. This time I whisper.

"What's happening?"

"We're being robbed. Or at least, that's how it is supposed to look."

Supposed to look?

His words send a shiver through me, and I roll them around in my mind, grasping for the deeper meaning buried beneath the surface of what he just said. Nothing is ever simple with Jack. Anxiety sloshes around in my gut, and I crane my head around to see him. The stabbing pain through the base of my skull makes me gasp. Warm blood trickles through my hair and down the back of my neck. I want to wipe it away, but I can't. Not with my hands clamped to this damned chair.

"What do you mean it's supposed to look like a robbery?" I ask in a voice that's barely a whisper.

"Like you don't know."

His razor sharp tone slices into me, and I'm afraid to ask what he means. There's a hardness—an edge to it that I know all too well—just another verbal scar in this ugly little war of ours.

Minutes tick by, and, little by little, the confusion evaporates, like dew in the morning sun. Still, his next words catch me completely off guard.

"How long have you been sleeping with him?"

I am breathless. My head reels from the blow.

"Who?" I manage at last.

An icy silence follows. My heart pounds, and I force myself to swallow, waiting for Jack to say more.

Another crash shakes the ceiling above us. I nearly jump out of my skin. I hold my breath in the chilling silence, waiting for Jack to speak.

"I saw him that time I picked you up from the school."

He spits the words out like an accusation. There's no point in playing dumb; we both know who he means.

"Kyle?"

Another frosty silence forms between us, and my head spins as I try to dredge up the details of that day.

My car had gotten a flat, and Jack arrived at the school,

fully pissed I had pulled him away from a meeting. I knew he didn't like being disturbed at work, and on any other day I would have dealt with the problem myself. The whole morning had been a disaster, and when I left school later than I should have, and found the flat tire, I didn't know what else to do. So I'd called.

Kyle's daughter, Megan, was in my fifth grade class. Megan's basketball game had just let out, and the two were leaving the school when Jack arrived—red-faced and ready to argue with me when sweet little Megan had called out her goodbye.

The timing was beyond horrible. I faked a smile and waved. She'd waved back.

And then there was Kyle, tall and angular, with a military bearing. He pulled his ball cap down over his thick brow and fixed me with a look my husband didn't miss.

Jack had interrogated me later, as I knew he would, and I'd done my best to brush the whole thing off. Kyle was just like that, I said. He was an odd duck; he truly was. But clearly Jack hadn't bought my story. Here he was bringing it up again.

Now.

"What does Kyle have to do with anything?" I ask, wiggling my hands to try to pry loose the bonds, but the sharp edges of the zip ties slice deeper into my skin, and I suck in my breath from the pain. Jack releases his breath loudly. I can feel the anger wafting off him like shimmering waves of desert heat.

"How long have you been sleeping with him?" he barks.

My eyes fly to the ceiling, and I wait for the inevitable sound of footsteps racing down the stairs in response to Jack's roar. I hear nothing. In a way, the silence is more disturbing than the sound of the house being ransacked. At least that helps me track his movements.

My husband swears, and I can feel him trying to fight his way free, but for once, he's every bit as stuck as I am. There's something satisfying about the thought.

Jack's a hard man to live with and always has been. He's commanding, successful, and driven. Once he seemed like everything I ever wanted in a man, a real life dream come true. How wrong I was.

A whirlwind courtship ensued, and we said our vows on a sandy beach. Naïvely, I thought he would take care of me forever. In his own way, I suppose he has. Fairy tales are for little girls, and reality is a fickle beast.

Growing up poor made me appreciate the fact that the money is plentiful with Jack, and I don't really want for anything. But it's lonely living with a man who cares more for his business than he does for his wife. I'm a pretty ornament to dangle from his arm when it's convenient, and a housemate and personal maid when it's not. Left alone night after night to wander the halls of an empty house, a wife gets to thinking.

Don't pretend you don't know what I mean.

"There's nothing going on between us," I say. I hold my breath and pray he believes me, but of course he does not.

"Then why is he here?"

"I don't know. He's got… problems."

"Problems?"

"He's not… stable." I grasp for the words, finally latching onto one that seems to fit best. Jack's harsh laugh shreds me.

"Unstable? No fucking shit. Leave it to you to hook up with some fucking nut job."

I cringe from another verbal blow.

"It's not like that."

"Oh, so now you're going to give me some bullshit story about how I'm never home. How I mistreat you? How somehow this is all my fault."

His words bubble like acid inside me, and I want to lash out. He knows I'm trapped. He knows the damned prenup he forced me to sign would strip me of everything, should I have the fool sense to leave him.

"How stupid do you think I am?" he asks then, and fear snakes through me, like mercury in my veins. Fast and toxic, it fills me until I think I will burst. "It's one thing for you to embarrass yourself, Mally—and subject yourself to the fallout you've earned—but now you've pulled me into this sordid situation, and all for some tawdry little affair. I thought you'd at least have better taste than a veteran with nothing more going for him than the ability to lift heavy things. I thought you'd do a better job of hiding your tracks."

"You've been checking my phone?"

Of course he has. It's the only way he could have known. I've been careful.

"Obviously." Ice forms on the single word and invades my heart.

There's not the tiniest part of my life that's mine; not my friends, my schedule, my bank account, and not even the way I dress. Jack controls it all. Or at least he believes that he does.

Angry tears leak from my eyes and burn down my cheeks, leaving trails of fire in their wake.

"It was just once, and I broke it off as soon as it happened. I swear that I did. I never meant for you to find out, Jack. Not like this."

"Shut up, Mally."

"Please, Jack."

"Shut up!"

He falls stonily silent, and my mind whirls as the whole, terrible situation plays out in my head.

Kyle.

He's upstairs. I can hear him. My gut wrenches tight, and I know it won't be long until his footsteps thunder down the stairs, and then…

"He's obsessed with me," I blurt out, like beans spilling out of a split bag and hitting a bare tile floor. "He went nuts when I broke it off. Texting me. Following me. I didn't know what to do."

"Good call, Mally. Letting him fester."

"What was I supposed to do?"

"You're goddamned lucky my hands are tied, or I'd…"

"Or you'd what? Hit me?" I'm suddenly brave in the knowledge that he can't reach me. "Like the blow to the back of my head? I probably have a concussion."

"You goaded me into it. You know you did."

All at once, I remember Kyle's fingers running down the angry bruises on my arms. Soft. Gentle as a whisper of air. I shudder at the memory of his touch.

Arguing with Jack is pointless, I know, even though it feels good to let go. The words are bursting in my mind. Somehow I stop them from leaking out, afraid of going too far.

"We've got to get out of here," Jack says. "Look around for something to use."

Like what? A knife? A weapon? I look around at the stuff that is piled halfway to the ceiling—evidence of our lavish lifestyle—and an image fills my mind. A bird trapped in a gilded cage. Flailing to get out. Desperate. Willing to hurt itself in the attempt.

"There," Jack hisses.

I crane my head to see what he's talking about and come up empty. The pain in my head stabs again, and I close my eyes, waiting for the flare to subside.

And then I hear it—the thump of Jack's chair on the floor. It shakes the mountains of crap. He does it again.

Each jump moves him inches away, and I hold my breath, gaze fixed to the ceiling, straining for a sound—some clue about what's happening above.

Jack moves again, and a box topples over, its contents tumbling to the floor in another vibrant crash.

"Stop," I cry. "What if he hears you?"

"What do you think he'll do?" Jack sneers.

I bite my tongue, knowing that whatever I say will not matter in the least. He's not listening. He doesn't care. My opinion has never mattered much before, and now is no different. Now I matter even less—a skin to be shed as the snake moves on.

Behind me, Jack jumps. The floor shakes again and again. Finally, I hear a crash and a crunch.

Jack grunts.

"What are you doing?"

I catch sight of his chair as it topples to the ground. Jack falls hard, too. His head crashes into the floor, and for a moment he is still.

The noise above us stops, and I hold my breath. Waiting.

Softly, Jack swears. He writhes on the ground and then suddenly is free.

At least one of his hands is.

He crawls across the floor, dragging himself along with his free hand; the rest of him is still bound to the chair. The wood scrapes with each agonizing inch. I hear the splintered edges scrape against the concrete. Jack gathers his strength and keeps moving.

I struggle, trying to thrash myself free, but the restraints hold me fast.

Jack reaches a toolbox shoved beneath a workbench. He paws at the contents inside. Metal clangs on metal until finally I hear it.

Footsteps on the stairs. Coming closer.

Adrenaline burns through me, and I know Jack hears it, too. He cocks his head and listens. The cords stand out on his neck. A grim resolve flattens his lips, and I know he's got a plan. I can see the wheels turning in his head, but before I can say a word, the door crashes open.

Kyle's broad-shouldered frame fills the doorway. Six-feet two-inches tall and powerfully built, he still looks like a marine. Hard. Lean. Cruel.

Kyle's ice blue eyes meet mine, and a jolt shivers through me. Primal. Thrilling—like I've touched a live wire and can't let go. Kyle says nothing. His gaze shifts to Jack, still lying on his side, tie wraps binding him to the broken chair.

He looks old. Worn. More like my father than my husband.

I can barely breathe. The tension expands in the room as neither man utters a word. Kyle shatters the stillness as he marches toward Jack, his boots ringing out on the floor.

Jack's jaw sets, and I see the sharp glint in his eye.

"You don't want this," he says to Kyle in a flaccid attempt to intimidate. His words have the opposite effect.

Kyle smiles a smile of pure menace.

"That's where you're wrong, Jackie boy. This is exactly what I want."

He reaches behind his back as if he's got all the time in the world, and for the first time, I see the gun tucked into the waistband of his fatigues. Just the sight of it sucks the air from my lungs. I can't speak, move or scream.

Jack lunges—his hand lightning fast. I see the glint of metal before he drives something deep into Kyle's thigh. Kyle screams. It's an animal sound filled with pain and fury, and my heart roars in my ears.

Kyle whirls away, beyond Jack's reach.

I see another flash. A knife, now, in Jack's hand. He slashes wildly downward at the zip ties binding him to the chair.

Fear twists in my gut. Blood oozes in a dark stain down Kyle's leg. His face is full of thunder; he straightens and limps across the floor, gun leveled at my husband's head. Blood drips down his pant leg onto his shoe.

Jack looks up, panic blazing bright in his eyes.

"I'll give you whatever you want," he blurts, ever the businessman trying to make a deal. Kyle cocks his head, the gun rock steady in his grip.

"What if this is what I want? You. Groveling. Begging for your life?"

"What about Mally?" Jack is desperate. Grasping at straws.

Kyle stops feet away, studying him like a biologist uncovering some new species of vermin.

"If the two of you want to be together then who am I to stand in your way?" Jack reasons.

Kyle's bark of laughter sends chills down my spine.

"You're giving her to me? Like she's a side of beef? How generous."

I can see Jack spinning, groping, and searching for the right angle to save himself. He shoots me a pleading look, but what can I do? Kyle holds all the power in his hand, and it's pointed straight at my husband's head.

"You're right about one thing," Kyle says in a slow midwestern drawl. "This is all about Mally and the things you've done to her."

"I've done to her? What have I done to her? When I found her she was nothing—just a washed-up beauty queen waiting tables at a run-down bar, attending some podunk community college trying to make something of herself. Everything she is now is what I've made her."

His words had lost their power to wound me years ago, but I see Kyle flinch. Fury contorts his face, and he stares down at Jack, his eyes brimming with contempt.

"You hit her. You abused her. And you dare tell me that you've never done her harm?"

"I never laid a hand on her." Kyle's shadow falls across Jack, and his terrorized gaze cuts to me. "Tell him, Mally. I've never hit you. I've never…"

Liar.

Kyle's jaw clenches tight, and I see the muscles jump in his lean face. He pulls back the hammer, and Jack dissolves into tears. Kyle turns back to me. Our eyes lock, and all I can hear is the hammering of my heart. Then Kyle squeezes the trigger.

My breath leaves me in a rush, and I turn away from the gory sight of my husband's head exploding. Blood and brains splatter the wall as I fight to catch my breath.

He did it. Oh my god, he did it.

I can hardly believe this has happened.

The smell of gunfire hangs in the air, and my ears ring from the blast.

Kyle is no longer looking at me. He's staring down at the bloody lump on the floor as if Jack is a piece of garbage. He taps the body with his foot and shakes his head.

"It's done."

There's no triumph in his voice, no jubilation. It's just a bland statement of fact.

I see the knife on the floor, just shy from where Jack lays. Kyle bends to retrieve it and then slowly walks my way.

I see the blade splattered with blood clutched in his hand, still glinting in the silver light.

He stops right in front of me. I suck in a breath and search his deep blue eyes.

His sudden smile is like the breaking of dawn after a long stormy night. He hunkers down, until we're eye to eye, still holding the blade.

I can hardly breathe with him here so close, as if his presence burns the oxygen from the air.

His gaze caresses me, as soft as a lover, and for a second I'm lost in his spell. He speaks, and the spell is broken.

"Well," he says.

I've been waiting years for this moment.

"Well, what are you waiting for? Untie me."

His breath hot on my cheek, the knife cuts through the zip ties like soft butter.

"You're wearing my favorite perfume."

"It seems fitting."

His laugh is a growl in the back of his throat, and he pulls me roughly to him. His mouth brands me. The kiss—deep and fierce, an open flame in the heat of his touch. His fingers tangle in the back of my hair, and I cry out.

His hand drops away. Blood coats the leather pads of his gloves, and Kyle frowns.

"Are you okay?"

"I'm fine."

"But Mally…" He trails off.

I shake out my hands and rise from my chair. My legs feel like rubber, and I sway for a second before regaining my balance. I can tell Kyle is brooding about the things Jack has done.

"It's over," I tell him, and he nods.

"I made you a promise. He will never touch you again."

"And he won't." I rub my wrists, the raw flesh burning like fire. "The zip ties were too tight," I complain.

Kyle examines the bloody crescents carved into each wrist, regret filling his face.

"Had to be. I had to make it look real."

"Then hit me," I say. He drops my hands. His expression grows dark.

"No."

"Hit me," I command in a voice hard as stone.

"No."

"You said it yourself, Kyle. It's got to look real."

"I don't care. If I hit you, I'm no better than him."

I chuckle somewhere deep in my throat and shake my head. My hand cups his cheek, and I pull his mouth down to mine. The tangle of our tongues sends an electric jolt through us both, and I hear Kyle moan.

"Pretend I'm him," I whisper.

Kyle pulls away. "You know I can't do that. I could nev-er..."

"Do it," I yell.

And he does. Kyle backhands me across the face and sends me reeling. A high-pitched whine drowns out every-thing as the world spins out of focus. A cut opens up on my cheek. I gasp and stumble back, nearly fall, until his hands reach out to catch me.

"I'm sorry," he says. His fingers stray to the cut as if somehow he can heal it with his touch. "I'm so sorry."

Head still fuzzy from the blow, I blink and force myself to smile, the flesh under my eye already starting to swell.

"I'm okay."

"I never want to be like him. You believe me, Mally, don't you?"

"Of course. We're a team now."

Satisfied, he takes a step back, and I survey the scene with a keen eye, wondering what story it will tell. For the first time I'm grateful the basement floor is bare concrete. Carpet would be so much harder to clean.

"Be careful where you step."

I remove my shoes and take the knife, my fingers close on the hilt.

"It has to look like he untied me."

Quickly we adjust the scene and manufacture evidence to match the story I will tell. When we're done, I stand over Jack, the pool of blood beneath his head starting to congeal.

I think I should feel something. Anger. Hatred. Regret.

But standing staring into his lifeless face I feel nothing except gratitude. As Kyle said, I'm finally free.

"The upstairs?"

"I did like you told me. It looks like it was robbed."

"And my jewelry?"

"I dumped it down the storm drain out back. They'll never find it."

"Good." I step back into my shoes.

"I was careful," he says as he breathes in my scent.

Kyle flattens his hand on my belly and pulls me against him. I arch back. He grinds into me, and I groan.

Then he spins me around in the steel bands of his arms and kisses me deep. My hands slide around his back. The hard, taut muscles of his shoulders are so very different than Jack's. My hands close on his waist.

"What's the first thing we're going to do with his money?" he whispers into my ear, sending shivers down the length of my spine.

"I've been thinking a lot about that," I say. And I have.

Quick and as deadly as lightning, I pull the gun from the band of his pants, point it at his face, and pull the trigger.

Another shot rings out. Kyle's eyes bulge, uncomprehending. His body flails backward, and he crashes to the floor. I hold my breath and tick off the seconds, keeping watch to make sure that he's dead.

He doesn't move. He doesn't breathe. I hover over him watching for some sign of life, but there is nothing, just the shocked look on his ridiculous face.

I drop the gun to the floor. It lands beside him with a hollow clang.

"First, I think I'll go to Paris," I tell him. "I've always wanted to see Paris in the spring."

A peaceful silence settles over the room, and I bite down hard on the inside of my cheek until the blood flows into my mouth. Tears spring to my eyes, and I let them come. Each one backs up my story.

"Jack," I breathe, fishing in my pocket for my cell phone. "Jack is dead."

I test the words. Adjust them. Until they sound just right.

By the time I call 911, my hands are shaking. My breaths come in ragged gasps.

"My husband," I cry into the phone. "Someone shot my husband. Oh god, oh god please. Hurry. I think he's dead."

"Calm down, ma'am, we're on our way. Now I need you to tell me what happened."

I cry something unintelligible into the phone. It slides from my hands and shatters on the cold concrete floor.

Then I crouch down beside my fallen husband and wait for the sirens to come. My forehead falls onto his chest.

My tears soak through his shirt like spring rain.

Q&A with Chris Patchell

Oh boy, was this one full of surprises. Deliciously devious! Do you ever feel bad about writing about people who are... just so bad?

LOL. I suppose I should. I used to think of myself as a nice girl from a sleepy little town in Canada, but it seems my alter ego writer self is not very nice at all. I think one of the big surprises for me, when I started writing these kinds of stories, was how much I love writing as the antagonist. As Stephen King says, even the bad guy is the hero of his own story.

What attracts you about writing mysteries and thrillers? What's tough and what's easy about this genre?

I wrote romances in my early twenties—fluffy stories with

happy endings tied up in neat little bows. And then life got busy—college, career, family. When I finally got back to writing again, my tastes had changed. I had changed, and so, I started writing something different. The minute I started working on my first thriller I was hooked. I love these fast-paced, high-stakes stories. Unraveling a plot is like creating an elaborate labyrinth, and it happens to be my very favorite thing about writing. Coming from a tech background, I'm analytical in nature. This is probably why plotting and pace come naturally to me. Character development and emotional arcs are much harder, so I spend more time on this aspect of my craft. My heroes tend to come from the "scratch and dent" section of life.

Any works in progress?

Absolutely. I've always got several projects on the go. Writing this shorter piece provided a welcome break in the editing cycle for my next novel. My agent and I are debating about the title. I call it *The Farm*. She calls it *Dark Harvest*. Whatever we end up calling the book, it will be the second in the Holt Foundation series. Seth, Marissa, and the cast of characters from the first book, *In the Dark*, investigate the disappearance of a pregnant woman who has gone missing. The police suspect the boyfriend is to blame, but the Holt Foundation fears there is a darker motive at play. With the missing woman's due date only weeks away, there is no time to waste if they are to save her and her baby.

Tell us where readers can find you and hear about your upcoming books.

Readers can follow me on my Facebook page at https://www.facebook.com/authorchrispatchell/. They can also signup for my newsletter on my author website at http://www.chrispatchell.com/.

Starter

by Samuel Peralta

"It's a perfect starter," he is saying to us.

I step into the house first, after the realtor, and she steps in behind me, her small hot hand clutched in mine.

~

A modest brick two-story on a thirty-five-foot lot frontage. Grass.

A tidy porch, an asphalt driveway turning into a busy thoroughfare that was once a quiet street.

On the right, one house away from a gaggle of shops—pharmacy, hairdresser, tanning salon, cafe.

On the left, four houses from a clutch of tombstones, an old cemetery across from a new supermarket.

~

I'd discovered a new Thai-Indonesian fusion restaurant in the west end, coaxed her to lunch a week ago. But all throughout, she'd dampened my triumph, pensive over *nasi goreng* and tea.

Then, without warning: "It isn't far from here, you know."

"What isn't far?"

"Where it all began."

~

Not far. Seeing the house stunned me, an apparition from her past, suddenly present. But the sign in front took us both aback—

FOR SALE

For days our conversation wound its way in and out and around that house for sale, wavering around letting it go and going further—until one day she told me she'd rung up a realtor, that we'd go there after work.

~

"Easy access, everything you need a short walk away," the realtor is saying.

I'm watching her. She's silent.

"The main floor refinished, fresh paint on the walls, the windows completely redone," he continues. "Everything like new."

But the memories are still there. Under the whitewash, plaster and paint, revenants linger.

I see it in her eyes, the way she circles around the perimeter of the empty room, now and again her right hand reaching up to brush the silent walls, as if they could speak.

I am her memory's accomplice. Each hesitant confession, all her Scheherazade stories, whispered to me nights over the years, coalescing into reality as we continue our ritual dance to the realtor's vapid incantation—

Living room… dining room… kitchen… bath…

Through every doorway another tormented ghost, in every open room another stab wound in her heart.

~

"Would you like to see upstairs?" the realtor asks.

She stops him and asks if she and I could talk alone. It's her first time to speak.

Always accommodating, the man takes out cigarettes and retreats to the backyard.

She takes my hand. As in a trance, she leads the way upstairs.

I count the number of stairs, every step up a step back into the past, and skip a beat when we reach the top at fourteen.

Our dance moves across the landing past two empty bedrooms and a bath before we reach the small, unremarkable room that was her own.

~

"Are you afraid?" he asked her, that first night, fourteen years ago. He twisted her arm, and she whimpered. No use pretending, as before, that she was asleep.

"No I'm not," she whispered.

"You should be," he said, unsheathing his belt. "You should be."

~

She leads me to the back wall and kneels down, traces remembrance on its surface.

Scuff marks where the bedposts scraped the wall.

The outline of a nonexistent bedframe.

The indentation of the legs still marring the floor.

The ceiling light, and how she willed herself to stare at it, to think of nothing else but the burning in her eyes.

~

She sifts the walls and floorboards as if through evidence, the archeology of her past, and here I am, belated witness to her truth.

Eleven years old again, she whimpers, pulls me close, a coverlet against the night.

~

And when she's found it all, proven to herself that it was real, an unimagined life, when she's sifted and catalogued the forensic minutiae of her innocence unravelling, she weeps—for who she was, for why she is, here in a whitewashed starter, where it all began.

Q&A with Samuel Peralta

This is an unusual and haunting story. Can you share how the idea came to you?

"Starter" is based on a true story. I had a troubled friend who confided to me a story about something that happened to her in her aunt and uncle's home. One day I found myself in her hometown, on business, and I happened to drive past the street she told me about, and there it was, just as she described in her story, but with a 'For Sale' sign in front. I never told her about it, and eventually we lost touch. I imagined this story as a way for her to face her ghosts.

What brought you to writing?

I've always been a storyteller, ever since I can remember. I remember keeping my younger brothers entertained for hours with stories I made up on the spot. Since then I've explored a variety of forms, from poetry to songs, from essays to short stories—and am now beginning a novel—but the thrill of telling a new story remains the same.

Do you have new works in progress?

I have a couple of speculative fiction pieces destined for magazines and anthologies. The titles may change, but *Sonata Vampirica* is a dialogue between a vampire and his lover; *A Love Song for the Apocalypse* explores one way the world could end; and *The Illustrated Robot* is a tribute to Ray Bradbury.

My biggest effort now is a novel destined for the box set *Dominion Rising*, a collection of original novels by a group of authors I'm proud to be associated with, coming out in 2017. I can't really say what my novel will be about, but I'm really excited about it, because it will be my debut novel.

Your background is quite varied. Please give us a short description of what you do, and how you manage to juggle work in so many different fields.

Many of my creative projects I view as missions to encourage other creatives and pioneers—whether in art or technology—and to spotlight them to a broader audience. That mission is what keeps me going.

Most people know me as a business development executive for a nuclear engineering company, or as a member of the Board of Directors of a Canadian nuclear industry association. But I also sit on the Boards of several resource firms pivoting to the high-technology area—in augmented reality, the Internet of Things, and in hybrid semiconductors.

I've had several successful start-ups in the past, in handheld computing and in III-V semiconductors, which have given me the experience to do this—as well as some freedom to write and independently publish books, including my *Future Chronicles* anthology series—www.smarturl.it/get-free-book —which has about 17 titles to date. I also support visual artists, particularly in independent film, having been involved in nearly 100 feature and short films so far.

Where can we find you?

For my literary projects - www.amazon.com/author/samuelperalta
For my film projects - www.imdb.com/name/nm6182058/
For my business projects - www.linkedin.com/in/samperalta

Pride

by Eric J. Gates

There were no sirens.

A lazy Sunday afternoon, sitting on the deck, watching the waves, people playing on the beach, sipping lemon tea, talking about the future.

"I think we should hand everything over to the kids and go find that house in the Caribbean we keep talking about." Todd McGee chuckled as his hands rubbed his knees. "At least it might help with this damned arthritis."

"What? The house in the Caribbean or the kids running the business?" replied his wife, Mary, refilling Todd's empty glass.

"Both, probably. We're getting too old for this, Mary, and we know it. It's a young person's game; well, young as in less than sixty."

"You feeling old again?"

"Mentally, no. It's just this body of mine is starting to protest all the abuse of the last forty years. I'm afraid one day I'm going to screw things up because I can't hack it anymore. No, my darling Mary, it's time we retired. The kids are more than capable of carrying on. Let's go spend some of the money we've got squirreled away."

"Sounds good. They'll both be back in a couple of weeks, so that's a great time to tell them."

"FBI! FREEZE!"

Green-garbed men swarmed onto the deck, automatic weapons pointed. Mary screamed. Todd started to rise.

"GET DOWN ON YOUR KNEES! DO IT NOW! ON YOUR KNEES! HANDS BEHIND YOUR HEAD!"

Todd glanced at his wife, then at the man in the dark suit emerging through the terrace door. He recognized the man. Knew of his obsession.

"GET ON YOUR KNEES NOW!"

The agent in the green fatigues and flak jacket shouting orders did not wait for Todd to comply. Mary could see the FBI SWAT team members were on edge. She was unaware their adrenaline had peaked as they breached the beachside house in Malibu, fueled in part by the pre-operation briefing two hours earlier.

* * *

"Make no mistake, this is the deadliest professional assassin on the planet. They call him the Lion. He's been responsible for over fifty kills, that we know of, in the last twenty years. He won't be taken easily. Do not be fooled by his appearance. If he has to kill you to escape, he won't hesitate. I want him alive, though. ALIVE, people. Remember that!"

The SWAT team commander looked at his men, a stern expression fixed on his face.

"You heard Senior Special Agent Thompson. Take no chances with the target. Use less-lethal unless no alternative is available. Got that?" There was a halfhearted grumble of assent from the other team members.

The team commander turned to the man in charge.

"SSA Thompson, just how dangerous is this guy? I mean, without the hype."

"Let me put it this way, I've been tracking him for the last fifteen years. Not once have I come this close. I'm not willing to allow the bastard to go free. If it looks like he might escape, I will be the one to put a bullet in him." Thompson grunted as he finished the last sentence.

* * *

The team commander had the target in his sights. The two-dimensional image of the photographs they had studied a couple of hours before was now replaced with three-dimensional reality.

He was an elderly man, greying hair, tanned face, an outdoors type. He looked to be in shape, sinews moving in strong arms as he levered himself from the deck lounger. He did not move quickly, as if about to make a break for it, but Thompson had insisted they not underestimate the man. The commander dropped his hand to the X26 Taser holstered at his waist. He extracted the Taser with his left hand, his right still pointing the MP5 submachine gun at their target. His thumb flicked the safety switch up, and raised the less-lethal weapon to eye level. Unknown to him, two of his colleagues were performing the very same actions. All three fired at once.

* * *

The barbs from the Tasers embedded themselves in Todd McGee's chest and back. His body went rigid as three, five-second electrical discharges ripped into his torso. A strangled cry escaped from taut lips. McGee fell forward onto the deck, thudding solidly against the wooden floor. Another scream from the woman alongside. Green-garbed figures rushed toward the fallen man. A SWAT officer roughly pushed the woman to the deck, holding her down with his knee as handcuffs were applied.

The SWAT team commander leaned over McGee and dragged his arms behind his back. He trapped one in place with his leg then applied the cuffs to the other. A final ratcheted click. Target secured.

Senior Special Agent Thompson approached and knelt beside the prone form of the man he had been chasing for most of his career with the FBI. He pulled the man's shoulder up to stare into his face.

Something was not right.

Thompson released the target's shoulder and placed his fingers on the fallen man's neck.

"MEDIC! Get a paramedic here now! I can't feel a pulse."

* * *

It had been one of the longest weeks in Mary McGee's life. In part, it was the shock of seeing her husband die so suddenly in front of her; her absolute helplessness as she stood handcuffed watching the paramedics trying to revive him on their Malibu deck. In part, it was waiting for the other shoe to drop.

The Coroner's report was a farce. Massive heart failure. No mention of any potential effect of the Tasers. It read as if it was the first salvo in an operation to cover the asses of all involved, especially the SWAT team.

The Memorial service, following the cremation of Todd's remains after they had been released by the Los Angeles County Coroner, had been a well-attended affair. Both their children had flown back in time. Todd and Mary's many friends, private and work-related, turned out in force.

There was one unwelcome attendee. Senior Special Agent Thompson from the FBI stood apart from the throng, his eyes moving over the faces in the crowd as though searching for a lost relative amongst the mourners. After the service finished, he was also the last one to approach Mary and her family to offer his condolences. Mary's response had been a slap that sounded like a gunshot in the quiet crematory at Valley Oaks. Thompson would probably book her now for assaulting a Federal Agent, she thought. He was that sort of bastard.

Friday she had a date at the FBI offices on Wilshire Boulevard in Los Angeles. Thompson had called earlier in the week saying they needed to interview her, part of the investigation he was heading, he said. He stated a date and time. Mary hung up without uttering a word.

The tall, whitish-gray building imposed its solidity as

they exited the cab. Mary's daughter had accompanied her. An anonymous agent met them in the foyer and escorted them to the bank of elevators. Mary watched as the numbers flashed by and the car whisked them upward to a meeting with the person she now considered her personal nemesis.

They were shown to a small conference room, not the bleak interview room she was expecting. Thompson made them wait over ten minutes during which time the escort tried to cover his embarrassment by bringing coffee and even a plate of cookies. He must have known what the meeting was about. As he left, he placed a new box of tissues on the table near the two women.

Thompson eventually showed up looking as though he had run up the stairs from the ground floor.

"Mrs. McGee, I'm sorry I'm late…"

"I'm sorry I'm here," she responded with caustic cynicism.

This brought a cough from the FBI man. He looked at the other, younger woman.

"You are the daughter, Tessa, right? I remember you from the cemetery." He held out a hand in greeting, a tight smile showing yellowed teeth. The hand was ignored.

"I'm here as my parent's legal representative. As you probably already know, we have filed complaints with the FBI's Office of Professional Responsibility and the Criminal Courts. I'm not even sure we should be meeting today…"

"I'm sorry for your loss, ladies, but there is an ongoing investigation. Until I hear otherwise, I intend to—"

Mary McGee slapped her palm down hard on the wooden tabletop, causing the coffee cups to rattle, the box of tissues to jump.

"Listen up, you bastard," she began in a low, menacing tone. "Have you no feelings, no remorse for what you've done? You and your men barge into my house and murder my husband in front of me. You didn't even formally arrest him. You electrocuted him; stopped his heart. No attempt to explain why you were there. The last time thugs like you walked the planet was in Nazi Germany. Your career is over, Thompson. If it's the last thing I do, I will see you locked away for this."

Tessa patted her mother's arm and embraced her as deep sobs filled the room. Thompson pushed the box of tissues closer. His action went unheeded by both women. Minutes dragged by. Mary controlled her grief and stared at the agent through red-rimmed eyes, wordlessly cursing the man.

Her daughter broke the mute tension in the room.

"We still don't know why you and the SWAT agents were there at my folks' house." It sounded like a statement, but was clearly a question. Any answer would be breaking protocol for an open investigation, but the piercing green eyes of the younger woman defeated Thompson's resolve.

"We were going to arrest Mr. McGee on several counts of premeditated murder."

"What! Murder?"

"Assassination, more like. We believe he is the professional killer for hire known as 'the Lion'."

"That's preposterous! How can you…?" She shook her head, long blond, sun-streaked tresses flicking over her shoulders, the archetypal Californian girl. "How the hell did you arrive at that conclusion? My father is a security consultant."

"We believe that was a cover for his illegal activities as an international assassin."

More head shaking.

"Based on what, dammit? Some hunch you had one morning while eating a bagel? I have looked into you, Senior Special Agent Thompson, and it seems you have a certain… *fixation* on this 'Lion' person. You've been on his case for years with no results. Time's running out for you, isn't it? What happened? Retirement looming, and no suspects? Your pride got the better of you? You pick the first candidate you can think of? How can you possibly connect my father to the work of a professional assassin? You searched my parent's house, I'm told, after you murdered my father. Did you find anything to back up your claims?"

"Ms. McGee, it's true the investigation was getting nowhere. That I will admit. That was certainly the case until I thought of contrasting travel itineraries with the dates and times of the killings we know about. That took a lot of computing power. We had to seek Homeland Security's help. Anyway, the analysis told us most people travelling on the dates in question from destinations near to where the assassinations took place would only show up in a low percentage of all the cases. A couple of the incidents on average. Just coincidences. We found we had a shortlist of a little over a hundred people who had traveled from more than one of those destinations within a few days of the killings. Your father's name appeared in over twenty percent of the cases. That is well beyond any casual probability I know of. He was our prime suspect. No one came near him in that analysis."

Tessa let out a short, derisive laugh.

"Where were these killings, Senior Special Agent? Conferences, hi-tech companies, private upscale estates?"

"Most of them…"

"My father was a security consultant, as I've already told you. He designed and improved the protection measures around those same buildings for those very same clients. He was paid to analyze the measures in place, to assess their effectiveness, to recommend improvements..."

"Yet the assassin's targets still died." A smug smile accompanied Thompson's statement.

"My father makes recommendations. People don't have to implement them, though. That's how it goes. I work for that company, too, as do my mother and brother. Does that make us suspects in your investigation as well?"

"What roles do your family members have in your father's company?" Thompson took out his notebook, flicked it open to a blank page, extracted his cheap disposable pen, and sat poised to write.

"My mother handles logistics. My brother Mark is the electronics and computer systems expert, and I cover the financials and contracts as well as being the company's lawyer. It's a family business."

Thompson finished his notes and looked at the two women. He opened his mouth to speak but was cut off by Mary.

"Agent Thompson..." she began.

"Senior Special Agent Thompson."

Mary treated the man's interruption as though he had not spoken.

"Are you married?"

The question threw the FBI man off his stride.

"What?"

"I asked if you were married?" she repeated, her voice heavy with forced patience.

"I was. Twice."

"What happened?"

"The job." He kept his replies short, evidently wary of saying more.

"Okay, now I understand." Mary glanced at her daughter, exchanging one of those looks lasting only a fraction of a second that women use to convey long messages. "That's why you don't understand exactly what you've done. You see, you haven't just murdered my husband, Agent Thompson, you've killed me, too."

She paused, letting her enigmatic statement filter through Thompson's brain.

"You have two failed marriages because of your job. You want to know why? It's because you treat your life with your partner as separate from whatever you do at work. You are in both universes, or at least you try to be, at first, but your partner isn't. Sooner or later your partner's exclusion from the other universe you inhabit will start to grate on their nerves. You will tend to use your other existence as a refuge from the rejection you feel at home. Then you'll end up spending far more time away from your marriage doing stuff related to your job. The result is usually divorce. You had no unity, no balance, no complicity in your life."

"I don't see where this is going…"

"Todd and I met a long time ago through our respective professions. We collaborated, then fell in love. We partnered not just as a married couple but in our professional lives, too. We supported each other constantly through all the problems our work threw in our way. We shared the triumphs and the failures. The highs and the lows. We were a unit, a single entity in many respects. That is why our marriage worked and lasted so long. Sure we argued; it was a sign we cared. Cared about what we did, and about each other. The quarrels also meant one of us hadn't subjugated the other, hadn't canceled the other's personality. Couples who never argue are not in a marriage; they're in a dictatorship. What you have done, Agent Thompson, is demolish that wonderful creation. Ruined what it took us decades to achieve in one moment of self-serving blindness. Our marriage was our business, our profession. You will not be forgiven for this."

"Are you threatening me Mrs. McGee?" His tone held menace.

"I wouldn't stoop so low, Thompson."

A nervous stillness invaded the room. For over half a minute no one spoke.

Tessa finally cleared her throat and started to stand.

"If that's all, Senior Special Agent, we'll be leaving."

Thompson said nothing.

The two women left the conference room and took the elevator to the ground floor. A few minutes later they boarded a cab heading north.

They traveled in silence. Other than to give the driver the address of an oyster restaurant on Ocean Drive in Santa Monica, neither woman spoke during the twenty-minute drive. The table had been reserved the day before. They sat alongside each other with their backs to the window and the view of the sea. That would make lip-reading through high-powered lenses almost impossible. The transparent plastic awning around the terrace outside also helped. Tessa removed a device that looked like a cell phone from her bag and surreptitiously attached it to the windowpane. She pushed the slider switch on one side and the jammer started up. It sent subtle vibrations through the glass and emitted a white-noise masking signal which, when combined, would make attempts to listen through laser or long-range microphones useless. The additional hubbub from other patrons would make their conversation as private as they could hope to achieve. They were almost certain Senior Special Agent Thompson would have detailed a surveillance crew to follow them. He was desperate to justify his actions as time ticked away to his retirement date. If he could show the death of Todd McGee had happened during the attempted arrest of a professional assassin, he would be vindicated, at least in his own eyes.

They placed their order, a half-dozen grilled oysters and the establishment's famous lobster roll for both. A bottle of cold Sauvignon Blanc from the Napa Valley. Tessa leaned close to her mother's ear and spoke in a low tone.

"Mom, can I ask you a question that's been on my mind for a while?"

"Sure."

"When you and Dad met and married, were you in love?"

The question, had it been asked by any other daughter of any other mother, might have seemed odd. However…

"At first our marriage was a convenient way to do business. As you know, some of our clients in the Arab countries frown on women in business, which makes it difficult to earn contracts there. Being married did make a difference though. For my work, it also meant people didn't look too closely at why I accompanied your father on his trips. My particular perspective allowed him to stand out in a very competitive industry and, at the same time, benefited me. We had been working as a married couple for almost four years before we realized we had fallen in love. Crazy, isn't it? They say arranged marriages are more solid than the more natural sort, and I guess ours was '*arranged*,' albeit by us. We certainly had a good one for almost forty years."

"I think it's rather sweet. Did Dad know what you did from the beginning?"

"Yes. His consultancy was failing. Clients not paying, that sort of thing. So when I came on the scene, we exploited those clients, and I was able to help by injecting cash into the legitimate side of the business. Symbiotic, I guess you could call it, but it worked well for both of us."

Tessa paused, running the meeting with Thompson through her mind. "What do you think he's going to do next?"

"Thompson? Well he's under a lot of pressure to conclude his investigation. You said he was retiring in eight weeks, right?"

Tessa nodded.

"Then he will probably pull out all the stops to prove his hunch about Todd was correct. We can expect agents following us twenty-four seven, our phones bugged, probably the house, too. You need to tell your brother to sweep every day, and nothing important is to be said indoors. They'll be digging into our bank accounts also, personal and the company. They won't find the offshore accounts. When their Office of Professional Responsibility starts to investigate Thompson's actions, that will make him even more inclined to do something stupid. It's going to be a difficult time for you and your brother. Are there any contracts in the next few weeks?"

"One. South Africa. I was prepping it when you called about Dad. I can put it on hold though, or even subcontract if necessary. Mark hasn't got anything scheduled for the next three months. The Hong Kong trip was to collect for the last job in Asia."

"Okay. That's good. Downtime for everyone..."

"But you're not going to stand idly by and let Thompson get away with what he did, are you, Mom?"

"Of course not! That man doesn't know what's coming his way. I need to tie up a few things first, though." She paused. "When you lose your life partner through natural causes, even accidental death, it must be devastating. When they are murdered right in front of your eyes... there are no words to describe what I feel right now. It's just a big, black emptiness."

* * *

It had been a long day for the FBI SWAT team. A joint raid with the Drug Enforcement Agency in the early hours of the morning led to seventeen arrests, all following an anonymous tip. Then, toward midday, another call from the same source had informed of a homegrown terrorist group planning an attack on a soft target, a shopping mall. They had been returning from the first call and were still geared up when the order to divert to the old Californian bungalow near the Los Angeles Memorial Coliseum had been received. That operation had netted them over a hundred kilos of ANFO explosive, several submachine guns, and six perps. With a huge sigh of relief, the team had trudged toward their Lenco Bearcat armored vehicle just in time to learn their unidentified informant had called in yet another tip. This time it was a self-storage locker containing Semtex explosive, placed there by a pro-ISIS group. The address given was not far from their last operation, so it was clear who was expected to respond. At least a storage locker was a fairly low-risk situation. They would secure the premises and wait for the FBI Bomb Techs to arrive. The place could be booby-trapped. The team was tired after the day's accumulated activity. Not the best time to be on top of their game.

They waited for thirty minutes before the Bomb Techs appeared, checked the locker in question, and pronounced it safe for a breach. There was Semtex inside, stacked in ubiquitous orange bricks in one of the far corners, but far fewer than the haul their caller had promised. Had they been less tired at this juncture, maybe, just maybe, they might have started to question the string of tips.

The FBI SWAT team commander waited until the Bomb Techs had loaded the explosives into their own transport before ordering a final sweep of the area. They already had the details about who had rented the unit, and another FBI team was on its way to the renter's address. It would turn out to be a false lead.

Finally, the call came to board their Bearcat truck and head back to base. The weary men climbed into the back of the vehicle as the commander took his seat up front with the driver. The three-hundred horsepower Caterpillar engine roared into life. The day was over for the team, at least that's what they hoped.

They had traveled just two blocks.

Ahead, a street junction.

A single figure walking near the intersection.

The Bearcat's driver slowed.

The pedestrian was an elderly woman wearing a floral

dress, oversized sunglasses, and an expansive straw hat with a large, bright-red, paper flower, something the few witnesses would focus on later in their descriptions rather than the woman's face. She stepped off the sidewalk into the path of the SWAT vehicle. The driver reacted by applying the brakes hard. The powered hydraulic ABS disk brakes squealed as they brought the seventeen-ton vehicle to a juddering halt. The woman's scream was lost inside the armored cocoon of the tactical truck. Her collapse into the middle of the road was visible to the driver and commander though.

"We never made contact! She must be deaf if she didn't hear us coming," said the driver.

"And blind," added the commander as he cracked open the passenger door.

The commander approached the fallen form and leaned over the old woman. He reached an arm around her waist and held her proffered left arm with his own right hand. He did not suspect anything until the microsecond before it was too late.

A cold, metal object jabbed under the bottom of his bulletproof combat vest. With a dull pop, a deadly projectile penetrated his torso below the sternum, raced upward through his left lung, smashed into his heart.

The woman took the strain of the man's weight easily, lifting him erect in a way that the driver thought the opposite to be true. Now matters speeded up. Shedding her elderly sloth, the old woman let go of the SWAT commander's corpse and, in two long strides, reached the open door of the Bearcat truck. She extended her arm and fired the Russian-made PSS Silent Pistol again. A headshot at the man behind the wheel. From inside the vehicle's cargo area, the other team members did not hear the firing weapon over the growl of the Bearcat's engine.

Another rush forward. Two steps up into the cabin. The hat flew away to reveal a younger face beneath.

"Hi boys. Remember me?" she said loud enough to draw the attention of the tired men in the back of the SWAT truck.

Four spherical, green M67 fragmentation grenades bounced into the cargo bay of the Bearcat. Instantly recognizable to the SWAT team, they induced sudden panic as the crew fought to open the rear doors and escape the deadly blast.

Four short seconds of yells, thuds, an inhuman scream. The half-inch of high-tech ballistic steel protecting the SWAT team from outside aggressors now made for an effective killing ground for the grenades' five-meter lethal blast radius.

Four seconds.

Time to await instant oblivion for some.

Time for the assassin to hurl herself toward the fallen commander's body, seeking shelter beneath his bulk from the hell unleashed.

* * *

Another week. Another cemetery. This time, multiple funerals with all the pomp the FBI could muster for their fallen. After the priest had said more words at the gravesites. After the piper had played 'Amazing Grace.' After the twenty-one gun salute. After the folding of flags and their subsequent conveyance to next of kin. After the lowering of the caskets. After the queue of people waiting to throw a handful of dirt into the open graves. After tears and sadness. After hugs and condolences. After almost all had departed. Only then had Senior Special Agent Ryan Thompson approached the gravesite of the commander of the FBI SWAT team. In all honesty, he had hardly known the man; could not say he was a friend. But then, SSA Thompson had so few he could include in that category.

The sun sliced through a cloudless blue sky, glinting off his prominently displayed FBI badge with its black band of mourning. Thompson squinted as he looked around at the now-empty last resting place for so many. He felt warm in his dark suit. Uncomfortable, perhaps, at this nearness to the end of the journey. Retirement would come soon, very soon. Another journey over, with nothing in particular to look forward to afterward. He stood, facing the hole in the ground, looking at the dirt-spattered wood below without really focusing his eyes. Thinking, musing on the last week.

Thursday, the day after the attack on the SWAT team, had been his birthday. Two colleagues had remembered and brought him a single cupcake with a lonely candle. He'd smiled and done his duty, then invited them for a drink and lunch. Both had refused with thanks, citing meetings for ongoing cases. A couple of cards appeared on his desk. One from his coworkers, indecipherable scribbles purporting to be from the rest of the office's occupants. One from someone in LAPD.

At home, he had received none. His smartphone had pinged indicating a notification. He had mail. Sitting in the inbox of his personal email account was a single electronic greeting card sent through a popular Internet site. It was addressed to him by his full, official title. FBI Senior Special Agent Ryan Thompson. It was not signed.

It read '*The Lion has avenged the murder of an innocent man.*'

He had stood there in the midst of the bustling office for over two minutes, staring at the single line of text. Then his training kicked in. He made a beeline for the Computer Forensics department and had the sending email address traced. Dead end. Just created for the purpose of requesting the greeting card. The card had been selected over a week before and had been scheduled for delivery that morning. The tech had woven his magic and somehow obtained the IP address of the computer used to send the card to the greetings service. He had laughed aloud when the results came back. The IP address was for his own laptop at home. He had not sent this, of that he was sure. How many might believe this amongst his colleagues was another matter.

So the Lion had chosen, or been contracted, to avenge Todd McGee's death by eliminating the SWAT team. There was only one candidate for the contractor in his mind. The widow. They had been running surveillance on the whole family since the arrest incident. He called the team assigned and was told all three, the mother, the daughter, and the son, had left the US two days before the attack on the SWAT team. Destination South America. Their Malibu home was up for sale. Paperwork had been put in to reregister their company, Todd McGee's business, in Panama. That just gave them an alibi for the attack. It didn't absolve them of possible responsibility for it.

Thompson shook his head. He had a feeling all the leads he thought he had on identifying the Lion were turning out to be so much smoke. He had identified the travel patterns of Todd McGee, forced his conclusions past his supervisor to get an arrest warrant approved, while all the time admitting to himself the nagging doubt he harbored. As the family had said, McGee's job could easily have taken him to those places. What also stood out was that McGee had traveled under his real name. Surely if he was the Lion he would have used a false identity. Then, some days after his death, the Lion had claimed responsibility for the slaying of the SWAT agents.

Was there more than one Lion? Should he go back to the NSA-supplied data and see who else had been traveling from the places where the assassinations had taken place? Had he overlooked something in his obsession to close this case before they put him out to pasture?

He feared becoming another ex-Fed pursuing a neurotic fixation on an old unsolved case until he died... or until his digging prompted the Lion to come for him, too. Should he just accept the situation as it was, forget about everything, pull up roots and move to Florida or Baja and spend his days fishing?

Thompson raised his head and let his eyes wander over the gravestones. His ears picked up the silence of the cemetery, broken only by the occasional chirping of birds and the fluttering of flags. Flags? He turned and followed the movement of the red, white and blue with his eyes. Six flags in all, stuck in the ground near plots, forming a rough line to the far side of the cemetery. Wait! There was a rag or something caught in a tree branch further out. His brain sorted the data into a recognizable pattern. The Flags, the rag. They were wind indicators. There was a sniper out there somewhere. The Lion.

Far off in the distance, he saw a single, bright flash of light. Almost immediately he heard a whining buzz, like a bee on steroids, getting louder. He became aware of a dull thud and felt motion. Thompson did not see the fifty-caliber bullet leave a fist-sized hole in his upper torso. He did not see the same projectile smash into the gray stone of a grave marker behind him. Did not watch the shards scatter, the plume of white dust linger in the air.

Senior Special Agent Ryan Thompson had been propelled backward into the open grave of the SWAT commander. The dirt thrown on top of the casket darkened as it soaked up the blood from his mangled corpse.

* * *

"Kill shot!" whispered Mark McGee from under the tarpaulin.

"One more bastard down," replied his sister, lying alongside. "It won't bring back Dad, or make Mom any less sad, but I must say it was satisfying. Fifteen hundred meters, give or take."

"Your eleventh confirmed kill with that thing."

In the darkness beneath the tarp she nodded. Both began to dismantle their equipment. Tessa removed the short magazine from beneath the rifle, then pulled back the bolt to eject the spent cartridge. She unscrewed the long suppressor from the RPA Rangemaster rifle, folded the stock along the weapon's left-hand side. They had to move with speed now. Despite the efficient sound suppressor, the rifle's large caliber had meant the shot would have been heard. It was only a matter of time before someone came to investigate.

Mark rolled out from the tarpaulin and dragged it off his sister. They had been lying on the roof of a mausoleum situated at the southern edge of the cemetery since before dawn. Waiting behind them, on the other side of the surrounding wall, was a red Honda Accord, the most popular car on Los Angeles roads this year, easy to mingle in unnoticed with traffic as they made their way north toward San Francisco and the freighter waiting to take them back to South America. North, opposite the direction in which the Feds would initially look.

Mark folded the tarp into a large black sports bag then held it open as Tessa placed the rifle, magazine, suppressor and spotter scope on top, covering them with the two sniper mats they had been using. The tarp, a potential source of DNA, would be burned within the hour; the weapon would be cleaned and returned to their cache for future use in jobs that brought them back to the States. A steady seven-hour drive up Interstate Five awaited, a reunion with their mother, then a slow ride for all on a container ship to Panama.

They made their way to the back of the roof, dropped the aluminum ladder to the ground, descended, used the ladder again to climb over the perimeter wall. The weapons bag was stowed out of sight in the trunk, and the folded ladder put in front of the back seat. They boarded the nondescript car and set off at a leisurely pace.

"Sis, do you think Thompson would have figured it out in the end?"

"I don't know. Maybe? Why? Are you asking me if I think this was justified?"

"No, hell, no. This wasn't about revenge, I get that. Mom needed to punish the people responsible for ending her marriage to Dad. She's gone from complete happiness to outright depression in less than a week. I'm worried about her."

"When we get back, I've been thinking of hiring an oceangoing cruiser to take us around the Caribbean for a couple of months. Perhaps spending time away from the rest of the world, taking things one day at a time, will help us all deal with Dad's passing."

"That's a great idea. Count me in."

"No Internet or phones. We'll check in with the news, if there is any, when we dock, wherever we happen to be. If the FBI ends up on our tail, we'll know about it soon enough."

"I guess I could live without being connected for a while. What about Thompson though? Would he have put the pieces together eventually?"

"That's academic now. Hell, Mark, had he been doing his job right in the first place, he should have realized that in any pride of lions, it's the females that do the hunting and killing."

Q&A with Eric J. Gates

I love stories that surprise the reader. This one takes you all the way to the end, and then has a big reveal that turns everything around. Did you know exactly where it was going the whole time?

Yes. My writing method involves starting at the end. If I can sit down and write the last chapter of a book, or last few paragraphs of a short story, then I know I have a solid premise. Then I work on the opening sequence. Once the start and finish of the journey are defined, I'm writing to an objective so the pace and direction of the tale is maintained.

Do you draw from your fascinating work background and your own international travels when coming up with new stories?

Very much so, particularly in this short story. Writing thrillers is, for me, taking the reader to places and events on the extremes of experience and making those situations real by grounding them in the mundane. We have all seen the kind of obsession that drives ordinary men, like the FBI agent in the tale, to make wrong calls, even if the scale of the consequences is not so deadly. By making this *extreme reading*, the thriller writer hooks the readers into the tale and plunges them into unknown territory.

What are you writing now?

I am currently working on *Chasing Shadows*, the sequel to *Leaving Shadows*, about the kidnap recover team that does occasional work for British Intelligence. In the sequel, they are on a mission to rescue a Canadian geologist being held in a West-African nation. However, they have not been told everything they need to know, and soon, matters take on a deadly turn.

After that, I'll be writing book 5 in "the CULL" series, *Blood Kill*. This will be the last in the series (for now?) and I've promise CULL fans that it's going to be explosive!

Where can readers find you to connect and learn about new books?

I can be contacted (email) directly through my website, or via Twitter, FaceBook and Goodreads. There are extracts from all my novels, interviews, and articles, as well as a competition in which anyone can win a character named after them in a future book (over fifteen winners so far)... and there are the Winks, inside secrets behind the pages of each of the books. I also run a blog where guest writers talk about distinct aspects of this crazy profession.

Links:

Website: www.ericjgates.com
Amazon Author page: www.amazon.com/Eric-J.-Gates/e/B0030H3Y3A/
Goodreads: www.goodreads.com/author/show/4078563.Eric_J_Gates
Blog: my-thrillers.blogspot.com/
Twitter: www.twitter.com/eThrillerWriter
Facebook: www.facebook.com/Eric.J.Gates/

Two Faces

by H.B. Moore

ONE

New York City, 1911

Sometimes I hear him whisper at night. And before I'm completely awake, when caught between the world of dreams and reality, I reach for Simon. As my hand touches the cold sheets and empty space, I awaken fully. And then I listen. If I'm very still, I can hear his movements in the attic above me. On the nights he tells me to lock him in there, he doesn't sleep. He wanders. He talks to himself. And sometimes, he cries. Tonight, he is silent.

This worries me the most. Because my greatest fear is that when I unlock the attic door in the morning to let my husband out into the light, he won't be there.

TWO

Sometime earlier

"Look at you, Vivian. You're beautiful in the morning," Simon tells me as he pulls me against him. I'm wearing nothing but a thin nightgown. We've just returned from our honeymoon in Paris and my new husband's desire for me hasn't lessened.

I wrap my arms about his bare shoulders and kiss his still damp cheek. I hadn't meant to walk in on him while he is shaving and completing his morning ritual, but I know his valet is out sick, so I am not as careful as usual about appearing in my sleep attire.

Simon Wood and I have only known each other a few short months, but I've been watching him for much longer. The moment he asked for a place on my dance card, I had let myself hope that the most eligible bachelor in New York City might choose me over the hundreds of swooning debutantes.

The Andersons' ball was one of the first of the season, and at the age of twenty, I'd been to plenty of balls, and was feeling a bit disgruntled that evening. It seemed the only men who paid attention to me were the ones green about the ears and not yet able to afford a wife, or older, widowed gentlemen who were looking only for a mother to their brats. Not that I didn't like children, or didn't wish for any of my own, I just didn't want to raise someone else's.

Now, as Simon's hands slide across my shoulders and down my back, I release a sigh. Simon is worth the death-glares I received that night at the ball and the malicious gossip that followed me every moment thereafter. I'd lost friends over him. My best friend, Elizabeth, was the hardest to lose, but if she couldn't be happy that Simon chose me over her, then I suppose she hadn't been a true friend after all.

For that's how I came to learn so much about Simon. Elizabeth was practically stalking him, reading every snippet of news in the society papers and even clipping out his pictures. Her obsession amused me at first, but when I saw him in person months before that first dance, I became smitten myself.

The weeks during which he courted me were a whirlwind, and even though I wrote every night in my diary, I still can't believe half of the events that happened. When Simon proposed marriage, musicales and dances throughout the city were canceled because if Simon Wood was no longer eligible, then there was no purpose for the matrons to spend money hosting an event that held no opportunity for their daughters.

As Simon begins to kiss me, I close my eyes with triumph. I have won Simon. He is mine now. My husband. And tonight we'll host an exclusive dinner party as the newest newlywed couple in New York City, and those in attendance will envy my good fortune.

THREE

The dinner is seven courses; nothing but the best for New York's elite. Both of my parents are in attendance along with my younger brother. The Andersons, the Phillips, and the Lovells have all been invited as well. Simon was quite particular about who would be invited tonight, and I have yet to discover the reason. The scent of money practically oozes from our guests, filling the dining room of our estate home with excitement and energy.

When Simon stands to offer a toast, the room falls quiet.

He flashes me a smile, then reaches for my hand. I lift my hand and settle it into his firm, warm grasp.

"Tonight I'd like to offer two toasts, one to my lovely bride," Simon announces.

Everyone smiles, and a few of the ladies make cooing sounds. I don't mind because Simon is gazing at me with all the adoration I could ever dream of. "Vivian, when I first saw you at the Anderson ball," he says and casts Mrs. Anderson an exaggerated wink, "I thought I had walked into paradise and spied an angel."

Mrs. Anderson giggles like a young girl, and my own heart soars.

I know it's impossible to be perfect, but Simon is perfect for me, and I feel so proud watching him as everyone else looks up to and admires him, not only for his business in the railroad industry but for the way he draws in people. He makes a striking, and at times, imposing figure, in his well-tailored suit, with his intense blue eyes contrasting against the deep black of his hair.

Simon continues praising me until I'm blushing, and then he says, "My next toast is to our guests tonight. I have a special announcement to make. I've successfully acquired Tanner Shipping and will add it to my business holdings. Because of this, I've invited each of you to this exclusive dinner to hear my proposal." His gaze moves about the table, including Mr. Anderson, Mr. Phillips, Mr. Lovell, and my parents. "I'm offering exclusive partnership equity to our guests here tonight."

Gasps echo around the table, and then everyone starts clapping. Mrs. Phillips wipes tears from her eyes. Mr. Lovell stands and folds Simon into a hug. As if on cue, our servers enter the dining room with two bottles of champagne and start pouring the sparkling liquid into crystal flutes.

I stare in wonder at Simon. He is the most generous, the most loving, and the most thoughtful man alive.

It isn't until hours later, when I'm alone in my bed for the first time since my wedding night, that the first doubt creeps in.

FOUR

"Simon?" I whisper as I walk through the doors separating our dual master bedchamber. Despite there being a *master* side and a *mistress* side, he's been spending the nights in my bed, curled against me, keeping me in his arms.

So it is with surprise that I awaken to an empty bed. Perhaps he couldn't sleep. My father is known for reading in the early hours of the morning when he can't sleep for one worry or another. Perhaps Simon is the same way, and now that we are off our honeymoon and his business decisions are facing him once again, his patterns have returned.

I pad barefooted across his bedchamber, but even in the glow of the moonlight spilling from the tall windows, I can see that his bed hasn't been slept in. The royal blue coverlet is as smooth as ever.

I'm grateful the servants' rooms are below the kitchen

stairs and they won't hear me creeping around. I don't relish the thought of running into one of them in the dark. Just to be sure, I light an oil lamp even though Simon had the house retrofitted with electric lights when he inherited from his father.

The shadows of the hallway leap away from me as I walk toward the top of the stairs. I peer down the wide staircase to see if there's light spilling from the library or the drawing room, but I see only dark doorways.

It is then I start to worry—the worry that many women have about their husbands who do not share their bed at night. I wonder if my new husband has a mistress, a woman whom I know nothing about, a woman whom he's missed this past month while we were in Europe, a woman he couldn't wait to get back to.

I fetch my stitching sampler from the drawing room and take it to my bedchamber, where I put my nervous hands to work as I try to calm my mind.

FIVE

The sky is just softening to gray when Simon comes in the front door. He's not even trying to be quiet. He's not stealing in like a guilty man hiding something. The door snaps as he shuts it, and he takes off his hat and removes his coat on his own. I am sitting at the top of the stairs, keeping vigil, as our butler Ronald won't rise for at least another hour.

"Simon," I say as he starts up the steps. "I've been worried about you."

He stops on the step and looks up. Even in the gray

dawn, I can see that his eyes are bloodshot. His white shirt beneath his vest is rumpled and stained. Alcohol? Lipstick? I rise to my feet.

And then he smiles—a slow smile that I love, a smile he reserves just for me.

"You waited up for me, my dear wife?"

I am breathless, doubts and questions colliding in my mind. "I did." Do I demand to know where he went? Am I to be a petulant wife?

He continues up the stairs, and as he nears, I smell a bit of brandy, but it's not overly strong. And he isn't swaying or stumbling like a drunkard. Before I can analyze what the marks on his sleeves might be, he wraps an arm about me and steers me down the hallway toward our bedchamber.

"You are sweet, Vivian, to worry about me so," Simon says in a low voice.

A pleasant shiver runs along my skin, warm at his touch, yet a bit of wariness accompanies it. I try another question. "Were you out walking? Perhaps riding? Thinking of your business dealings?"

His laugh is soft. "Yes, I was," he says, not exactly answering my question. "And now I've made you lose sleep." He stops me and spins me toward him. I nearly drop the oil lamp that has long since burned out. The corridor is dim, the only light coming from the space by the stairs. But his blue eyes are bright enough to capture my own. His eyes look less tired now, and perhaps I've imagined the redness I thought I saw.

"I can't have my bride miss her beauty sleep," he says, kissing me on the forehead then pulling me close. "In the future, when I become a wanderer in the night, do not worry."

I don't know what he means about being a wanderer. He leads me by the hand back to our bedchamber, and even as I finally fall asleep in the new dawn of morning, I can't forget my apprehension.

SIX

The invitations are endless, and I sort through them by making two piles as I sit in my private drawing room. In the first pile go invitations that I must—or want—to accept, which consists mostly of ladies' luncheons. The second pile comprises invitations that I'll consult with Simon about.

We have been back in New York for two months now, and the hot stickiness of summer is in full bloom. Simon was gone again last night and twice the week before. I said nothing to him, but this morning I discovered that he'd crawled back into his own bed. And with noon approaching, I finally hear him walking around upstairs. I straighten the stacks and then wait.

I tell myself I should be glad that I'm the one who Simon seeks out first thing when he awakens, and that he is always pleased to see me. Frankly, he spoils me, but he still hasn't told me what he's doing on the nights he leaves.

"Vivian," Simon's voice sails through the room, and I rise from my chair to greet him. He crosses to me, and kisses my cheek, lingering for a moment, and I feel tingles rush through me.

I try to tamp them down, because I should focus on discovering where my husband goes at night. But Simon has a way of making me forget what my intentions are, and I become swept up in all that is him.

"Invitations?" he asks, stepping toward the desk where my two neat piles lay.

I explain the separated piles, and he quirks a brow at me in amusement, then he sorts through the invitations for the ladies' luncheons. "Mrs. Lovell's is tomorrow afternoon," he observes. "Are you going to her home?"

"Yes, I'd like to," I say, wondering at his interest. "Her husband is soon to be one of your partners."

"Correct," Simon says with a smile, setting the invitation back on the stack. "She is a quiet woman, very withdrawn. I think she could use a friend."

My husband is very observant and very sweet. "I quite agree," I say. And we spend the next half hour going through the rest of the invitations and deciding which ones we are able to accept.

By the time Simon leaves my drawing room, he has promised to accompany me to the Phillips for an evening musicale. "I'll return before the appointed hour." He gives me a quick kiss, then is gone.

I smile to myself, pleased with my married life for the most part. I push any further worries to the back of my mind.

SEVEN

"Simon," I call out in a breathless voice as I enter his bedchamber. I have run up the stairs, my full skirts clutched in my hand. He is with his valet, John, preparing for the evening musicale, and both men turn.

I look from one to another, and Simon says to John, "I'll call for you in a moment."

John nods, glances at me, then exits the room.

"I've just returned from visiting with Mrs. Lovell," I say, even though I now think of her as poor Bethany.

Simon's blue gaze is curious as he watches me, listening.

"As you suggested, I took extra care to befriend her, and we spent time together after the other women had left the luncheon," I say, remembering the beautiful white and gold parlor we sat in while we shared our backgrounds. "It was when she was pointing out the miniature portraits of her family members that I noticed a dark bruising above her wrists. When I asked her about it, she acted as if she didn't know what I was talking about."

Simon grasped my hand, concern in his gaze, and I found myself clinging to his strong warm fingers.

"When I pressed my case, Bethany broke down," I say, tears coming to my own eyes, and my voice hitching with emotion. "She told me that her husband… Mr. Lovell… can be quite strict and controlling."

My shoulders begin to shake, and I start to cry, thinking of how awful Bethany's married life has been. She is so sweet and elegant and her husband seems so dignified. But all is not always as it appears.

Simon pulls me into his arms and holds me, whispering soothing words.

"I'll find a way to speak to Mr. Lovell," he says. "But for now, your friendship will be invaluable to Mrs. Lovell."

I nod against Simon's chest, knowing that he'll have to change into a fresh shirt. I've quite soiled his current one. Somehow I need to pull myself together, trust in my husband, and attend the Phillips' musicale as if we have no concerns in the world.

EIGHT

The silence wakes me, and I turn immediately toward Simon to find his side of the bed empty. He is gone. I push up onto my elbows and scan the dark room. The moon is waning tonight, and there's only a sliver of light across the floor. The door adjoining our bedchamber is closed, but I can't remember if it was open or closed when we tumbled into bed the night before, Simon scooping me into his arms and kissing me.

I listen to the sounds of the house for a moment and hear nothing. I know that it's futile to look in the library or his adjoining bedchamber. My husband must be on one of his night walks.

I pull the covers about me and close my eyes, trying to get back to sleep so that I'm not a tired hostess for all the commitments I have the following day. But my mind will not rest, and my stomach twists and turns at the questions running through my head as I wonder what Simon does on his nightly walks.

And then I hear a quiet click. I sit up again, not moving, not breathing, but listening intently. A creak, then a whisper of cloth, and a light spills beneath the crack of Simon's door.

Before I can talk myself out of it, I climb out of bed and reach for my robe. Tying it securely about me, I walk barefoot across my floor and open the adjoining door. My breath stalls at the sight of my husband, his shirt stripped and discarded on the floor, and his naked back sporting several prominent bruises. He's bent over the washbasin, scrubbing his face.

I gasp, and the sound causes him to turn. His eyes are wild, his hair a mess, his jaw clenched, his lips twisted, and there are more bruises on his neck.

"What's happened?" I say, rooted to the place where I stand in the doorway. He reminds me of a wild animal, and fear shoots through me—fear of my own husband. "Were you mugged?"

His eyes flash away from me, and his gaze goes to the shirt on the floor. I look at the shirt as well, and a new horror rises in my throat. A great deal of blood stains the shirt.

"Simon?" I whisper. My body has started to tremble.

He's looking at me again, and something almost imperceptible changes in his eyes. They are calmer now, and his face relaxes back into something that I recognize. He reaches for a nearby towel and rubs it along his face and neck. "Yes," he says in a raspy voice. "I was mugged near the park."

"Oh my poor dear." I move toward him.

He holds up his hand. "I need to get cleaned up."

I hang back as he dips his hands into the water time and time again and proceeds to clean his face, neck, and torso. And when he is finally clean and has dried himself, he picks up the discarded shirt and rolls it into a tight bundle. "I should burn this."

"What happened, Simon?" I ask, still trembling from distress that my husband was attacked and injured. What if the outcome had been worse?

"I didn't get a good look at the man." He glances at me before he opens the door to the hallway. "I'll return in a moment."

I sink onto the edge of his bed while I wait. I look over at the basin of water, darkened now with his washing off of dirt and blood. The sight of it constricts my stomach enough that I think I might grow sick. I look away and focus on my breathing. But that only makes my head throb.

When Simon returns, it seems that ages have passed, and he takes my hand, pulling me to my feet. He leads me into my bedroom. It's a long time before I fall asleep to my husband's steady breathing.

NINE

Mrs. Phillips calls on me soon after the breakfast hour. I am surprised to have a visitor so early, but when I see her pale face, I shoo the maid out of the drawing room.

"It's so terrible," Mrs. Phillips says, her round form quivering as tears spill down her cheeks.

"Whatever has happened?" I cross to her and take her hands in mine.

"Mr. Lovell—have you not heard?" she asks.

I shake my head and wonder what news she's brought. My heart starts to pound before she speaks again.

"He was found strangled in the stable behind his house," Mrs. Phillips says in a choked voice.

The first thought that cuts through my mind is sympathy for his wife Bethany. Although her husband was abusing her, as a widow she will be devastated.

"The police have yet to find the… murderer," Mrs. Phillips' tone drops to a whisper on the last word.

I shudder along with her, and then it's as if the sky has suddenly filled with clouds, and the drawing room had grown dark. When Simon returned last night, he had bruises on his neck. Had the same man who'd killed Mr. Lovell attacked my Simon? Had I almost lost my husband?

Simon promised me he would put in a report with the police this morning. Perhaps he is there now and they're comparing the two events.

I lead Mrs. Phillips to the sofa, and we sit together, clasping hands, as we try to decide how to help our friend Bethany Lovell.

A maid knocks and enters, bringing the society paper as I've asked her to do each morning.

The headlines scream the announcement of Mr. Lovell's tragic death. I scan the two articles on the front page. One details how Mr. Lovell's body was discovered, another says that there are several suspects, including Mrs. Lovell. Not for a moment do I think that someone as sweet and shy as Bethany could commit murder.

I turn to Mrs. Phillips. "We must stop the delivery of the newspapers to the Lovell's home for the time being," I say. "News of the investigation and other details of her husband's death printed in the papers will be too distressing."

"I can send a note to the newspaper office," Mrs. Phillips says, drying her eyes.

"What about Bethany's family?" I ask. "What sort of help does she have?"

"Her parents and father-in-law are in good health." Mrs.

Phillips says. "They will be putting together the funeral arrangements."

"We must be Bethany's support then." Firm resolve courses through me. While the Lovell family members take care of the details of the funeral, I can be Bethany's friend.

TEN

"I don't want you over there," Simon tells me that afternoon as I am preparing to visit Bethany.

I turn from my vanity mirror. "Why ever not? She's grieving and needs a friend."

Simon crosses the room and places his warm hands on my shoulders. He leans down to kiss my cheek. "You may write to her, but the house and grounds are still an investigation area for the police. Until they finish their examination, it's not a good idea for us to be there in the way."

What he says makes sense but I feel sorry for Bethany, in that mansion of hers, unable to receive friends who would comfort her. "I'll send her a note then," I say, wondering if I can be satisfied with just that.

I look up at Simon, wondering why he is home so early.

"Did you meet with the police?" I ask.

His eyes seem to blank out for a moment, and then he says, "I did. I gave them as many details as I could, but I'm afraid I can't identify the man."

I take a deep breath. "What if the man who attacked you was the one who killed Mr. Lovell?" My voice cracks as the emotions spills out.

Simon's smile is soft, and he draws me to my feet and

wraps me in his arms. When he is holding me like this, it's hard to remember my fears and worries. When I'm in Simon's arms everything is all right in my world.

"Whoever it was, the police are now on the lookout." He runs a hand along my back in a comforting motion, and I close my eyes and try to forget my fears. Here, now, my husband is safe. I need to be grateful for that. "Promise me you'll stay away from the Lovell's home for now," he says again.

If I wasn't feeling so relaxed, I might have protested. As it is, I'm determined to send a note right away to Bethany. But Simon distracts me, and before I know it, it's time to prepare for our dinner guests. Although such a terrible thing happened in the Lovell family, Simon tells me that we must continue forward with all of our plans.

I feel odd about hosting guests when I can't imagine what Bethany is going through. She and her husband were supposed to come tonight as well. But it takes only moments for the maids to clear away the two extra place settings.

ELEVEN

The music, the laughter, and the combined scents of ladies' perfumes begin to create a throbbing in my head. I've drunk too much wine, that I know with assurance. And I've smiled for far too long, pretending that I'm enjoying our guests and that I'm not begging inside for them to go home.

The men are in deep conversation, likely discussing the Lovells, and the women are discussing the upcoming horse race—the first of the season.

My gaze flits to Simon, to see how he is faring. His eyes are bright and attentive, his posture erect, his high collar hiding his bruised neck, and I realize that perhaps I'm the only one in the room feeling weighed down. I desperately want to make my excuses and return to my bedchamber, but as hostess, I cannot. Finally, when the midnight hour draws near, our guests make their motions to leave and it's all I can do not to push them out the door. After the last goodbyes are given, Simon touches my elbow. "I'll be up later."

As a recent bride, I should probably feel affronted, but my weariness overrides any other potential emotion. "Goodnight, love," I say, and start up the stairs.

I pause once halfway up the stairs, catching my breath as if I'm overtired, and wonder if I'm becoming ill. Continuing up the stairs, I think I might sleep in my gown and not take the time to remove it before crawling into bed. The shock and the emotions of the day have taken their toll.

I open the bedchamber door, and as I reach the bed, I realize I've walked into Simon's room. My foot knocks against something hard beneath his bed, and I bite back a sharp cry. I move, slowly, and turn on the lamp by his bed, then crouch down.

It's only a book. Probably something that Simon has been reading in bed in the mornings. I pick up the book and turn it over, curious to see that both sides are blank. There is no title. So I open the pages, expecting to see rows of black inked text. But it's a handwritten ledger of sorts.

No. Not a ledger, but a diary.

I begin to read and know that while I'm reading Simon's handwriting, I do not recognize the voice of the person writing. Some pages are very rushed and disjointed. Many words are spelled wrong, as if the person hasn't even graduated from primary school. I turn to the next page, and the writing becomes more and more sloppy.

Perhaps it isn't Simon's handwriting after all, for on the second page, the words are chilling. But then the script becomes neater and more legible. I sink to the bed and re-read the page, as if to convince myself that I read the words right the first time. He describes in detail the murders that have happened around the city, as if he's a reporter or a police officer. As if he knows even the most minute details.

I turn page after page of accounts. I am no longer tired, every bit of my body is on alert, but my head continues to throb. When I arrive at the last written page, my breath stalls. Simon has written about Mr. Lovell. Here, the handwriting is unmistakable.

Cause of death: asphyxiation by strangulation

Time of death: 2:15 in the morning

James Lovell and I argued about his treatment of his wife, which had been brought to my attention by my own wife. James laughed at first and tried to deny his abusive ways. But when I plied him with more brandy, his tongue became loose. It took only a half hour for James to tell me in detail the way that he keeps his home in order. I was angry upon arrival at the Lovell home, but then I became livid. I changed the subject to the new stallion James purchased last week. Even though it was well after midnight, I convinced him to show me his stables. It was there that I took the opportunity to avenge a helpless woman.

The door to the bedchamber swings open, and I snap the book closed. Simon stands there, staring at me.

"Simon," I whisper, rising to my feet. "What is this?" I hold out the book as if it's a repugnant thing.

He clicks the door shut. In two strides, he's crossed the room and snatched the book from my fingers.

We stare at each other for a moment, and in his eyes I see a depth I haven't seen before, or more accurately, a darkness. The seed of suspicion and doubt that had germinated in my stomach now sprouts. "You…" I can't seem to speak the words.

Instead, Simon speaks them for me. "I killed James Lovell." He holds the book up. "And others, but only those who deserve to die. Only those the police ignore."

My mouth opens and then closes as my limbs grow heavy, numb. My husband is a murderer. A confessed killer.

Simon takes a step back from me, and smoothly opens the top drawer of his dresser, his eyes on me. And I watch with horror as he withdraws a revolver. Am I about to be his next victim?

"No, Simon," I say, wanting to scream, but my voice won't cooperate. I'm not sure who will hear me and come running anyway. The servants' quarters are beneath the kitchen. Too far and too deep to hear a woman's scream.

Simon's mouth twists into an ugly smile and he says, "You would think I'd use this to kill my own wife?"

How can I answer this? How can any wife of a murderer answer?

With his dark gaze steady on mine, he turns the revolver upon himself.

TWELVE

This time my scream is piercing. I lunge for Simon, unsure of what I might accomplish. My strength against him is no match. I slam into his arm, and he staggers backward, but he doesn't fall. Instead of pushing me off, he grasps me around the waist. "What are you doing, Vivian?" he growls.

"Don't shoot yourself," I sob. "Please." I fumble for the revolver, which he still grips in one hand. I've never handled a gun, and the cold steel is hard, smooth, unforgiving. Deadly.

He lets me take the revolver from him, and once I have it, I don't know what to do with it. I can feel his gaze on me though, and I can hear his short staccato breaths. My legs tremble as I walk to the bureau and set the revolver inside the drawer, then slide it shut.

I take a deep breath, letting it travel the length of my body, then turn to face the man I no longer know.

"What have you done?" I whisper. *What have I done?* If I hadn't pressed Bethany for information about her bruises, then shared it with Simon, would Mr. Lovell still be alive? *No*, I tell myself. My confession to Simon cannot be considered an accomplice to his terrible deed. Perhaps he didn't write the truth. Perhaps he wrote some twisted tale. The diary is on the floor between us now. "Did you write the truth?"

Simon bends to pick up the book, keeping his eyes on the blank leather bound cover. "I will buy a home in the country for you. You may decorate it however you like, host parties and events, invite your friends. I will remain here."

His eyes finally lift to meet mine. The color is less dark now, more of the blue that I used to know and love. The hardness has softened into pain and vulnerability.

"How can you do those things?" I say, my voice cracking. I wonder if I will every truly catch my breath or speak normally again. "They are innocent—"

"*None* of them are innocent," Simon cuts in, his tone a harsh thing. He takes a step toward me and stops when I back up against the bureau. "None of the people I've… taken out… are innocent. They are despicable humans, not fit for living."

I bring a trembling hand up to my mouth, not believing, not understanding. "So you… just kill them? Who do you think you are, *God*?"

His eyes grow hard again and become so dark they're almost black. "God has nothing to do with this—and that's why *I* must do something. I cannot sleep, I cannot eat, I cannot live with myself until justice is done."

I wrap my arms about my torso as hot tears slip down my cheeks. "What happens when you're caught?" I look at the diary still clutched in his hand. "You've written it all down, as if you want to be discovered."

I wait for his anger, for his denial, but instead, he turns slowly from me and crosses to the windows. Pulling back the heavy drapes, he stares out into the darkness.

I watch him. I study the lines of his back, the broadness of his shoulders, and the arms that have held me many times. The tilt of his head is so familiar, the color of his skin, and the slight curl of his hair at the nape of his neck. His suit is immaculately tailored, and he runs a million-dollar business. Yet… I try to reconcile the Simon I know intimately with the Simon he is to the New York City public and the Simon who wrote such terrible revelations in that diary.

"I don't want to be discovered," he says in a voice so low that I almost don't hear it. "I don't want to go to prison or to die slowly in an insane asylum." He turns to face me then and tosses the diary onto the bed between us. "That's what will happen, Vivian, if I'm discovered." He pauses a heartbeat. "Will you turn me in?"

My Simon is looking at me. His blue eyes are intense, but not hard. His mouth is slightly open, and the shadow of whiskers paints his face. His hands hang at his sides, empty and waiting. For me.

And then I know my decision.

"I won't turn you in," I whisper. "But you can't…" I blink back the tears and swallow my sob. "You can't keep killing. *Promise* me."

He holds my gaze for so long that I wonder if he'll answer. Or if he'll send me away to the country after all. If this is the end of our marriage.

He turns toward the window again. And it's then that I notice that his hands are shaking. My heart tugs toward him, but I don't allow myself to move. How is it possible that I feel compassion for a man who could do such things? It's as if my heart is a foreigner in its own body.

When he finally speaks, his words are simple. "I promise, Vivian. But you will have to lock me up on the nights when vengeance heats up my blood and won't let my mind rest."

THIRTEEN

"Lock me up tonight," Simon tells me, and I can't look him in the eye. Those blue eyes that only remind me of his intelligence and love have now become a gray blur because of my tears.

"Lock you up?" I ask. It's seems a cruel request, both for him and for me. But I have to remind myself that the man standing before me is a murderer. "How?"

The edge of his mouth lifts. "You won't have to force me with a revolver, if that's what you're asking. Just don't let me out. No matter what."

He steps toward me, and this time I don't retreat. I allow him to encircle me with the arms that I once trusted, although now, I am unsure. Perhaps I am in shock. Perhaps I am dreaming.

I feel my body meld with his, and a deep well of grief starts inside of me—grief for my shattered illusions. My husband is not the man society thinks him to be. But he is still my Simon, I tell myself. And he needs my help.

I could leave. I could return to my parents. I could live in the country as he suggests. Or I can remain by his side as his wife, while I fulfill his request.

"Come," he says in a soft voice. He releases me and takes my hand with his hand that has killed many men. The strength of his fingers has a different meaning now.

Without a word, I walk with him out of his bedchamber and down the corridor until we reach the far end. He opens the door to the narrow staircase leading to the attic, and we ascend together, clasping hands, with Simon leading the way.

He takes down the key that sits on top of the door-frame, then opens the door. Dust tickles my senses as we step into the attic room. Crates are stacked in one corner, and two high windows let in the light of the moon. The air is dry and musty, and I look around for a place for Simon to sleep, hardly believing that he could be comfortable up here.

But when I look at him and see the darkening of his eyes, I want to leave his presence. I am afraid of my own husband.

"Go now," he says, handing over the key and stepping back from me.

Whatever is happening inside of him, even I cannot stop it. This I realize as I hurry out of the attic space and shut the door, firmly turning the lock with my key. Simon hits the door just as I start down the first step. The sound reverberates through my entire being and I gasp.

"Simon!" I call. "What's wrong?"

"Just go!" he calls back, his voice an anguished cry. Another thud against the door.

The sound startles me into action. Sobs tear against my throat as I practically stumble down the steps to the second floor of the house. I race along the corridor, my heart pounding blood against my ears.

I fling myself onto my bed and tug the covers up over my head, blocking out all light from the moon. But no matter how hard I press my hands against my ears, I can still hear the distant banging against the door in the attic. I don't know how long it takes my husband to go silent or how long it takes me to fall asleep, but when I next awake the sunlight is streaming through my windows.

FOURTEEN

I scramble out of bed and barely remember to grab a robe. Then I rush to the attic stairs, hoping that one of the maids doesn't see me hurrying down the hallway. At the top of the steps, I unlock the door, my heart pounding so hard I can barely hear my own breathing.

"Simon?" I whisper into the filtered light of the attic.

Then I see him. He's curled up on the floor, not moving.

"Simon?" I say again, this time louder.

He stirs and opens his eyes. When he sees me, it takes him a moment to focus… and to remember.

"Are you all right?" I ask, rushing to his side and kneeling down in the dust.

He rises to an elbow and pulls me against him. Burying his face against my neck, he says, "I need to drag a mattress up here."

I exhale. I had been so afraid last night, for myself, for Simon, for our future. But here he is, *safe*. And I am safe.

I nestle against him and sigh away all my questions. I have many things to ask him, about his rage last night, about his justifications for killing another person, about our future together. But for now, I will let my husband of two faces hold me in his arms.

And tomorrow night, and possibly the next, I'll lock him once again in the attic until he can be strong enough to keep his demon inside.

Q&A with H.B. Moore

I loved the feeling of old-time elegance mixed with chilling violence that this story evokes. What inspired this plot?

I wanted to write about a husband/wife relationship that could endure an extreme challenge in which the spouses make unexpected, complicated choices. My choice for the turn-of-the century setting creates many advantages for my characters as well as limitations for the law and police force. Evidence and proof are harder to come by and criminals can be much more elusive. Author friend Simon Wood and I decided to add each others names into an upcoming story. Because Simon writes pretty scary stuff, I told him he'd be the villain in my story. But the character-Simon had a mind of his own, and even though the entire story is told through the wife's viewpoint, Simon turned out to be someone you'd always "hope" would be on your side.

Do you ever scare yourself when you write stories?

Like most writers, my imagination can be very vivid, and if I'm not careful, I could probably let things spiral quite deeply and lose any desire to turn off lights or leave the house. Writing an intense or scary scene isn't nearly as impactful as reading one—in which you don't know the outcome—and I absolutely don't read scary stuff at bedtime, or when it's nighttime, or when my husband is out of town, or...

Is "Two Faces" similar to your other writing? What are you working on currently?

I write in several genres including thrillers, science fiction (YA), romance, women's fiction, and light paranormal. I'd say the mood of "Two Faces" is close to my Gothic romance *Heart of the Ocean*, which is in 1840's New England. My best villain is found in my historical thriller *Daughters of Jared*. And for those who enjoy fast-paced intense thrillers, *Slave Queen* is my newest release. Currently, I'm working on another thriller called *The Killing Curse* which deals with honor killings in the Middle East.

Where can readers find you and learn more about new releases?

Visit my website to for all updates. Be sure to sign up for my newsletter and receive a free e-book: www.hbmoore.com Or join my Fans of H.B. Moore group on Facebook: www.facebook.com/groups/37783537691/

Loving Frankie

by Patrice Fitzgerald

Her stomach hurt a lot now. She moved a bit to try to get into a more comfortable position.

Who was going to pick up Shannon? Well, she was a resourceful girl. She had lots of friends. Way more friends than Faith had at her age. Faith never brought other girls home when she was young.

But Shannon would be fine. If her mom didn't show up after Saturday band practice, she'd ask someone to drive her home.

So that was off her mind. Shannon would be okay.

Dylan… hmm. Dylan was at soccer. He loved that game. Loved running down the field. Loved showing off to the other guys. Loved looking at the other guys, truth be told.

That was okay with Faith. She loved her boy. Would love him no matter what. But Frankie… well, it was going to be hard for Frankie to accept his son. He was slow to catch on about Dylan, but he would, and soon. Dylan was only 13. Her baby boy.

When his dad found out how he was, well… it's hard to say how it would go. Would it be blows or disgust? Or both?

Actually, if it came to blows it would go bad for Frankie. Dylan was a tall kid, already, and strong for his age.

Fathers forget. By the time their sons are old enough to dare to strike back, the dads have lost the advantage. Frankie would find that out.

But not just yet.

That was a couple of years off. Not something to be all doom and gloom about now.

Faith shifted to ease the pain. She looked at the decorative tile on the side of the bathroom wall, just above the level her head was now. There was a name for it. Listello. And the color… aubergine? That's right. Very elegant. Frankie put it in last spring when they redid the master bath.

How long had she been sitting on the bathroom floor looking up at the listello?

She and Frankie had a very nice house. Something Faith was proud of. Just like she was proud of her beautiful children, so successful and popular.

She could hear Frankie pacing outside the bathroom. He probably felt bad about her stomach. He ought to.

Not a real sympathetic guy, her Frankie. But, oh boy, she loved him.

The door edged open and she could see Frankie peeking in. He saw her there on the floor, but he didn't say anything. He still had that look. She called it his Mr. Hard look. He was still angry.

Such a foolish man. It was going to go bad for him.

Funny thing. One of the things she loved about Frankie was that little boy in him. Actually, he was mostly little boy. Full of enthusiasm and energy a lot of the time. Fun to be with. Most of the time.

But when he got mad. Oh boy! Like a toddler with a tantrum. She smiled, thinking of him like a toddler throwing his toys against the wall. Pretty funny that she should be smiling thinking of Frankie right now.

Frankie had always needed someone to take care of him. And that's what she did. Indulge his whims and pick up the toys after he messed everything up.

Her bond to Frankie was more than love. It was need. She needed him for all that playfulness. And he needed her for everything.

They both had flaws. His flaw was his Mr. Hard part. And Faith's flaw was loving him.

The door to the bathroom opened. Frankie came in, his eyes different now. He wasn't Mr. Hard anymore. He was Mr. Soft. That was the look that came after. The look when his brain seemed to wake up again.

"Oh my God, Faithie. Oh my God."

He rushed over to her side where she was lying propped against the wall. He almost slipped on the blood. She smelled the stink coming from her gut. She was embarrassed at her smell.

She wondered what he had done with the knife.

"Oh my God Faithie. What happened? Oh my God." He pulled her against his chest, blood and all. It hurt a lot, but it also felt good.

Oh but she loved her Frankie.

"Don't die on me," he said, rocking her against him. "Don't you dare die on me. What would I do without you?"

What would he do? Faith didn't know. Somehow she couldn't worry about that any more.

She wondered where she would go. Heaven, of course. Right? She'd been good.

But had she? Would a better woman have made it impossible for Frankie to get to this place, sitting on the bloody bathroom floor rocking his dying wife?

She didn't know any more. She had done her best. She had stayed with him. That had felt like love.

One time Mrs. Cunningham up the street had seen Faith with a black eye under her sunglasses and told her to go talk to the priest. But what point was there in talking? Faith knew what the priest would say. A wife's place was with her husband, no matter what.

So here she was.

And where would Frankie go? Jail, of course. That would be hard on the kids.

Shannon would help, though. So together. Nothing like her mom. Always very brave and independent—no boyfriend, at sixteen, even though she was a beautiful girl. Faith was proud of that in her. Her independence. Shannon looked at the boys who hovered around her like she didn't want them to get too close.

It was easy to understand why.

Shannon would make it like a family for Dylan. Dad in jail, Mom gone. They would go to Nancy, of course. Nancy, Faith's little sister who had always worried that this day would come.

She had been right. It was coming all along. From the moment on their honeymoon when Frankie had punched Faith in the gut, it had been coming. Nancy knew it. And Faith knew it, even though she pretended not to. Only Frankie hadn't known.

What was it, amnesia with him?

Faith sighed. His need to hug her even now was a bit selfish, it occurred to her. Shouldn't he be calling 911?

Strangely, it didn't matter much to her now. It was probably too late.

That the kids—Shannon—would see her like this… well, that was awful. But nothing for it now. Faith could feel a sort of liquid peace replacing her usual need to fix everything for everyone. It was kind of nice, this helplessness. Let someone else do it, for once.

Suddenly Frankie dropped her and stood up.

"Jesus, Faithie, what am I gonna do?" He ran his fingers through what was left of his hair. "I can't call anyone. You understand."

His eyes met hers for a moment. "You understand, I know."

He leaned down and pulled some hairs away from her face. Her face was sticky. "Always my biggest fan, Faith. What am I gonna do without you?"

Faith wanted to say something. She opened her mouth, but words would not come out.

She thought of the story she'd heard in religion class, years ago. About one of the saints being beheaded… John the Baptist? One of them.

Kind of a gory story, actually. As his head bounced away from the chopping block, his mouth said, "Jesus, Jesus, Jesus." She wanted to do something dramatic like that. Something to mark the end.

She wanted to say, "I love you," or just, "Frankie." But nothing would come out.

She thought of what was to come. Her in Heaven… what would that be like? Frankie in jail, probably. And then… in Hell?

She didn't like to think of him in Hell. She wanted him to be with her. After all, if they were in Heaven or Hell or anywhere together, he couldn't hurt her any more. She wouldn't have a body, right? So he could punch her or stick a knife in her gut and twist it while he was throwing a Mr. Hard tantrum and he wouldn't ruin anything.

Faith looked at Frankie as he backed out of the bathroom, giving her one last injured gaze.

If she could have laughed, she would have.

He was mad at her.

He was mad at *her*. For dying.

Jesus. Jesus, Frankie.

Jesus.

Q&A with Patrice Fitzgerald

This one sort of creeps up on you. Did you know what the story was when you started?

I did. The whole family and the entire scenario sort of unfolded. I think I actually had a stomach ache myself, and I started thinking about this woman who felt the same way… that's what we writers are like, always thinking, "what if…?"

Have you written a lot of mysteries?

No, actually! I've written a few short stories that are suspenseful in flavor, especially in the science fiction realm, but no true mysteries. Although there is one book I started that's supposed to be the first volume in a cozy mystery series, and I may get back to it someday. I do publish another author (she's in this collection—Jerilyn Dufresne) and she writes a fabulous mystery series about Samantha (Sam) Darling.

You're a publisher too?

Yes. I publish books for a couple of authors—one is Anne Kelleher, who writes the Tilton Chartwell mysteries and has a story in this anthology—through my niche publishing company. I'm the producer and editor for this new Mostly Murder suspense anthology series as well as a space opera series, Beyond the Stars. And of course I publish books under my own name plus a couple of pseudonyms I use for the steamier stuff.

I'm an attorney as well, though I don't practice any longer… I got so good at it that I don't have to practice. Ba dump bump!

And I'm an actual diva—I sing opera, jazz, and Broadway in shows with my husband, who is also a singer.

Are you asking yourself these questions?

Why yes! Yes I am. One of my many duties as the editor. Fortunately, I find myself very amusing to talk to, so it's no problem.

What are you working on now?

As soon as I publish this anthology, I will be looking at submissions for the fourth volume of my space opera anthology, *Beyond the Stars: New Worlds, New Suns*. I have a short story due next month for a WOOL-based anthology to be produced by Samuel Peralta, and I've made a good start on the first book in my space pirates saga, *O Captain*. Lots percolating!

Where can we find you?

I have a slightly neglected website at www.PatriceFitzgerald.com and you can find me under my real name on Facebook at all hours of the night. If you do, tell me I should stop posting and go to bed.

In Sickness and in Murder

by B.A. Spangler

My wife is a murderer.

She's not a bad person, but she *is* a killer. I'd come to learn that painful truth while investigating the death of a homeless man. As the lead detective on the case, I broke every rule, every promise, every law I'd vowed to uphold. After all, up until then, the greatest thing I'd ever done in my life was to love my wife, and we have vows too.

I was convinced she'd killed the homeless man in self-defense. Only, she didn't stay at the scene like you're supposed to. She didn't scream for help or call the police or wait to tell her side of the story.

Instead, she ran.

At some point, she'd even gotten rid of whatever evidence there might have been. But she missed some of it—she just didn't know it at the time. It was the way the homeless man had died that clued me onto the fact that something was off. The Captain and my colleagues didn't see what I did. They looked uncaringly at the crime scene, missing it, dismissing it much the same way the homeless man had been dismissed. In my career, I'd seen dozens of murders—a hundred maybe. I'd seen mortal wounds, self-inflicted wounds, and I'd seen my share of defensive wounds. But what I saw in the alley that night told me a very different story. What might have started as self-defense had ended up a murder.

Later, when I discovered my wife's involvement, I turned a blind eye. For the first time in my career, I saw what I wanted to see, lying to myself, convincing myself that she'd done what she had to do to survive. So I guess I shouldn't have been all that surprised when she killed again. But I was, and now another man is dead.

My name is Steve Sholes. I'm a detective, a husband, and a father. My wife is Amy Sholes. We met in a romantic, storybook fashion, finding one another amidst a sea of stirring lights and sweaty bodies, rocking and thumping to a hard dance-club beat. Seeing her was like having a taste of honey—sweet and wanting me want more. The world disappeared around us, and we played a flirty game, swaying slowly and talking softly. Before I knew it, we'd found ourselves in an intimate bubble where we quickly fell in love. We fit. We were the puzzle pieces that completed the picture we both wanted to see. And it was a beautiful picture.

Then came the day when she walked into our home, her face flushed a deep crimson red, her clothes torn, her hands and knees scuffed and blood-stained in a way that triggered alarms in my head. She'd told me she'd had an accident, she'd tripped and fallen while leaving the library. She laughed sheepishly at her own clumsiness, but I could hear her forcing the tone and trying to make light of the scene in front of me.

I wish I'd been more careful then, but the detective in me came out like a Dr. Jekyll to his Mr. Hyde. I barraged her with question after question, prodding and probing, unable to stop myself in searching for an answer she refused to reveal. She held to her story, though, and the intuition that told me she was the victim of a robbery or maybe an attempted rape was dismissed. Thinking back, if I hadn't been home, if I hadn't seen her walk into our kitchen in the state she was in, I would never have been able to place her at the scene of the murder. Amy did a good job of cleaning up after herself, but in her haste, she left the buttons from her blouse that the homeless man had seized in his hand, clutching them in a death grip as his life spilled from his neck. The image of Amy stayed fresh in my mind for days. Her hair pulled out, the scratches, her torn clothes. There are some images that remain forever.

Being the lead detective, I got a call from the coroner, asking that I meet him at the morgue. I had no idea what it was he wanted to show me, but if he was calling, then he had to have found something worth a look. I was eager to prove to the Captain, and to everyone else, that the case was more than just a few homeless caught up in a knife fight over a bottle of rotgut.

The memory of that day is as cold as the air that had rushed past me when I entered the room where the dead speak. I remember how I jumped at the sound of the doors shutting behind me and how the coroner held back his laughter. To him, I had to have looked out of place—I rarely visit the morgue, preferring to read the reports rather than stand in a room and stare at dead bodies. I was a tourist in a strange city, and I hated the smell of the place too. I hated the refrigerator cold even more.

"Put this on," Walter Nolan had instructed and handed me a small container of what he called an *odor inhibitor cream*. He spoke with a slight lisp and dabbed his upper lip, adding, "It makes the room smell like vanilla." I waved off the cream, deciding to breathe shallowly. I was eager to see what he'd found and didn't plan to stay long.

"Did you find something?" I'd asked.

"Well, I heard from the Captain, and the thinking in this case is it might be a robbery gone bad… maybe two homeless fighting?" he began as he opened the morgue's refrigerator door. The handle clanked, and one of the hinges protested before the dark interior revealed two blue feet through a frosty vapor. A toe-tag hung limply like an ornament from the dead man's left foot, showing the date and time of death as best estimated by our findings at the crime scene.

"A robbery, yes," I answered, watching him take the body out of the refrigerator. I heard the squeal of metal as the tray carrying the homeless man slid into place, locking with a loud clack.

The man had been dead two days, and even with the refrigeration, the smell made my stomach lurch. A taste of bile rose into the back of my throat. I clenched my jaw and nearly gagged, but held it back. He was an older man, and the dirt on his face made him look like some kind of ancient refugee, but the paperwork identified him as being in his early fifties. My eyes shifted to the wounds on his neck which had already turned as black as road tar, save for a few spatters of blood on his face and chest that had dried thin and showed a hint of red. His skin was paper thin and riddled with a heavy traffic of bluish veins that branched in long sweeps from his head to his toes. But what was most surprising was how frail the man was. Beneath the heap of shirts and coats he'd worn, he was as thin as a rail.

I stepped around the body, taking to the other side so that Walter and I were facing one another.

"I kept the evidence as is, wanted you to see it," he told me as he slipped on a pair of latex gloves, snapping the rubbery lips against his wrists.

"Help me out Walter," I said and reluctantly leaned closer. "What am I looking at?"

"They're right there," he answered with a light guffaw. I frowned, uninterested in the humor. His smile waned as he turned the homeless man's hand to face the ceiling. The joints in the dead man's wrist hollered in protest like the refrigerator door. "You got an evidence bag on you?"

I showed Walter the plastic evidence bag—the space left to write in the chain of custody still blank. I'd learned early in my career to carry a few spare bags whenever investigating a case.

Walter pried apart the dead man's fist, pulling away the fingers and filling the room with another set of grating pops. In the homeless man's palm I saw two buttons. The sight of them was almost bizarre, and I had to blink away the shock, believing my mind must be playing tricks on me. I recognized the buttons. My heart stopped then, the evidence bag slipping from my fingers. An image rushed into my mind like a kick in the head. I saw Amy standing in our kitchen, telling me she'd fallen. This had to be a mistake.

"Sorry," I managed to mutter and picked up the bag, pitching it open like a hungry mouth. He plunked the blouse's buttons into the evidence bag like ice cubes into a stiff drink and then closed the dead man's hand for a final time.

"Your evidence," he said with a smile, handing over the buttons. "Doubt there are many homeless wearing a woman's blouse. I betcha didn't expect to see that. Huh?"

"Nope," I answered, sealing the bag, my voice gravelly. "I suppose that does change things a bit."

"Well, that's for you to figure out. I just write the reports and send them over."

"Thanks, Walter."

The picture of what had happened was suddenly becoming very clear—the images of the library and the alley piecing together. I rushed out of the morgue, escaping the cold and the smell, the truth about Amy's accident chasing me like a predator. I heaved my breakfast, throwing it up onto a corner wall. Walter followed me out of the room and put his hand on my back.

"Just need a minute, please," I told him, hoping he'd leave and take the smell of the dead with him. "I'll be okay."

"Everyone picks this corner," he said. "Always this corner. I'll get it cleaned up. And if I find anything else, I'll let you know."

I heaved again, giving him a cue to leave. He mumbled a few more words, but my ears were thumping with the sound of my heartbeat.

Knowing my wife had been there, knowing that she'd nearly sawed the man's head clear off his neck, knowing that she'd lied about it all... the truth tore me up.

I spent the next five minutes trying to catch my breath and clear the sting from my eyes. I also spent the time justifying what Amy had done. Maybe what she did and the way she did it wasn't all that bad. Was it?

I had come up with a dirt-simple plan. I had the buttons from her blouse in my breast pocket. The evidence that could convict her was close to my heart, and it was there they'd stay. The normal procedure to follow is for us to submit all evidence to our forensics lab for analysis. There's a lot that we can't see, but those sciency nuts with their scopes and million-dollar pieces of equipment, they see everything.

When I got back to my desk, I swiped errantly at the sweat on my forehead and forced myself to breathe. And for the first time in what might have been minutes, I did breathe. I almost broke down and cried too, but held it in long enough to sit before my legs gave out. I also did something I thought would end the homeless man's case forever, closing it like Walter had closed the dead man's clenched hand. I stuffed the bag with the bloody buttons deep into my desk drawer, where nobody would ever go looking.

Had this been the murder of someone else, questions about the recovered evidence would have come up. But this was a homeless man, and nobody was going to miss him. Charlie, my boss and the Captain of our small police department, had stopped by my desk a week or so later to ask about the evidence. By then, the coroner's report had been written, read and processed along with the ton of other daily reports that flow through our small police station. I remembered feeling nervous, tapping my foot beneath my desk while he leafed through a collection of ratty case files. But I also remembered feeling confident about handling any inconvenient questions.

"That homeless man... evidence is still not showing up at the lab. You gonna take care of that?" he'd asked, slipping his finger into a folder. I gave him a quizzical look, even though I knew exactly what he was talking about. "Dead guy in the alley. You know, the one that *effed* up our dinner plans with the wives at Romeo's."

And it had. Amy and I were supposed to have a dinner date that evening. But across from the restaurant there was the dark alley, and in that alley were the remains of what Amy had left behind.

"I'm on it," I told him.

He flipped open another case folder and rocked back and forth the way he sometimes did when waiting impatiently.

"Anything else?"

"Nah. Suppose not. It's not like there's a rush on that one anyway," he answered, depositing three new case files onto my desk. "Get on these too, when you can. And tell your missus we'll reschedule that dinner."

"Got it," I answered—a sigh of relief leaving my lips unnoticed. But the buttons remained where they were, and the homeless man's body was later cremated and disposed of. Nobody came forward. Nobody called the station. Nobody asked about the homeless man. It was as I expected: nobody would miss him.

* * *

After a few weeks, the homeless man, his murder, and any evidence were all but forgotten. Amy's wounds healed, scabbing over and then flaking until her skin turned a bright pink. Her scars eventually faded and disappeared like a memory, but I didn't forget. I couldn't forget.

I realized I'd made myself an accomplice—a partner in her crime. I'd broken the law. Scratch that, I'm breaking the law with each day that I continue to sit on the evidence. *Obstruction of Justice* means an immediate release from my position. It also means I'd lose my badge and gun. My career would be ruined. If convicted, I could go to prison. And prison is no place for a cop.

I protected Amy by hiding the truth, but I should have pushed the issue, should have pushed her to do the right thing. I should have shown her the buttons, the evidence she'd left behind. I could have convinced her to come forward and explain how she'd been attacked and had been forced to defend herself. She'd say it was her life or the homeless man's—nobody would have questioned her. If I'd done what I was supposed to, she would have walked away from it all, free.

I'd never be able to explain why I held onto the evidence, though. A detective at my level just doesn't forget about evidence sitting in his desk drawer. How would Charlie and the district attorney react? I think they'd see through any of my excuses. At best, my career would be over, and I'd face a light prison sentence. But if the DA wanted to, he could put me away for a long time, using me to make an example of some *zero-tolerance* corruption bullshit.

So, what did I do? Nothing. That's a sour pill to swallow when considering that I'm now partly responsible for another man's death. And I'm not at all sure I can cover up Amy's second murder. I'm not at all sure I should. It crushed my soul just thinking she could have done this again, but like I said, we took vows, and somewhere in those many word-filled commitments, I remember saying: *In sickness and in health.*

* * *

By the time of Amy's second murder, I was no longer working homicide. A gunshot wound ended my days on the streets. I could still contribute—even participate in a few investigations (mostly older, unsolved, cases)—but I no longer had the legs for the type of door-to-door work needed to cover the homicide beat.

Jenna White was the detective in charge now, overseeing many of the new cases. She often jumped between missing persons and homicide, since one case led to the other frequently enough. Nobody in the department had the experience she had—given the fact that she'd lost her daughter to a kidnapping a few years earlier. Maybe it was the past that gave her a hard look and an even harder demeanor, but she saw through everything and connected clues that were invisible to the rest of us. Without a doubt, she was one of the better detectives and not just hanging around to collect a paycheck.

"Morning," Jenna said, passing my desk, the smell of fresh coffee following her. With her summer-red hair, she wore a striped top that matched her gray slacks and as usual, she kept just enough buttons open to keep things interesting. The tune she was humming told me that today was going to be one of her *better* days.

She'd confided in me once about her days—and how the

bad settled in on most while the good occasionally made a brief appearance. Today would be a good day because the past would forget about her, or she'd forget about the past. I wasn't sure how she'd worded it, but the net result was the same: today was a better day. She sat down at the desk next to me, the song she was humming slipped softly from her lips. "Good day, Sunshine…"

"Beatles?" I asked, recognizing the melody. She smiled, and a light flush came to her face. I smiled back, glad to see her more cheerful. She was an excellent detective, but that's all she was, having given up on most everything else in her life. "Good song, haven't heard it in years."

"Beatles marathon on the radio," she admitted, turning to face her computer. The top of her shirt separated just enough to catch my attention. I couldn't help but notice, but I turned back to my screen and to my thoughts about the man Amy murdered. When Jenna's screen came alive—a glow showing on her face—I peered over for a glance. As suspected, she *was* working the case that had me up nights: the murder of Garret Williams. Like the buttons and the homeless man, it was the evidence found on his body that could produce the biggest clue—Amy's ring. My Amy.

I'd only seen it one time before, but I recognized it immediately. And once I recognized the it, I knew that my one chance at saving Amy, saving us, would be to steal the ring before Jenna reviewed the collected evidence. I just had to figure out how to get it without being caught.

To make matters worse, Garret Williams was one of us, a police detective. My wife had murdered a cop. That's capital murder, meaning a lot of eyes on the case and eligibility for the death penalty. Complicating the case, Garret wasn't just any cop; we had worked together. He'd been to my house—he had met my kids and had met Amy. She didn't just kill some random stranger this time. But why was Amy even with him? What was the connection? I closed my eyes, cringing, my gut chewing on a million terrible thoughts.

Amy's ring—a gaudy, ugly and nearly indescribable thing—was something I'd come upon quite by accident. She'd said it was a gift, a friendship ring, and that I shouldn't make fun of it. We were struggling back then, having just lost a baby, and when I saw her expression, I could see how important the ring was to her, and I had the crazy idea of buying a pendant or earrings to match. Without Amy knowing, I'd snapped a picture of her ring and started my search in hopes of finding any jewelry to match. The station was the safest place to do a discreet online search for similar jewelry, and that's when Jenna got a memorable glimpse of Amy's ring. Standing behind me, staring at my screen and shaking her head, Jenna quickly agreed; it was one of the ugliest rings she'd ever seen.

"Sentiment does have a way of making things beautiful," she'd said, placing her hand on my shoulder. "But ugly is ugly, and I doubt you'll find anything to *pretty-up* that much ugly."

"Funny," I'd replied in a warning tone. "Don't you have some cases to catch up on?"

It was the smallest of exchanges, the kind that fills our days—often spoken in passing and easily forgotten. But like I said, Jenna was an excellent detective, and that meant she was dangerous, too. I knew once the ring showed up in the evidence, she'd know who it was that killed Garret Williams.

* * *

"Steve, you okay?" Jenna asked, noticing my hands at work kneading my thigh. "You're going at it kinda hard."

I shook my head, saying nothing and rapped my leg impatiently like an animal chewing on a dead limb. Since the shooting, I'd lost most of the feeling and mobility there. While the doctors made no promises of what might or might not return, I'd also made no plans of letting my hopes up. I decided this would be the best it was going to get and that I needed to live with the handicap. Smacking and picking at the tender muscles was a habit I'd formed, stirring a wave of pins and needles and ridding any momentary numbness. And, like a smoker, I'd also found the habit helped me to think.

"Good days... and bad days," I said, hoping she'd pick up on the meaning. "Ya know?"

"I do," she answered plainly, but her eyes showed concern. "Let me know if there's anything I can do." Jenna turned her focus to her screen and clicked through the reports on the Williams case, selecting the coroner's folder and a collection of files. I recognized the summary and scene reports as well as the autopsy, but I couldn't be sure when the ring had been collected or if any pictures had been taken yet. I leaned in some more, trying not to get noticed. In the case of the homeless man and the buttons, I'd swiped the buttons before forensics received them. With no photographs and no analysis, there'd been no evidence. The same could be true for Amy's ring.

I mirrored Jenna's moves, clicking to open the same reports. Our computer screens became a carbon copies of one another. I searched for any pictures across the different folders, scanning the file names, recognizing our station's template files and the occasional spreadsheets for crime-scene inventory. But I found no image files. I'd leaned too far, putting an unfamiliar strain on my leg. I tried ignoring the needling sensation, but sweat beaded on the back of my neck—a response to the lightning turning my skin into electricity. I shook but held my place a moment longer.

A quick click and preview of the spreadsheets, and I saw no line items describing Amy's ring. I dropped forward, perspiration running down my nose, my lungs cramped for air. I had a chance of getting the ring before any processing could be done. I knew the guard who manned the evidence cage, Jimmy Blume—a drinking buddy from our academy days. He owed me for helping him pass, but did he owe me enough to let me into the cage? It was near noon, and I knew he didn't inventory new cases until after lunch. A new flash of lightning rode up my leg and into my crotch, causing me to double over and groan.

"Are you sure you're okay?" Jenna asked. I couldn't speak. I couldn't move. I'd had worse, but this was bad. She stood to come over, and I jabbed my hand out, crashing down on my mouse to close the windows on my screen before she noticed the Williams case files. "Steve, you're really sweating. Should I get some help?"

I shook my head, strangely thankful to have an excuse for getting up. "I think I'll have to walk off the spasms," I told her, swiping at my brow. "Will do me some good to move."

"Okay. If it's not too much when you get back, would you mind helping me go over some of this?" she asked, nudging her chin toward her screen. "Not sure I'm seeing everything."

"Sure thing," I said and pushed up on my desk, struggling to stand. The standing up was just an excuse to go to the evidence locker, but the pain was real.

* * *

Jimmy Blume was a monster of a man. I'd often thought he might be too big to be a cop. Maybe standing guard at the evidence locker was the perfect job for him. Big, and not necessarily bright, he had an equally big heart, making it easy for me to want to help him at the Academy. While most in our class had moved on to become detectives, Jimmy floundered. By now, I think he'd worked every beat there was to work wearing the uniform. And, as it turned out, Jimmy's assignment at the station as a guard over the evidence locker might just be one of the luckiest happenstance moments in my life.

"Mr. Blume!" I yelled, startling him from his usual slumped posture. He dropped a crinkled newspaper and stood at attention. I shook my hands and limped out of the narrow hallway's dim light, adding, "Just me, Jimmy. Relax."

"Scared me is all," he answered sheepishly. "Gets too quiet down here."

"Any good news in the world?" I asked, pulling the newspaper around. The headline was a few days old, and the corners of the paper had already begun to fray. Curious, I lifted the front page to find a Marvel comic book beneath. I gave Jimmy a stern look. He bit his lip and furrowed his brow. "I think I like what you're reading better than what's in the newspaper."

"Not gonna say nothing?"

"What you read in the cage, stays in the cage," I answered, knocking my hand against the metal. I turned the comic book back around to face him.

"Thank you, Steve," he gave me one of his simpler smiles. "I get bored sometimes, and I like the pictures."

I nodded my understanding and leaned onto my good leg, trying not to wince. Lifting up onto the plank of wood that separated us, I scanned the room behind Jimmy. The evidence locker was more like a room than a cage, but I guess the name was a fit across all police stations. The door separating the outside from the inside was the Dutch door variety, divided in the middle with the top open and the bottom made to accommodate a small table for receiving and signing out the evidence. A small metal fence covered the open areas and gave us an excuse to call it the cage. Inside, I saw a well-worn chair where Jimmy sat, the seat sagging under a flattened cushion. The rest of the room was filled with rows and rows of shelves stretching front to back and rising from the floor to the ceiling. There was a step stool in the corner—the handle caked in a thin layer of dust. Jimmy could touch the ceiling easily enough, so he'd likely never had a need for the stool.

"Checking something out?" he asked, readying a clipboard and clicking the end of a pen.

"Not sure," I answered while I continued to survey the room. In the corner, near his chair, I saw what I was looking for. An old cardboard box, the words 'Received' scrawled across the front. The box was filled with slender envelopes and thick, chunky bags. It was the evidence waiting to be inventoried. Amy's ring was in there somewhere. There was a pinched feeling in my gut—anxious and gnawing. I breathed a heavy sigh and prepared myself. I was about to break the law again, and, like before, it didn't sit well.

I looked Jimmy straight in the eyes. He glanced away, uncertain. After a moment, his gaze wandered back, and I could sense that he was uncomfortable. After shifting about, he finally asked, "What? You gonna say something to the Captain 'bout my reading?"

I shook my head again, reassuring him. "Jimmy, I've got to ask a favor," I told him and directed my focus to the box next to his chair. "Evidence hasn't been checked in yet?"

"Not till this afternoon—" he began and shifted uncomfortably again. "—after lunch. Same time, every day. Captain's order so I don't forget to do it. Why?"

He sounded protective, but I wasted no time and got to the point, "Need to see one of them bags," I told him.

"Not supposed to do that, Steve," he answered. "Once it's in the box, I have to inventory the items before anyone's allowed to check 'em out."

"I only need it for a couple of minutes," I said, lifting my voice in hopes of persuading him. "Hey, Jimmy, who's always helping you when they can?"

Jimmy dipped his chin and picked at the frayed newspaper. "You do," he answered, sounding dutiful. "You promise? Only a few minutes, right?"

"A few minutes," I answered and clapped his arm. "Damn, Jimmy, got some muscle in your arms... have you been working out?"

He smiled, distracted by the comment, and lumbered toward the box, snatching it from the floor in a single, swift motion. "I lift the weights at the gym sometimes. After my—"

"The Williams case," I interrupted, knowing I was pressed for time.

"Williams case?" he asked, shaking his head. "That one's not checked in yet... was told it'd be in this afternoon."

"What do you mean?" I asked, raising my voice. I took hold of the table and felt my arms go tight. "Should be here! Check again, Jimmy!"

A momentary look of hurt came over Jimmy's face, but it quickly turned to anger as he dropped the box and rose up, straightening his back and squaring his shoulders with the door. Jimmy always slouched. I'd forgotten about that. Standing as he was now—defensive and on guard—he filled the doorframe. I shrunk back onto my heels.

"Hard of hearing?" he asked, a peculiar look in his eyes as he wondered about the saying or what he was supposed to say next.

"Okay," I told him and motioned to settle down. "Sorry. Captain wanted something checked early. It's my ass too, you know."

"Then you need to talk to Detective White," he scolded, his voice becoming soft as he returned to his usual slouch.

My heart sank. The energy in me drained in a single wave. "Detective White has the evidence?"

Jimmy nodded and flipped the corner of the newspaper to open his comic book, dismissing me. "Said she'd bring it by this afternoon. Needed to review something first." My legs turned to mush, and I fell forward onto the half-door and tried to brace myself.

"Steve? Is it a heart attack? I'm sorry I raised my voice to you. I didn't mean nothing by it."

"You're good," I told him, patting his arm again.

"Thanks for giving the evidence a look. I'll talk to Detective White."

With nothing in hand and nothing else to say, I turned around and limped away. And as I entered the dark hallway, I heard the chair groan beneath Jimmy's weight.

Jenna White had the evidence. She had the ring, and I knew why it was she wanted my help.

* * *

The stairs leading back to my desk felt wobbly and abysmally impossible to climb. I gripped the railing, my knuckles turning white, and slid each foot upward a step at a time. It was torture. As the doorway neared, I saw the faces of my children. I saw the sad years ahead without their mother; a feeling of betrayal nestled in every memory like a parasite. I imagined being a single father—driving lessons and proms and graduations. Alone.

But what if Amy mentioned the homeless man? What if, during her arrest and interview, she decided to confess everything? An image of her ugly ring slammed into my skull like a bullet and nearly toppled me over. The doorway blurred, and the steps went out of focus. I hiccupped, and the sour taste of metal filled my mouth. My chest collapsed under the force of an invisible weight. For a moment, I thought Jimmy might be right. I thought that maybe I was having a heart attack.

I had to protect myself, too, and make this work. Get the ring and make it all go away. I'd have to ask Jenna to forget what she'd seen. Ask her to break the law and let a murderer go.

"Steve?" I heard Jenna say. Her voice sounded distant, but my vision had begun to clear. *I'm having a panic attack,* I told myself as I forced my eyes to focus. My breathing came in rasps, and my heart walloped like a drum thumping mercilessly in my ears. "Steve, I think I need to get you home."

"Help me to my desk," I said, reaching my free hand toward her voice. Her slender fingers found mine, warm and sturdy. She clutched my hand and braced my arm, letting me lean onto her as we limped together toward my chair. "I'll be fine in a few minutes."

"This is more than your leg, isn't it?" she asked and helped me to my seat. The view of my desk remained hidden in a gray blur while my heart slowed and eased back to a steady rhythm. I heard the sound of water and once again felt Jenna's warm touch as she cradled my hand and led me to a cool glass. The station's humid air had already turned the surface outside wet. She patted my head with a paper towel and asked, "PTSD?"

Post Traumatic Stress Disorder. I hadn't considered the diagnosis, but having been shot and almost died, I probably should have thought of it.

"Something like that," I answered. "More about the pain, though. Still a struggle. I should have used the elevator. I know better, but just don't trust that old rattling cage."

"Color is coming back. You look a little better," she said, pressing her palm against my chest. "Pulse isn't as thready either."

"I'll be fine," I told her, feeling the warmth of her skin near mine. I suddenly felt uncomfortable with her so close to me. "Appreciate the helping hand."

"Can we talk, now?" she asked. Immediately, my eyes

focused like laser beams on a target, and all woes ailing my body were dismissed as I mentally prepared for what was coming. "Found something on the Williams case that I need you to look at."

"Sure," I said, playing along, and then eased my chair around as she went back to her computer. She opened her desk drawer and pulled on an evidence bag, lifting it and placing it carefully onto my desk. I moved my keyboard and mouse out of the way while scanning through the clear plastic for what had been collected from the Willams murder. "You do know this should have been checked in."

Her face emptied and her expression was replaced with concern as though she'd made a mistake. "I had some work to do that couldn't wait. I had to confirm something first."

"Well, I doubt the mistake is fatal, but normal procedure is to inventory the evidence first and then check it out."

"Oh," she said, her hand on the lip of the bag while her eyes darted from me to the stairs and to the evidence room.

"Every station processes evidence a bit differently, and you didn't know. I can take it to Jimmy," I offered, and pinched the plastic between my fingers, seizing on the opportunity.

Jenna frowned and put on a latex glove, ignoring my offer. "You already know what I'm going to show you. Don't you?" she opened the bag and began to fish through the contents. A moment later, Jenna revealed Amy's ring. "This is your wife's ring. I recognized it out in the field when searching the victim's pockets. It's the one you were trying to match for a gift."

I dipped my chin and leaned back into my chair, shrugging as though unsure. She cocked her head and frowned, annoyed by my response. We'd seen the same reaction time and time again when interviewing suspects who tried to feign ignorance to prove innocence. A twinge of embarrassment came to me, knowing she'd see through my attempt. It wouldn't get me far anyway. It was Amy's ring in Jenna's hand—gaudy and big and with plenty of room for a partial fingerprint—there was no denying it. And it would be her epithelials they'd find to match a DNA study once the crime lab completed an analysis. I shrugged again and added, "I don't know what you want me to say, Jenna."

"Tell me I'm wrong!" she answered, sounding alarmed and raising her voice. The station quieted, and I felt the sudden stare of upturned faces and signaled for her to lower her voice. She took to her chair, pulling it close enough to me that we were facing one another and sitting knee to knee. "Tell me how absolutely impossible it is that your wife's ring ended up on a dead man's body... Damn it, Steve, tell me something I can use, so I don't have to arrest your wife!"

"Give me the ring," I begged. I kept my voice steady and in a whisper, but it shook as I spoke. "Forget you ever saw it. Please, Jenna. The evidence hasn't been checked in yet. Nobody would ever have to know."

"Steve," she answered, straightening her back and shaking her head as if I'd slapped her. I found her eyes and saw the disappointment in them. I turned away in shame like a sinner facing judgment. "Steve, I can't do that! You know I could never do that."

My chin trembled as the stark images of my broken family returned. "I know," I muttered. "I'm sorry, but I had to ask."

She stared at me for a moment, and I held her gaze.

"Let's get another sample," she said, lifting her voice and breathing life into the possibility of saving my family. "As odd as it sounds, Williams having the ring could be a mere coincidence with an equally sick timing. He could've picked it up at your house. Right? Regardless, we'd still need another DNA sample from your wife. Some hair to compare for a match."

"I can do that," I answered, adding hope to my words. And I could too. I could go home, take some hair from my daughter's hairbrush or even my mother's or even the dog. It didn't matter where the hair sample came from, as long as Jenna thought it was Amy's. "Give me an hour. I'll bring it to you."

"I have to check this in first and get forensics started," she said while I watched Amy's ring disappear into the evidence bag. "And Steve, you do understand, I'll have to go with you and perform the collection."

My heart sank again. Of course, she'd go with me. It was her case. It was her evidence to collect. "I understand," I told her and turned back to log off of my computer.

* * *

I drove to our home, giving Jenna an opportunity to prepare the paperwork while I tried to think of a way out of this. But my mind emptied. I couldn't concentrate. Everything was a sudden distraction. The cab of my pickup truck filled with Jenna's smell, adding to the strangeness, adding to the surreal feelings of what we were about to do. I stayed below the speed limit, reaching the middle of town and Romeo's restaurant where an old work truck in front of us came to an abrupt stop—the sloppy grunts of its diesel motor spewing black smoke, choking the air with a soiled cloud. I stomped on my brakes, sending Jenna's cell phone to the floor with a thud.

"Damn!" she scolded. "Can't afford to break another one of these."

"Sorry about that," I offered as she unbuckled her seat-belt and dipped below the dash to find it. When the top of her head cleared the passenger window, I looked out the cab's window to the restaurant I'd taken Amy on most of our anniversaries and celebrations. Romeo's parking lot was packed for lunch, and in the mix of lunch goers, I found Amy's car. "She's out. She's out of the house." At least our timing was good. We could get in and out of my house in a few minutes.

"What's that?" Jenna asked, returning to her seat and cleaning off her cell phone. "Couldn't hear you."

"Not important," I answered, shaking my head while I drove around the stalled truck.

"Steve, listen—" Jenna began in that same assuring voice I'd heard at the station. "I want you to know I'm on your side with this one. I want to clear your wife. But what if she did it? Have you considered that?"

I shook my head, intending to show disbelief. But in my heart, I knew she'd killed Garret Williams. I just didn't know why. Jenna leaned forward, waiting for me to answer. My chest thumped hard, and the nauseous feelings from anxiety returned.

"I want to believe she didn't do this," I finally said, admitting more than I should have while saying little. I quickly rephrased what I said to, "I have to believe she didn't do this."

Jenna touched my arm, laying her hand on mine the way people do when comforting one another at a hospital or a funeral. Is that what this was? Waiting for my wife's death? It sure felt that way. "Let's get what we need and then clear your wife of the case."

We were minutes from my front door and passed over Neshaminy Creek. I felt the urge to turn off the road, but my ideas couldn't see around the corners and come up with what to do next. I kept to the speed limit as my mind numbed. The town's houses and road signs melted away, trickling into nothingness as I found myself following Jenna and her directions.

It was hopeless.

* * *

What began as the longest minutes of my life soon became hours and then days. Detective Jenna White had entered my home where I'd directed her to our bathroom and to where my wife's hairbrush lay near the sink. With the faucet sounding a steady drip, I watched helplessly as the detective collected the hair samples. The days that followed—days of waiting and wondering—were some of the longest and loneliest I'd ever had. When the forensics report came back confirming Amy's DNA as a match to what was found at the scene of the Williams murder, I thought about taking Amy and the kids and running.

But I couldn't do that. It was with great pain that I finally decided that we were done. I couldn't help Amy any more. I *wouldn't* help her any more.

The message from Jenna came to me during a weekend

away with Amy—a getaway weekend we had planned some time ago to help us get past the loss of our baby. It was drinks and food and long walks on the beach. The idea was to put a spark back into our relationship, but if the Detective got her way, I'd be going home alone.

"Can you wait until we get back to town?" I texted a reply to Jenna. A stiff breeze came up behind me, surrounding me with the smell of the beach and sea. "Let me bring her in." I peered up in time to see Amy approach. It was our last day, and she wanted a walk in the surf before the sun disappeared behind the crisp line of the horizon.

"Can't do that, Steve," Jenna texted. "We're driving in and will be there in a few minutes."

Amy's bare feet rubbed against the walkway, catching my attention. I dropped the phone back into my pocket. Her face was hard to see against the sky while the last of the day's buttery sunlight showed through the thin fabric of her sundress.

"Who's that?" she asked, tapping my pocket. Her face came up to mine and our lips met briefly, and she took hold of my hand. "You know the rules. No business. No work. This is our time."

"Just my mom," I told her, glancing over my shoulder to listen for the approach of police cars. "She wanted to tell me the kids were good."

We reached the break of water, the surf turning foamy as it tumbled and ran toward our feet. The seawater was cold, and my toes instantly disappeared into the wet sand as the current drew the water back into the ocean. The taste of salt found my lips as the surf rushed over my feet again, warmer this time. Amy grabbed my hand, wove her fingers with mine, and reached up to my lips. She was trying to be romantic, but romance was the furthest thing from my mind. I didn't hesitate, though. I didn't say a word. I kissed her, playing along, waiting for the arrest to go down. But I was dying inside.

I kissed her as tenderly as though we'd just discovered we were in love. I had to remind myself that I was holding a killer, a murderer.

In sickness and in health, I heard in my head.

A wave crashed onto our feet. Amy leaped back playfully, pulling my arms to follow her. I followed, but by now I'd heard the first of the police vehicles approach, saw a faint reflection of blue and red on one of the sandy dunes.

"I love you," she told me and pressed her hand against my leg, against the wound that had almost ended my life. "And I love that you've done so much to change. You're going to be the best damn district attorney this town has ever had."

I swallowed hard—my mouth had become as dry as the sand. I put on a smile as Amy kissed me again. I wanted to die.

Another sound came then, car doors slamming and a radio's static rasp and police chatter. But the noise drifted in the wind along with gulls calling and waves breaking. Amy didn't notice. I held her, knowing what was coming and thinking suddenly that she might run. She returned my hug, fitting her body to mine the way she always did.

But when the sounds came again, Amy heard them. Instinctively, I held her, as distant voices called across the beach and hard-soled shoes clomped through the sand.

"What's going on?" Amy asked, looking confused. She wrenched herself free, stepping away from me as a half-dozen people dressed in dark suits and police uniforms surrounded us.

"Amy..." I pleaded in a calm tone.

But she ignored me. A scowl came over her face, and she stared at the police like a cornered animal.

"Amy, you've got to go with them."

"Steve! What's going on?" she cried.

She spun around to run, finding Detective Jenna White standing there. Their eyes locked as everyone came to rest where they stood. Amy froze, her legs shin deep in the breaking surf while some of the officers stood guarding us, and others waded into the water, blocking Amy from the ocean. The daylight was fading fast, and I motioned for Jenna to get on with it. The last thing I wanted to see happen was Amy diving into the water and disappearing into the night.

As if Amy had heard my thoughts, she moved deeper into the ocean, her body cutting the glimmer of sunlight as it carved a thin line of red and orange across the water's surface.

"Amy Sholes?" Detective Jenna White asked. Her voice was deep and sounded formal. On cue, the surrounding officers stepped closer.

Amy flinched when she heard her name. She searched past the detective, finding my eyes. I shrank back and wanted to run, feeling I'd betrayed my wife. *She's a murderer*, I reminded myself again. But in my heart, I didn't care. I loved her.

I'm sorry, I mouthed. She turned away, a distant look in her eyes and the questions in her expression fading. She searched the ocean, swallowing hard against tears that seemed to tell me the truth about Garret Williams. But why she killed him was still a mystery—the obvious answer, an affair, was impossible for me to believe.

Amy turned back again, looking lost in deciding what to do. And in her face I could see her spirit dying. She knew she'd been caught. And then I saw anger and resentment beaming toward me. It was my turn to look away.

"Yes," Amy answered the detective. "My name is Amy Sholes."

It felt as though my legs were going to give, and I braced myself, favoring my good leg as I braved a step away from my wife, giving the officers the room they'd need to place handcuffs on her. Amy stood alone.

At once, she lunged for me, but the officers were well trained and were triggered by her actions. Jenna raised her hands, stopping the officers mid-step like a dog trainer signaling the animals to halt.

"Stand down!" I screamed in a voice that was shaky with emotion. I scanned the officer's stone faces and then Detective White's, pleading with her in my mind to make this easy.

Detective White nodded.

"Babe?" Amy asked, her eyes turning soft and beautiful again. "Why?"

She began to cry, and I wanted to go to her, to hold her, to tell her everything would be okay. I felt my heart break for a millionth time as tears welled and fell. Amy didn't say anything else, but instead she squared her shoulders and straightened her back.

"Amy, you have to go with them," I told her. I kept my voice deep and empty. And then I gave her one final look as a husband. I filled my eyes with love for her and repeated our vows in my head. I turned away after that and fixed a look on the sun setting behind a ridge in the west.

"Amy Sholes." I heard Detective White direct again. I heard Amy's sobbing voice and then the sounds of splashing and of a body diving into the ocean. The officers raced passed me and waded into the ocean after my wife, rescuing her from drowning herself.

"Please, Amy," I shouted without turning around, but I knew she couldn't hear me. "Go with them. I can't... I won't help you."

"Amy Sholes, you are under the arrest for the murder of Garret Williams," I heard Detective White say, adding the final words that closed the door on our life together.

"In sickness and in murder," I muttered sadly and walked away.

Q&A with B.A. Spangler

I have a feeling there's more to the story of the murdering Mrs. Sholes. Is this connected to some of your other books?

"In Sickness and in Murder" is a short story based on my series, *An Affair with Murder*. The story came to me while finishing the second book of the series. *An Affair with Murder* centers around Amy Sholes—a mother and wife and who just happens to be a serial killer. I thought it would make for an interesting read, switching perspectives and giving readers the same point of view Amy's husband had when he discovered that his wife was a murderer.

Anything in your background that led you to write mysteries? Or were you just drawn to the genre as a fan yourself?

Like many writers, I write in multiple genres, favoring the types of stories I love to read. Some are science fiction, while others are mysteries. This is my first series in crime mysteries.

Any works in progress?

The first draft of book 3 in the series is complete and should be available in early 2017. I'm also working up a new kidnapping mystery with one of the characters from the short story, Detective Jenna White.

Let us know where readers can be in touch and find out about new books.

My website, writtenbybrian.com and Facebook page are the best places to stay in touch with me.

Nun of Your Business

by Jerilyn Dufresne

I never thought when I left the convent that I'd be killed by a husband I didn't know I had.

When Mother Evangela allowed me to take a leave of absence to discern if being a nun was my true vocation, I was scared, even though I'd requested the leave. My knees shook as I took off the veil and habit. And I swear my whole body shook as I walked out the door dressed like a civilian. But I relaxed as soon as I put my hand through my short, curly, red hair… and I laughed as I felt the wind ruffle it.

I hardly had time to take a breath before it happened.

A nondescript black limo pulled up, the darkened window went down, and a guy in the passenger seat said, "You Sister Mary Jordan?"

There was nothing else I could do but say yes. Even

though I was in civvies, I was still a sister, bound by my temporary vows.

"Get in," he commanded in a voice from The Sopranos.

Again, I thought, what else could I do? My upbringing had taught me that these kinds of cars weren't scary, but were "normal" vehicles in my family's business. Besides, I couldn't outrun a car, especially in the clunky shoes I was wearing. I didn't have a cell phone to call for help, and there was no one around I could turn to.

The back door opened as if by magic, and I ducked to slide in.

The back seat wasn't empty.

"Joey!" I smiled and hugged my twin brother.

"Jordie," he said. "Lookin' good."

I probably should have already told you that my family is connected. Yeah, in that way, and for many years. They have various specialties, but Papa always said they didn't do "wet work"—for the uninitiated, that means they don't kill people—a fact I always appreciated.

"Still playing Robin Hood?" I asked him.

"Yeah," he chuckled, "rob from the rich and give to the family." His dark eyes shone, and his smile revealed perfect teeth. Too perfect.

Sitting back in the seat, I asked him, "How did you know I'd be walking out today? I didn't know myself until Mother Evangela finally said yes."

"Let's just say Papa had a deal with the nunnery. He'd give them a sizable chunk of money—clean money—if they'd report on you every now and then. You know Pops has always had a thing about control."

"Yes, I know. One of the reasons I joined the convent.

As much as I love everyone in the family, I didn't like being treated as a princess."

Joey leaned over and touched my shoulder. "Jordana, you'll always be our princess, no matter where you live. You're the only girl in the family. We can't help it."

"Okay," I said as I shrugged my shoulder away. "Tell me why he kept tabs and why you picked me up."

"That I can't say." At my look, he added, "Papa will tell you. It's not my place."

"And when will I see Papa?"

"Right now," a booming voice said from the driver's seat.

The car pulled to the curb, and the driver turned around.

"Papa!" As angry as I was, I was overjoyed to see my dad.

We both jumped out of the car, me a little quicker, and met behind the limo. I was engulfed in a hug that helped describe why he was called Orso, the Italian word for bear. He was indeed a great bear of a man. I called him a "Teddy Bear," but others might have suggested he was more of a grizzly.

After the hug, I hit him in the chest, "Papa, why are you keeping tabs on me?"

"It's not simple, *cara mia*. Not simple at all." He put his arm around me. "Let's have lunch. We'll talk."

I knew I wouldn't win this argument with him. So I didn't say anything.

Joey had exchanged seats with Papa, and Papa was now sitting with me.

"Why did you want to leave the convent?"

I could tell my father was using his "gentle" voice, reserved for children and for me.

"I didn't really leave," I answered. "It's just that I have some doubts. And I thought I could think more clearly if I got away for awhile." I looked at his face, lined with concern. "Do you understand?"

"I don't know, Jordana. I never really understood why you joined in the first place. However, I do know I'm happy to see you and actually happy you are free."

When he saw my face, he added, "You know what I mean. Free, as in the ability to roam about freely and, of course, to visit with me."

"But there's something in particular you want to talk to me about." I didn't have the patience to wait too long.

"Yes, and I'll tell you when we sit down to eat."

When Papa made a decision, it was usually a done deal with no negotiating, no compromising. The only exception had been when I decided to enter the convent. He accepted my choice, especially after I reminded him that I was over 18 and could make my own decisions.

So on the way to the restaurant we spoke about family things. Real family, not "THE FAMILY." All my brothers were doing well, most of them in the family business. Mama was at home cooking a welcome dinner for me for later tonight. Uncles, aunts, and cousins were all happy with their lives. Everything seemed fine.

We finally got to Cara Mia, the restaurant Papa bought when I was born and named after the endearment he used for me—"My Dear." I always considered it mine, even though I had no financial interest in the place.

"It's good to be here," I said as I looked around the familiar warm room.

Papa beamed.

"It's just too bad Mama isn't here, but I suppose I'll see her soon?"

He answered my question with a nod.

It was only then I noticed that the restaurant was empty except for one server. I assumed there was someone in the kitchen cooking for us.

"I ordered already," Papa said before I could venture a question. "I need to talk to you privately."

Joey and the other guy in the car were also absent. I was almost scared, except I knew Papa would never do anything to hurt me.

"We're going to eat first," he asserted.

I long ago learned to choose my battles. This was not a hill I was willing to die on, so I just smiled.

The meal was exquisite: veal scallopini, pasta with mushroom sauce, a salad with olives, pimentos, and salami. Although it was a little too hearty for me after my convent fare, which had been plain but serviceable. Everything was covered with freshly shaved Parmesan. With it we had a red table wine, which was a far cry from the communion wine I tasted every day at Mass.

Like someone who overindulged on Thanksgiving, I pushed myself back from the table a bit then gave an uncharacteristic burp.

My father laughed, which pleased me to no end.

Finally I said, "Now, Papa." This time it wasn't a question.

"Sure." He motioned for the server to fill our glasses and then excused him from the room. He looked around to make sure we were truly alone.

"Okay, *cara*, I have a confession to make."

"Papa, I'm not a priest."

He scrunched up his face. "Not that kind of confession." He pulled his chair over near my side of the table and touched my hand.

"I have to tell you a story." And so he did.

"Many years ago, when you were a little girl, we got in a turf war with the Moselli family. You won't remember it; you were maybe four or five. It was bad. Some people were getting hurt, even killed." He held my hand a little tighter. "I know I told you we don't kill in our branch of The Family, but there were exceptions at that time." He let go of my hand and took a drink of wine.

After a sigh, he continued. "It's not something I'm proud of."

At this point he stopped making eye contact with me, causing me some concern. Again, I was scared, but not really of Papa. I was scared of something unknown that might threaten me, like the boogeyman when I was a kid.

"It got so bad that other families intervened and told us we had to stop. It was hurting everyone's businesses, and that wouldn't be tolerated." He glanced at me so briefly I almost missed it. "Sal Moselli and I didn't trust each other. Still don't. However, we had to do something to cement a peace deal. Something that was unprecedented."

He stopped. I thought he would never talk again. This time I took a drink of wine—a healthy one.

I said, "Go on, Papa. Tell me the rest. Tell me why you're talking about all this now. Why now? And what does it have to do with me?"

"First, I want to tell you that if you hadn't walked out of the convent voluntarily, I would have gotten you to leave in a year or so."

I didn't want to tell him that he couldn't have made me leave if I hadn't wanted to. That would just have challenged him. So I didn't say anything.

"In order to broker the peace, both Sal and I offered our child in marriage to the other one. We joined our families. Even though I still distrusted him and disliked him, I couldn't harm any of his kids. They were now mine as well, as much as I hated it."

I couldn't be still. "I don't remember anyone getting married back then. All my brothers were too young."

He shook his head very slowly and said, "Not your brothers."

I stood up and I knew my mouth dropped open as I stared at Papa. I pounded my fist on the table, "You did not marry me off when I was five years old. That's obscene." As much as I hated it, I began crying. Papa always thought crying showed weakness.

"Just so you know," I said, "I'm not crying because I'm weak. I'm crying because I am full of rage." I spat out the last part. Then just as quickly, the anger released, leaving only hurt. "How could you do this to me?"

"At the time, I was desperate." He put his hand lovingly on my arm. "Plus I never thought Sal would insist on consummation."

"What? I have to have sex?" I practically yelled it. "I've taken a temporary vow of chastity."

"That's why I'm glad this whole thing happened now, while your vows are temporary instead of permanent. You can easily be released from them. I checked with the priest at St. Teresa's."

"Maybe I can be easily released. That doesn't mean I

want to be. I took this time to think about my calling, my vocation. I'm not ready to leave for good."

"I'm sorry, *cara mia*. If you don't consummate the marriage with Sal, Jr., it will cause another war, more deaths. And I'm also sorry to say that this time it will be on your head."

"What," I screamed. I jumped up and headed out of the room. That's when I found out that Joey and Nameless were right outside the door.

Joey, showing pain in his eyes, grabbed me and said, "I'm sorry, Jordie. I'm really sorry. I can't let you go."

Betrayed by both my father and my twin brother, I just gave up and quit fighting. I allowed Joey to escort me back to Papa.

Without acknowledging that I'd left, Papa said, "Sal thinks we need grandchildren in common in order to keep the peace going for the next generations. I think it's a good idea."

"So not only am I to have sex with a guy I've never met, but I'm to bear him children? This is unconscionable."

"You met him," Papa said. He paused. "At your wedding."

"There was really a wedding when I was five? No wonder I've blocked it out." Although most girls dreamed of getting married and would have loved a ceremony at that age, even at five I felt the call to be a nun. "Did we kiss? Did anything else happen?"

Then it hit me. "That's ridiculous. How could you get a priest to marry us at five?"

"Well, Sal Jr. was seven."

"Still crazy." I was adamant. "How did you get a priest to marry us?"

"You can pretty much get anyone to do anything." That's all he said by way of explanation.

"But it can't be legal. Not in this state. Certainly not in the Church. I was too young to give legal consent."

"It's legal and binding within the two families, and that's all that matters."

I could tell this was one of those times where I had no choice in the matter. Papa had made up his mind, and he was intractable.

So there I was, surrounded by goons. Yeah, that's how I saw my dad, brother, and Nameless at that moment. What was I to do?

"All right. I'll do it for the family." I hung my head, and hoped Papa was buying what I was selling.

He was pathetically happy. He held my head, kissed me on both cheeks, and said, "We'll plan a celebration for tomorrow. Tonight you eat Mama's cooking. Tomorrow you celebrate with your husband."

"I don't think I can be exempted from my vows by tomorrow." I really wanted to buy some time, so I could figure out how to stop this farce, and return to the life I had chosen. All I wanted in that second was to go back to my life in the convent.

"Don't worry about that. I've got that covered."

I had no idea what he meant, but I didn't like the implication, not one little bit.

"I want Mama. I want my mom." My eyes welled with tears again. Some were left from my anger and hurt, but some were because I missed my warm, sweet Mama.

"Sure, hon," Papa said, as if I'd never screamed at him. Was he this easily fooled? Did he really think I'd give up this easily?

"Joey, go with her and make sure she's okay."

Right then, I knew. Papa wasn't fooled at all. He was sending my brother to be my bodyguard. I also knew that if I left while Joey was in charge of me, there would be hell to pay for him. As angry as I was, Joey was not just my brother, he was my twin. We'd always been close, and I'd missed him horribly.

Another kiss from Papa, and we were on our way.

When we got in the car, the first thing I said was, "Is the car bugged? Are you bugged?"

He shook his head.

"That's not good enough, Joey. Say it."

"No, Jord. The car's not bugged. I'm not bugged. He can't hear what we're saying."

"Then why in the hell are you doing this to me?" The hurt ran even deeper that my Joey would betray me.

I knew the answer but wanted to hear him say it.

"Because I think it's the right thing to do."

"Whoa!" I said. "I can't believe it. I thought you were doing it because you were scared of Pop."

"Well, there's that." Joey gave a half smile as he expertly wove in and out of traffic on the way home. He got serious again. "By doing this one thing, Jordana, you can make peace between two warring families. There's been peace the last 20 years, but it was kind of unreal, waiting for you and Sal, Jr. to, you know, do it." He blushed as he said it.

Our home wasn't far from the restaurant. It was palatial by the standards of the neighborhood—a lot of acreage and a huge house surrounded by a fence, with a guard at the gate. Yeah, that's the place I grew up.

A guy I didn't recognize waved us through, and we drove

the winding road to the front of the house. Normally Joey would have parked in the garage, but this was probably considered an important occasion, the only daughter returning home.

There she stood in the doorway, wiping her hands on her apron, beaming, a stereotypical Italian mama and grandma.

"Jordana!"

"Mama!"

Both were said at exactly the same time.

Joey stayed with me as I followed Mama into the kitchen.

She was still beautiful, although I noticed a few gray hairs had crept into the black mane she always had, and now she wore it in a bun.

Mama chattered about a lot of inconsequential things. She seemed nervous.

I picked up a bowl of pea pods and started shelling.

"What's wrong, Ma?"

"Nothing, *cara*, nothing."

But I didn't believe her.

I turned to my twin. "Joey, will you please give me a moment alone with Ma? I swear that I won't try to leave."

He nodded, but said, "Even if you tried to leave, you couldn't. Dad's got a man at each door."

I was stunned. "He must think I'm some kind of escape artist." I looked Joey straight in the eye. "Why doesn't he trust me?" This wasn't the Papa I loved.

Joey looked around to make sure no one else was listening. "This is a lot bigger than Dad let on to you. That's all I'll say."

With that, he left the kitchen, but I could sense he was nearby.

I touched Mama's arm so she would look at me.

"Tell me. Please. What in the world is going on? I feel like Alice in Wonderland."

She hesitated, then looked around like Joey had, "I don't know what your Papa told you."

I then repeated what Papa had said.

"Nothing more. I can say nothing more." She put down the pasta and turned to me. Mama took my head in her hands like Papa had done a short time ago. "I love you, *cara mia*."

"It doesn't feel like anyone loves me, Ma."

At that I ran up to my room and heard Joey following me. I threw myself on my childhood bed, sobbing. Joey didn't come in, but I did hear him say, "I'm sorry."

My head whirled with thoughts. I felt unloved at that moment, abandoned even by God. I pulled myself up, then knelt by my bed, as I'd done most of my life, and I prayed.

Nothing felt right, though. I felt like I was losing myself. Going from nun to wife in a few minutes was more than I could handle.

I must have slept, because the next thing I knew Joey shook me and said it was time for dinner.

Papa was really the only one who talked. He spoke of plans, parties, celebrations, and even the consummation. He was the puppeteer, and I was his own little Pinocchio.

Who was this man? And what had he done to my beloved Papa?

Finally, I interrupted him.

"When do I meet him?"

"Tomorrow at the celebration," Dad said.

"No. I want to meet him tonight. Privately." This was a hill I was willing to die on. "Tonight," I repeated.

Papa knew when I wouldn't budge, and it was my turn to be intractable.

He looked at his watch, then beckoned to a man who was standing at the dining room door. Papa whispered in the man's ear, and the guy took off.

I would meet Sal, Jr. tonight.

The rest of the meal was uneventful, although it was not a cheerful homecoming.

I said to Mama, "I was coming here today anyway to get some better clothes. I can't really wear this," indicating the out-of-date outfit supplied by the convent. How I'd longed to wear fashionable clothing and high heels again.

When I got back to my room and opened the closet, however, I was surprised to see that nothing interested me. I finally chose a pair of jeans, black sneakers, and a blue pull-over.

"I don't really care if he likes me or thinks I'm pretty," I said aloud to myself. But secretly, I did care. If I had to marry, I wanted him to be nice. I wanted him to think I was lovely. I hadn't thought about marriage for myself ever, really, but now it was kind of fun fantasizing about a prince to go with this princess.

While I waited for Sal to arrive, I thought about him. Was he tall, dark and handsome? He didn't really have to be tall, since I wasn't. But handsome would be nice, or even just cute. Kind was the most important.

I didn't want to talk to Papa, because I still didn't understand the importance of this whole arrangement. How could he sell me like this? Sure, peace was what I wanted, but it wasn't like he and Sal, Sr. were kings of adjoining countries. They were mafiosi, controlling jobs, information, people, and money.

Dad knocked on my door. "May I come in, Jordana?"

I didn't answer, and he walked in slowly. He sat on my bed and watched as I walked around the room, touching various favorite objects of my childhood.

He said, "I told your Mama that she made this into a shrine for you."

"She's so proud that I went to the convent."'

"I was too, even though I fought it. It was because I knew it would have to end some day, if I couldn't convince Sal to change his mind."

I finally turned to him, "You mean you tried?"

"Of course. I'm not heartless." He looked down at his hands. "It was an ugly time. A time that needed to end. At that point the only way to stop the war was to give in to Sal's demands. I hated every minute of it."

I looked at him. For the first time I saw an old, tired man.

He continued. "I'd killed people. I hadn't done that before and I haven't done it since. Some of my own people were killed. I had to stop the bloodshed. You were the sacrifice." Tears fell. "My favorite child. I sacrificed you."

Suddenly, I felt the weight of the decision. And I felt responsibility, too.

"Will the war really start again if I don't submit to this agreement?"

"I'm afraid so, *cara*. Sal is ruthless and without a conscience."

I went to him and knelt before him. I took his hands,

forcing him to look at me, as he had done earlier to me. "I forgive you, Papa."

At that he sobbed. He'd never done that before, at least not in my presence.

"Let me fix my face, and we can go down." I went into my bathroom and searched for some make-up. It had been a few years since I'd worn it, but I thought it would be appropriate now. As I tried to apply it correctly, I longed for the plain bathrooms of the old convent, filled with tile and white porcelain. I longed for simplicity where I didn't have to make decisions that affected people's lives.

Finally, I said, "I'm ready."

We walked downstairs, my hand through his arm. As we descended I asked, "Is the marriage really and truly legal?"

"Probably not. I thought we'd have a quick ceremony to seal the deal before you yourself seal the deal."

He chuckled and I blushed, but I was happy to see he was back to his old self.

It was then I noticed two men standing at the bottom of the stairs. One was grizzled, with a beard, and features that hid his age. His face showed no emotion. The other was handsome and slim. He was grinning from ear to ear.

Under my breath, I prayed, "Please let him be Sal, oh God. Please let him be Sal."

As we got near them, the handsome one said, "Gee, Sal, you sure got a pretty one."

I stumbled on the stair. Sal, Jr. was indeed a younger version of his hateful father, in looks anyway. I silently prayed that he was kind.

He was not.

My father introduced us, and I smiled tentatively at the bearded one.

Sal glared. He said, "I heard you wanna talk. Let's do it."

Papa ushered us into the study. At my adamant insistence he left us alone.

"So whaddaya want?"

He sounded like a 40s gangster movie. He looked like he belonged in one, too.

"I wanted to meet you." I indicated a chair for him to sit in. "Did you know about this before now?"

"Sure," he said. "My pops told me when I was a kid. Pissed me off, I tell ya. Havin' to marry someone you don't know. I told him, 'This is America. You can't do that here.' But he told me about the turf war and all that crap. So whaddaya gonna do? I mean, we're gonna keep people from gettin' killed off." He picked something out of a side tooth, then ate it. "At least you're pretty."

I didn't know whether to thank him or throw up. So I said nothing.

He, however, wanted to keep talking. "So I figured we'd have sex a lot, you'd have a kid, and then we could get a divorce. A kid is what they want. Something in common, so they couldn't fight." He leered at me. "A lot of sex."

"Yeah, I don't know..."

He continued. "It don't mean we have to stop living our own lives. I figure I'll still have my girlfriend, and you can do whatever it is you do. We'll keep up the, whachacallit, pretenses." He appeared proud of finding the right word. He puffed up his chest a bit, and that's when I first noticed how young he truly was. Only two years older than me, so still in his twenties. However, I felt much, much older than him.

I suddenly wished wise old Mother Evangela was here. I needed counsel. This was a nightmare. Now I wanted to be a nun more than anything in the world, and I couldn't be.

"Okay, listen. I don't want a big wedding tomorrow. I just want our family there to witness the quick re-ceremony, and then we'll have a fast dinner with them, and off we'll go to the honeymoon suite."

He grinned. "You're pretty anxious to have sex."

"I'm pretty anxious to get it over with," I said. "I don't want to do this, Sal. And it's got nothing to do with you." That was my first lie to him. "I'm a nun. I want to stay a nun. I don't want to be a married woman, have sex, and have a kid. There's nothing wrong with that," I assured him. "It's great. It's just not for me. I've wanted to be a nun since I was a little kid. Do you understand?

"Yeah, not really," he said. "I can't understand anyone not wanting to have sex."

"Well, of course, I would want to have sex if I weren't a nun," I said. "It's just that I can't have sex and still be a nun. Do you understand now?"

"Yeah, I guess so." He seemed calmer and less scary now.

"Tell me about your girlfriend," I said.

"What? Why?"

"Well, you seem to care about her if you want to stay with her even while we go through this sham marriage."

And so he told me about Delores. They'd been together since high school. They had a son, but couldn't get married because of the previous agreement between our dads.

"This just sucks," I said.

"Do nuns talk that way?"

"Sometimes," I laughed. "Sometimes I say even worse things. I'm human."

An idea was germinating, but I needed time to cement the plan. "Sal, do me a favor. Go out and have some wine with everyone. They're probably in the kitchen. Be nice to people. Smile like there's no problem. Lie if you have to."

"But…"

"Yeah, I guess nuns lie, too. Sorry. Just do it. I think I have a plan that can get us both out of this mess."

He did as I said, and his smile was real. Suddenly he looked like the nice guy I'd hoped he'd be.

The first thing I did was kneel down again. I asked for forgiveness for the hoax I was about to perpetrate. I asked forgiveness for lying and asking others to lie. But most of all, I asked for the rest of my plan to come together.

Then, I went to Papa's desk and fired up the computer. I searched for a few things that didn't pan out. Then finally, I hit the jackpot.

I yelled for Papa and Sal, Jr. to join me.

When they did, Sal was still smiling, and Papa looked confused.

"Pa, I have a plan that will allow me to go back to the convent and still keep the peace. Want to hear it?"

"Sure, but this sounds crazy," he said.

"It is."

So I told both of them what I'd planned. Sal was enthusiastic, but Papa was adamantly against it.

"You might really die," he said.

"Maybe, but only for a minute. I trust you to make sure I don't." Then I changed the subject, "Do you have any doctors on your payroll?" At his nod, I asked, "Do you have any coroners?"

"One," he said.

"One is all we need." I clapped my hands and giggled like a schoolgirl. In fact, that's just how I felt. Like an oppressive weight had been lifted off me, and I could breathe again.

So we set out to put the plan in motion.

The next morning, our immediate families met at St. Teresa's. A priest I didn't know stood at the front of the church. There was no Mass, no music, just immediate family and a few of Papa's close friends. And with that, there were still way too many people there for my taste. It was good to recognize my brothers and sisters-in-law, as well as nieces and nephews. Joey was the only one of the boys who wasn't married, and he didn't bring his girlfriend in honor of my protestations.

Papa didn't give me away. We just all walked in, and I went all the way to the altar and Sal, Jr. joined me. As I looked at him, I thought, "How could I ever have compared him to his father? There's nothing ugly about him. He must have been putting on an act when I first met him."

And then, voila, we were married.

We didn't kiss, and we didn't hold hands as we walked down the aisle. In fact, he went in the car with his family, and I went with mine. The reception, if it could be called that, was at the restaurant in the private room. This time the restaurant was filled with people, many of them calling out to Papa, Mama, Joey and me, and some expressing concern about the Mosellis being there. Papa quieted them down with a quick handshake or a pat on the back. He always did know how to work a room.

Both the family heads insisted that Sal, Jr. and I sit at the head of the table, like a real bride and groom. We played our parts well, although without enthusiasm. At one point, we were toasted by our fathers, and they both tried to go first. My papa graciously allowed Sal Moselli to lead the way, then gave his toast.

Then it was time to cut the cake. There was no time for a real wedding cake, so a server just brought one from the kitchen that was on the menu for the restaurant that night. I cut my piece of the cake without looking at it and fed Sal. He licked his lips and then put a piece of the cake in my mouth.

Immediately I put my fingers to my throat, as if that would help me breathe. I felt my body turn into one big hive and my throat close. That's all I remember of the incident. To almost everyone there, I had died. And I did die, for a fraction of a second.

Dad and Sal took turns filling me in later. Mama was so upset that she couldn't even listen. First of all, I'd made sure that Cara Mia's specialty cake was on the menu tonight—Strawberry Surprise. And most everyone was surprised when I collapsed. My parents and brothers knew I was deathly allergic to strawberries, but the server and my new husband supposedly hadn't known until it was too late.

Papa said he and the doctor immediately ran to me, telling everyone but Sal, Jr. to move away and give the doctor room. The doctor yelled, "I called 9-1-1," so no one else would do it.

Apparently Mama gave an Oscar-worthy performance pretending to faint and keeping my brothers busy with her.

Sal did a great job of being a worried new husband, while at the same time screaming to everyone to move back and give me some air. While this was happening, the doctor was able to quickly gave me a shot of epinephrine and adrenaline to get my heart started again while reducing the swelling so I could breathe.

Mama wailed so loudly when she woke from her "faint" that no one heard my big intake of breath as the medicine worked its magic. Soon two EMTs arrived and carted me off with the doctor in tow.

I became aware of things in the ambulance, and the doctor assured me I was fine and that the scheme had gone according to plan. He actually looked as if he had enjoyed it.

The ambulance dropped me at a designated corner, and soon my husband was there to get me. I still felt wobbly, and he helped me into the car.

Sal smiled at me as he followed my instructions to drive to the back entrance of the convent. We were safely off the street, and no one could see us.

"That was a great idea to have our fingers crossed when we said our vows."

I said, "It probably wasn't legal anyway, because we were coerced." At his look of uncertainty, I changed it to, "We were forced, so we weren't really going to be married because we didn't mean it."

"Ah," he said. "Well, I'm sorry I had to kill you so we could get out of this thing."

"Yeah, I'm sorry, too. But it looked like a total accident, so no one is going to be the wiser. Your dad will stick with the peace plan, because we did get married, and my dad held up his end of the bargain. He won't seek revenge on the Mosellis even though you killed me… sort of. You're now my dad's son-in-law, and there can be no fighting between the families." I gave a huge sigh. "I only wish we could have told someone besides just my mom and dad, and, of course, the doctor and coroner, but my brothers have big mouths, especially when they're drinking. I couldn't trust that they would keep it secret."

I added, "And I wish I could be at my memorial service when Dad gets mad at me for being cremated when that's not what he wanted for me." I laughed at the thought.

"I'll be there, and I think my tears might be real. You're really something," Sal said.

I leaned over and gave him a surprisingly pleasant kiss.

"Hey, you're gonna make me change my mind here." He laughed as he said it.

"I do want to tell you something before I go. What I wished for in a husband was that, above all else, he be kind. You are indeed kind."

His smile was warm as he opened the car door for me. My smile was even warmer.

And that is how I, a dead woman, walked into the convent and into my own happily ever after.

Q&A with Jerilyn Dufresne

This story is lighter than many others in this collection. Would you characterize "Nun of Your Business" as a "cozy" mystery, rather than the typical dark mystery--sometimes referred to as "hardboiled"?

Yes, it is a cozy mystery. I'm happy you noticed. Although I enjoy reading all kinds of mysteries, from hardboiled to cozy to paranormal to whatever, I truly love writing cozies with a hint of humor.

Do you always know where you're going as you write a mystery, or do you figure it out along with the reader as the story unfolds?

I wish I could say I knew where a story was going when I began it. It would make my writing life easier. However, I start with a basic idea—in this case, a young nun whose father was in the mafia. I thought that was an interesting concept and then I just started writing. I enjoyed Sr. Mary Jordan so much that I'm planning on writing another series with her as the protagonist. When I write, the characters decide what's going to happen. I usually don't even know who is going to die or who the murderer is until the characters tell me. This is probably called "flying by the seat of my pants." But it works for me.

Do you have any works in progress?

Yes, I do. Currently I'm writing book seven in the Sam Darling mystery series. It's called *Who Dies Next?* All the books take place in my hometown of Quincy, Illinois. Sam is a busybody who has a psychic connection with her dog. Her husband is the Chief of Detectives in town, and that makes it easier for her to follow her nose—right into trouble. They're all available from Amazon, Barnes and Noble, and other providers, both in ebook and paperback.

How can readers be in touch with you and find out about new releases?

I'm on Facebook as Author Jerilyn Dufresne. Please "Like" my page and you'll be able to see information about my new releases. I also have a website, jerilyndufresne.com, and a mailing list available at smarturl.it/DarlingMysteryNews

The Long Haul

by Josh Hayes

One

Mary Lancaster glared at the clock.

Only 6:29 a.m. Two weeks in a row her husband had been out of bed before 7:00, without so much as a kiss on the forehead or an "I love you." It was getting ridiculous.

I'm going to say something to him today.

She sat up, then winced at the pain along her spine, reaching back to massage the scar. The surgery that had fused her upper vertebra was supposed to have relieved the ache, but even after a year, it was still very much present.

The shower shut off and a few minutes later David stepped out, a towel around his waist. He grabbed the clothes off the back of the chair and dressed without a word. It seemed as though they'd grown further apart over these last few weeks, but she couldn't put her finger on why. He'd been on the road without a break for almost three weeks straight. She feared that the gulf they had worked so hard to repair over the last year was slowing reappearing in their lives.

"Another early run today?" Mary asked, trying to keep the frustration out of her voice.

"Mm-hmm," he said, bending over to lace up his boots.

"I thought you didn't pick up till this afternoon?"

"Bill called in," David said, standing.

Mary frowned. She didn't remember the phone ringing. "So you have to cover?"

"Yeah. Pulling two today."

She took a deep breath, biting back her frustration. Her spine pulsed again. *It won't help to get upset.* "Going to be late then?"

"Probably."

"Dan really needs to find someone else for all these extra runs."

David shrugged. "The extra money's good."

"It would be nice to spend some time together, too. We were pretty good about that for a few months, but now…" She trailed off, as he turned to her, eyes tired. Immediately she felt childish. He'd been doing his best, working long hours, trying to keep them above water, keeping the debt collectors off their backs. But even so…

He held her gaze for a moment, then said, "I'm sorry. Work's been crazy, I know, but it's going to get better."

"Okay."

"Gotta run, I'll see you later."

He was through the door and down the stairs a moment later and he hadn't said, "I love you."

The deep rumble of the rig sounded in the driveway, air brakes hissing as they disengaged. She crossed to the small window and watched as the bright red cab pulled out of the drive, made a wide turn around her maroon Ford Focus parked at the curb, then disappeared down the street.

She blew out a frustrated breath, slapping the window frame. "God, this is so stupid! It's been a freaking year!"

The pain in her spine flared and she cursed again, reaching back to massage the scar.

"Phantom pain will be normal for a while," was what the doctor had said. Of course, he'd said a lot of things, hadn't he? Made promises, said things that were so believable at the time. Looking back on his words now, she could see them for the come-on lines they were, and scolded herself for being so stupid. He'd told her the surgery was necessary, that it would rid her of the excruciating pain. He'd also told her that he loved her, and could give her more happiness than she'd ever known.

What a joke, she thought, rubbing her stinging palm.

Two

Mary spent the morning watching the local news, before moving on to The Price is Right. Drew was just about to present the Final Showcase when the two-tone chime of the doorbell echoed through the house.

She frowned, glancing over her shoulder. She craned her head back to look into the entryway and saw a dark silhouette standing on the front stoop.

She watched and waited, willing whoever it was to go away. She didn't want to buy a vacuum. Didn't need anyone to ask her if she'd had the chance to meet her Lord and Savior. Didn't need anything but quiet, alone time.

The doorbell rang again.

"Oh my god, what do you want?" Mary growled, pushing herself off the couch.

She opened the door to a short, balding man wearing a FedEx jacket. "Can I help you?"

The man smiled. "Good morning, ma'am. I've got a letter here for David Lancaster. Needs a signature."

"That's my husband."

"Good enough." He held out an envelope. There was a small pink receipt attached to it. He held out a pen. "Just sign by the X, please."

She read the name stamped across the top: Central Plains National Bank. She looked past the deliveryman, at her Focus in the street, wondering if the bank was sending a repossession notice. That would be just her luck.

"What is it?" She asked, taking the envelope.

The man chuckled. "Sorry, ma'am, I just deliver."

Mary signed and handed it back.

"Thanks, have a good day," he said as he handed her the receipt.

She ignored him and read over the address information a second time, making sure there hadn't been a mix-up, then pulled the rip-tab on the back. Inside she found a form letter, printed on Central Plains National Bank letterhead, addressed to David.

Dear Mr. Lancaster,

We'd like to congratulate you on making the final

payment on your 2012 CHEVROLET TAHOE. Acct# 614538274. It was a pleasure to serve you, and we hope that you will consider us for any of your future financial needs.

If you have any questions or concerns, please don't hesitate to call.

Sincerely,
Audra Wies, CPA, Senior Manager Liabilities and Loans
Central Plains National Bank
316-989-7848
Awies@cpna.org

Mary read it again. She looked up at her Focus parked at the curb, the replacement for the Tahoe she'd totaled in the wreck. But her Tahoe had been almost 15 years old, and it had been paid off for years.

It had to be some kind of mistake.

Calling David was her first instinct. She cursed as the call went straight to voicemail and hung up without leaving a message.

"Come on," she said, trying a second time.

Voicemail again.

"For heaven's sake," Mary told the phone before hanging up again.

She read the letter again, then dialed the number printed near the bottom.

After a single ring, a computerized voice answered the call. Mary rolled her eyes and listened.

Three

After three menu replays and two failed attempts, a real human being finally answered the phone.

"Hello, this is Karen, how can I help you today?"

Mary took a deep breath. "Yes, hi, my name is Mary Lancaster. My husband David and I have a car loan through your bank for a Ford Focus, and I wanted to ask you a couple of questions about the account."

"Certainly, ma'am, can I have your birth date, please?"

"June 2, 1983."

"And password for the account?"

"Sardine Sandwiches," Mary told her, shaking her head at David's ridiculous choice of security phrases.

Another pause and key clicks.

"Okay," the woman said, drawing out the word. "Here we are, yep, a 2011 Focus, maroon. What can I help you with?"

"Do you show any other vehicles on the account?"

"No… no I don't see anything else. I mean, there's your home loan, but that's it."

"You don't show a 2012 Tahoe listed at all?"

"No, no I don't, I'm sorry."

What the hell? Mary read over the information on the letter again, convinced she was missing something. "Can you try something else for me? Can you look up a different account number?"

"Of course."

Mary recited the numbers on the letter.

There was a pause. "Hmm, I might have punched them in wrong, let me read them back to you."

Mary ran her finger along the numbers as the woman read them aloud. When she finished, Mary said, "Yep, that's right."

"Well, that's strange." There was another pause. "I'm sorry, ma'am, can I put you on hold for just one second?"

Mary sighed. "Yes, that's fine."

When the elevator music started playing Mary cursed aloud. She hated calling banks, hated not being able to see what the person on the other end of the phone saw. It made her feel like a child who wasn't allowed to listen in to her parents' conversations. It was her money after all—she should be allowed access to all the information.

A minute later the teller came back on the line, cutting off the music halfway through its second repeat. "Okay, ma'am, I'm sorry about the wait. I was just trying to do a little research into the account. Unfortunately, I wasn't able to find your name listed anywhere on the account."

"What does that mean? If my husband set up an account I should have access to it. We've been banking there together for almost twelve years. When was it opened? Is the Tahoe the only thing listed on it?"

"I'm really sorry, ma'am, but without your name actually being on the account, I can't release any of the information to you."

"Oh, that's bullshit."

"I'm sorry, ma'am, I really am. I wish there was something I could do."

"Is there manager there? I'd like to talk with the manager please."

There was a pause. "I'm sorry, ma'am, it looks like she's stepped out for the moment. Would you like me to forward you to her voicemail?"

"Of course she's not there. This is ridiculous. Fine, transfer me over."

"Thank you very much, ma'am. Have a good day."

The line beeped twice before Mary could respond and moment later the branch manager's voicemail recording started. Frustrated and angry, Mary hung up without leaving a message.

Four

"I'm sorry, but we can't tell you anything about your husband's account," Mary mimicked, pacing around the living room. "Such bullshit. Leave a voicemail? Right, cause that's going to do a lot of good. Like she's going to call me back. Shitty customer service is what it is, plain and simple. That's my money in that account, damn it!"

She had been complaining aloud for almost fifteen minutes after hanging up the phone and had worked herself to the point of screaming with frustration. Her scar flared with a white-hot pain, which only fueled her anger. The idea of David keeping secrets from her knotted her up inside. Memories of the hours they'd spent in therapy, piecing their lives back together, flooded through her mind. It had been her affair that had led to the sessions in the first place, but they'd both promised never to keep secrets from each other again, and here he was, spending money that they didn't have, to buy a car that she knew nothing about.

In the end, Mary decided that a phone call just wouldn't work. She showered, dressed, and was on the road twenty minutes later. By the time she pulled into the bank parking lot, her fingers were sore from gripping the wheel.

She was led into a side office, where two small chairs faced a wooden desk. A placard, sitting among piles of papers, told Mary that Elizabeth Haskins was an extremely disorganized person.

Ten minutes later, a middle-aged woman in a pantsuit came into the office, smiling. She smelled of tomato sauce and cheap perfume.

"Mrs. Lancaster, so sorry to keep you waiting." She extended a hand and introduced herself. "I'm Elizabeth Haskins. I understand you're having some issues with your account."

"Yes," Mary said, placing the letter on top of a stack of folders. "I received this letter today, but when I called, I was told that the bank couldn't give me any information about it. Obviously there's been some kind of a mix up, because we don't own a Tahoe any more. It was totaled in an accident over a year ago."

"Oh, my. I'm very sorry to hear that," Mrs. Haskins said, looking over the documents.

"I want to know if this is a legit deal, or if there's just been some kind of mistake or misprint or something. And why am I not listed on the account? David and I have a joint account here—we have for years."

"Hmm," the banker said, brushing some loose papers from her keyboard. "Let me see what I can find out." After a few minutes of working, she frowned. "Huh. Well, now that is very strange."

"What is?" Mary asked, leaning forward.

Mrs. Haskins angled the screen slightly, just enough

so that Mary couldn't see it. "Well, I see that you and your husband do indeed have an account with us, but unfortunately, this account," she held up the payoff letter, "isn't associated with your joint account. It's completely separate."

"So what does that mean?"

"It means I'm not able to discuss the account information with you, unless Mr. Lancaster adds you to the account, of course."

Anger exploded out of Mary before she even knew it was coming. "I don't understand what is so difficult about this! He's my husband! We've been married for twelve years and banked here for at least that long. I know his social security number, his date of birth, how tall he is, hell, I know he has a birthmark on his left butt-cheek that looks like the state of Florida!"

Mrs. Haskins held up her hands. "I'm very sorry, Mrs. Lancaster, I didn't mean to offend you. It's just that our bank has very specific policies about how and *who* we can divulge account information to." Her eyes looked away as she continued.

"I can see that you're on the other accounts, but unfortunately we can only release account information to account holders or authorized agents, and your husband's name is the only name on the account."

"That's right—my husband. I'm his wife. That means you can talk to me."

"I'm sorry ma'am, but I can't do that."

"That's bullshit."

The banker straightened in her chair, putting her hands in her lap. "As I said, I am very sorry for the confusion, but we value the privacy of our clients here above everything else. I wish there was something I could do. I'm sorry. Perhaps this is something you should take up with Mr. Lancaster."

Mary suddenly realized how this entire thing looked and felt her cheeks flush. Tears threatened to seep out, and she had to clasp her hands together to keep them from shaking.

"Forget it," Mary said. She grabbed the letter and left as quickly as she could.

Five

"What a bitch!" Mary shouted. She slapped the wheel with her palm, but not as hard as she could, and the reluctance to strike full-force made her feel silly. Her only recourse was to blast the radio and scream "Since U Been Gone" at the top of her lungs.

Rain began to sprinkle against the windshield as Mary white-knuckled the Focus back onto the freeway. Several minutes later, the Flying J Truck Stop appeared as she crested a hill, its billboard inviting weary motorists to stop, refuel, and buy third-rate car radios. The diner, attached to the north end of the truck stop, reminded her of her first date with David. He'd insisted that the French toast at the Flying J was world class, and after a reluctant first bite, she'd finished all of hers and part of his.

Mary thought of another first "date," and immediately feelings of shame and anger came rushing in. Her doctor had wined and dined her at Angelo's, the elegant Italian place two towns over, which was a far cry from the truck stop. The exclusive nature of Angelo's made it ideal for their secret romance. Much like the bank; if you weren't a member, you weren't permitted access.

She pushed those memories out of her mind, grimacing at the twinge of pain that shot up her back, seemingly as an echo of the affair. She was the one who had strayed; but her feelings of regret were all mixed up with anger at David over his silence, his punishing work schedule, and now this thing with the bank account.

The line of semis at the back of the diner caught Mary's attention. *Son of a bitch*, she thought, shaking her head. Thoughts of David's secret crept back into her mind.

When he'd first started driving the rig and making all those cross-country hauls, she hadn't liked it at all. Every time he'd have to stop off at a motel or rest stop, Mary would imagine him hooking up with some roadside skank. It had taken her almost a year to get over the unjustified suspicions, and in the end, she had been the one who had been unfaithful. She wondered how long it would take for David to truly forgive her.

The thoughts of her own indiscretions stilled her anger slightly. *Do I really have the right to be mad at him?* Mary asked herself. There could be a perfectly reasonable explanation for…

"What the hell?"

Her foot came off the gas and she leaned forward, squinting at the long line of semis, thinking her eyes were playing tricks on her. They weren't. At the end of the row, David's distinct red, white and blue "D" painted on the air dam above the cab stuck out like a sore thumb.

A horn blared, bringing her back to the road as a pick-up passed her on the right, its driver flipping her the bird.

Another horn blared behind her as she pulled off at the last minute, slowing to maneuver through the busy lot.

As she drove to the back, arguments and accusations began to fill her mind. She would catch him completely off-guard and find out just what the hell was going on.

He better have some good answers—

She slammed the brakes hard, sending the car and her body lurching forward. Mary felt her stomach turn and time seemed to stop. She forgot all about the letter, all about the bank account, all about the questions she wanted answered. A fire erupted inside her as she saw her husband standing at the back of his rig, talking very closely, and very secretively, with another woman.

The woman wore a pale blue dress, the hem several inches above her knee, and matching high heels. Long blonde hair fell down past her shoulders. She had a slender but athletic frame and a pair of breasts that strained the low-cut neckline to its limits.

A hurricane of thoughts flooded Mary's brain as she sat there in silence staring as the pair shared their moment. Every now and then the woman would glance around as if she was worried about being seen. Memories of doing the same thing at restaurants, and even while riding in the doctor's car, flashed through Mary's mind. Memories of keeping her eyes open for friends or acquaintances, praying David wouldn't somehow discover them.

In the end, he'd never actually seen them together, but the guilt had finally become too much for her to bear. When she'd finally revealed the truth to him, the look of betrayal and hurt on his face had nearly taken her to her knees. After months of therapy, David had finally said that he forgave her. But seeing him here now, all but embracing another woman, she realized that those words had obviously been lies.

The sudden wail of a police siren made her jump. She cursed and glanced over her shoulder. A massive, sleeper-cab Freightliner rolled to a stop several car-lengths back, a black and white Crown Victoria pulling in behind, lights flashing.

She let out a long breath as she turned back to her husband, and almost vomited at what she saw. David had pulled the woman close, embracing her. Both were looking in Mary's direction. For a second, Mary thought they were looking straight at her, but then realized they were watching the trooper behind her. After what seemed like an eternity, they exchanged a glance, then separated, stepping back from each other. The woman said something, then turned and walked away.

Mary watched as she climbed into a black Chevy Tahoe.

"That son of a bitch."

The SUV pulled away a second later, disappearing around the front of the truck stop. David's rig rumbled and shook briefly as he pulled out of his spot, followed the Tahoe around the building, and headed for the highway.

As if on cue, the dark clouds opened up and sheets of drenching rain pounded down on her. Mary sat there listening to the rain, trying to understand.

Despite having seen the evidence with her own eyes, Mary couldn't believe it. After everything they'd been through, she hadn't thought David capable of something like this.

Apparently, she'd been wrong.

Six

David was already out of bed when Mary woke up the next morning. She'd heard him come in, had even felt him crawl into bed after he'd showered, but the choice words she'd rehearsed to cut him down and tear any excuse to pieces didn't come. She had lain there awake, listening to him breathe, wondering what he'd been doing and who he'd been doing it with.

Mary couldn't remember when she'd finally drifted off, but when she opened her eyes the next morning the smell of coffee was already wafting up from downstairs. David was heading out early yet again. Heading out again to see *her*.

She found David at the table, reading the paper, a cup of coffee in his hand. He looked up as she stepped into their small kitchen. She scanned his deep blue eyes, looking for any sign of guilt. She saw none.

"Morning," he said, taking a sip.

"Morning," Mary echoed, hoping she didn't sound as furious as she felt. "You're up early again."

"Yeah. Wanted to try and get the yard mowed before it rained again."

"Good idea."

Mary filled her own mug, adding large amounts of sugar and cream before turning to face her husband. She held the mug close, smelling the dark aroma, watching him, wondering just what was going through his mind. He didn't seem nervous. In fact, he seemed fairly relaxed and normal. But, then again, by the end of her own affair, it had become such an everyday thing that it had started to seem normal. Guilt and regret were no longer dominating her thoughts.

"So, I was thinking," Mary said, finally. "I'm kind of ready for a new car."

David's eyes shot up to meet hers. He seemed to study her for a moment. "A new car?"

"Yeah, it's been a little while, and I'm sure we're pretty close to paying off the Ford. I really miss my Tahoe. Maybe we could trade the car in or something and find me another one."

David held her gaze for a minute, then took another sip of coffee. "We still have another two years to pay on the Ford."

Mary shrugged, trying to keep her tone light. "I know, I just figured, maybe we can go look. Maybe I could run to the bank and see what they can do for us."

"No," David said, a little too forcefully. He paused a moment, then continued. "I mean, yeah, that's an idea. I'm just not sure we can afford the payment right now."

Mary let her shoulders drop. "It's just that my back is really starting to act up in that thing. I think the Tahoe would be much more comfortable and better for my back."

"Yeah, I can see that."

Mary considered him for a moment, wisps of steam curling up between them. She could probably push this further, but part of her really wanted to catch them red-handed. She wanted to see the look on that bitch's face when she found them. She would bide her time, although it was killing her.

David arched an eyebrow. "What?"

"Nothing, forget it, it's nothing." Mary heard the words she said, but didn't agree with them. A second later she said, "It's just—"

A particularly high-pitched version of Thunderstruck by

ACDC echoed around the kitchen, making them both start. David cursed and fished the phone from his pants pocket. He frowned, checking the caller ID, then gave Mary a furtive look and moved into the living room as he answered.

"Hello?"

Mary waited until he rounded the corner, then quietly stood and moved to the doorway, holding her breath as she listened. *That woman sure has some balls to call the house, especially when she knows I'm here.*

"Yeah, Dan, what's up?" There was a pause. "No, I told you… I don't… of course I'm worried about that… No she doesn't…" He groaned. "Fine. Fine. But after this… yeah. Bye."

Mary dashed back to the counter, bumping the table as she went. David's mug rattled, spilling coffee onto the checkered tablecloth.

"What's wrong?" she asked as he came back in.

"Dan," David said, pointing to the phone. "Needs me to take a load up to Salina, rush job."

"What the hell, David," she said. "It's your day off. It's his company, let him handle it."

"He's the boss, that's not his job."

"But it's your day off!"

David held his hands up in surrender. "Look, I'm sorry. It won't take very long. It's a short hop up to Salina and back, shouldn't take more than a few hours. Maybe we can go to dinner or something later."

"Ugh, you always do this. You always say maybe we can do something later and we never end up doing anything!"

"Look, Mary, I'm sorry. It's my job. I can't just tell the guy no, he's my boss."

"Which, obviously, is more important than your wife."

"Oh, come on, now you're just being dramatic."

Mary pushed herself off the counter. "Dramatic? I'm dramatic? Because I want to spend time with my husband, I'm being dramatic? Fine, just do whatever the hell you want to do, you always do anyway."

"Are you freaking kidding me? I work my ass off twenty-four-seven and what the hell have you done?" David shouted, moving around her. He snatched up his thermos and opened the back door. "Oh, that's right. All you did was fuck your doctor."

The door slammed, leaving Mary alone in the quite kitchen, mouth open, shocked. Blood pounded in her ears as she replayed what he'd said over and over. David hadn't mentioned the affair in almost a year, not since the last therapy session when he'd finally been able to say, "I forgive you." Hell, even during the thick of it, he'd never come out right and said anything about it like that. Never those words.

He'd always been a loving, caring husband. She'd remembered his face when the medics were loading her up into the ambulance. Even with all the chaos going on around her, his words kept her going, made her feel safe.

"It's going to be okay."

When she'd learned about the damage to her spine, learned that she would need surgery to repair it, his words got her through it.

"It's going to be okay."

Even after. When she'd finally confessed about the affair with the doctor. Told him she didn't know why it happened, it just kind of… happened. Told him about how she had been vulnerable, and in pain, and the doctor had seemed to offer solace and healing. And even love. Told him how she was so, so sorry.

Even after all that, he'd still been there.

"It's going to be okay."

And now, today, after everything she'd seen in the last two days, she wasn't quite sure that it could ever be okay again.

Seven

Her blood boiled. She wanted to scream at him for being a worthless, insensitive asshole. Tell him what a piece of shit he was. But somewhere in the back of her mind, she knew he was right. She'd done a terrible thing and he'd stood by her. He'd supported her and loved her. He'd put in untold hours driving to all four corners of the country, trying to earn enough money to keep them afloat. She'd insisted on returning to work, but David had refused.

"You've been through enough," he'd said. "You need time to recover and heal."

But money wasn't the only thing she needed. She needed him, too. She wanted to hold him again, to feel him close.

"Son of a bitch," she muttered. Thoughts of holding him brought back the scene from the truck stop, and that Blue Bitch. Her anger and rage washed back over her like a flood.

David might have been loving and caring, at one time, but none of that mattered now. How could it matter when he was leaving everyday to go be with her? For a brief second, Mary could imagine that David had experienced these same feelings after he discovered the affair. But it didn't matter what he'd thought, or how he'd felt—because now he was the one betraying their vows. It wasn't like he got a free pass just because she'd made a mistake.

Filled with a new determination, Mary picked up the phone, surprised that she remembered the number, and dialed. After two rings a woman, who sounded overly happy and thrilled to be working this early in the morning, answered.

"Lawrence and Son's Freightlines, Amenia speaking, how can I direct your call?"

"Dan Lawrence, please."

"Just one moment."

The line clicked over and for the second time in as many days, Mary was left listening to elevator music. As she listened to the tinny excuse for a classical score, she went over exactly what she was going to say to David's boss, preparing just the right words and arguments. A moment later, the line clicked again and a man's voice came through the receiver.

"This is Dan."

Mary forgot her well planned verbal attack and said, "You're a real piece of work, Dan! I know that David isn't the only driver you have on stand by. It's his day off, for Christ's sake."

"Whoa, whoa, hold on. Mary, is that you?"

"Oh, come on, you know damn well who this is, and I'm tired of you constantly sending David out. He has plenty of responsibilities besides hauling loads for you."

"Mary, I—"

"Don't feed me any shit, either, I'm not in the mood at all."

"Now, hold on a minute, Mary. Slow down. What's going on?"

Mary took a breath, collecting herself. "I want to know why you keep sending my husband out on all these last minute hauls."

"David?"

"Oh, for shit's sake, yes David. He hasn't had a day off in over three weeks."

Dan hesitated. "Mary, I… I really don't know what you're talking about."

"Don't play games with me, Dan, you know damn well what I'm talking about. You just called him in not ten minutes ago."

The voice on the other end stammered slightly. "Mary, I—I'm sorry, but I don't have any idea what you're talking about. David hasn't worked for me in over six months."

Eight

Mary's mouth opened, but the vicious retort she'd prepared caught in her throat. She stared at the phone, looking at the number, assuring herself she'd dialed correctly.

"You're lying."

"Mary, is everything okay?"

"You're lying," she said again, mind racing. "You called him. I've seen the numbers on his phone, seen the money deposited in our accounts. Hell, I've even seen his log books."

"Honestly, Mary," Dan said. "I'm sorry, but David hasn't worked here in months. I had to let him go, he missed too much work. I wanted to keep him on, honest. I tried my best, but he just missed too many days. Corporate initiated the termination. Said they had to fill the spot with someone who'd show up and drive."

"Impossible," Mary said. "Yeah, he missed a few days here and there, but he's never stopped driving. Dan, you called him just this morning."

"I promise you I didn't."

"Okay, Dan, if he's not working for you, who's he been hauling for?"

"Look, Mary, he's not hauling for us. Maybe he's doing some freelance work, I don't know. Maybe you should take that up with him."

Mary stared out the kitchen window, at the empty place in the drive where David parked his rig. Trying to make sense of it all. Why would Dan lie to her? Hell, why would David lie to her?

"Mary?"

She hung up without another word.

Nine

She didn't know exactly how long she'd been driving, didn't know why she'd even started in the first place, but she found herself pulling into the Flying J all the same. She drove past the semis, parked in a row behind in the back. David's rig was nowhere to be found, but, then again, she hadn't expected it to be there.

She stopped near the diner's entrance, looked in at the people eating, and thought back to their first date. She could still smell the French toast, could practically taste it.

Her stomach grumbled, reminding her she hadn't eaten yet. What the hell. She didn't know what to do next... she didn't even know where he was. She wasn't ready to call him—something in her knew he would just stonewall again—lie through his teeth. She had to come up with a plan to force him to be honest with her about the car, the woman... and the six months of living some kind of fake life. Maybe some food would help her think.

She found a seat at one of the booths next to the window. A second later the waitress, an older woman with greying hair, appeared next to her, smiling. The nametag above her pocket said Beth.

"Can I get you anything, hun?"

"I think some French toast."

Beth's smile faded momentarily. "Oh, I'm sorry hun, we've just run out of that."

"Of course," Mary muttered.

"Can it get you anything else?"

Frustrated, Mary waved a hand through the air. "No, thanks. Just coffee."

The woman away and an idea struck Mary. "Wait."

Mary fumbled with her phone, brought up Facebook and scrolled until she found what she was looking for. She held it up for Beth to see. "Have you ever seen this man before?"

Beth slipped her half-moon glasses up over her nose and studied the image. "Who? David? Of course I do. Such a sweetie."

Mary's stomach turned. "What do you mean *of course*?"

"Comes in all the time. Coffee, lots of cream, and coconut cream pie."

"Are you sure?"

"Absolutely. Usually comes in with his sister…" she looked up, through the window lost in thought. "Mira, I think. Is that right? Mira?"

Mary's heart pounded in her chest. Her teeth clenched together, Mary felt her grip tightening on the phone, threatening to crack it.

"Are you okay?"

Mary shook herself. *Get yourself together.* "Fine. Mira; shorter gal, dark brown hair, kind of skanky looking?"

Beth's eyebrows rose, as if she'd just made a very important connection. She took her glasses off, let them hang from the strap around her neck and looked down the bridge of her nose at Mary. "Not his sister then."

"Not his sister," Mary repeated.

"Huh," Beth said, dropping down into the booth opposite Mary. "Well, that certainly explains a few things."

"Oh?"

"There was just always… something off about them, I guess. Now that I think about it, they were always looking around, like they were looking for someone. You know?"

"How often did they come in together?"

"Oh," Beth drew out the word and looked up, as if the answer to Mary's question was written on the ceiling. "Probably every few days or so. Came in this morning, matter of fact. Sat right over there."

Mary glanced in the direction she indicated. "They were here today?"

"Yep, came in around eight or so, didn't stay very long. Thought I heard them talking about the Kite Flyer, but I could be wrong. These things aren't what they used to be," Beth said, pointing to her ears.

Mary straightened. "What's the Kite Flyer?"

"Old rest stop about forty miles north of here. Been out of business for years, nothing up there now but dirt roads and farmland."

Ten

The Kite Flyer wasn't just old and abandoned; it almost didn't exist anymore. The sign, an old metal statue of a kite flying above the building, had completely rusted over. Mary was surprised it was still standing.

As Mary pulled into the lot, a lump grew in her throat. She couldn't decide if she was more angry or afraid. There was no sign of David's rig or the black Tahoe she'd seen the day before. A single dirt road led away from the station to the West, vanishing in the hazy distance.

Well, you've come this far, Mary thought.

She pulled onto the dirt road and headed west. Seven miles down the road a row of trees appeared, running the length of the road, which elbowed to the left and up to an old white farmhouse. The whole scene was like something out of a movie; wide front pouch, white wood siding, small windows. Several large trees surrounded the place; one even had a rope swing hanging from its branches. Two outbuildings flanked the house and there was a small carport and a large red barn on the far side.

Mary's breath caught in her throat when she caught sight of the familiar air dam poking up from behind the barn, the red, white and blue letter "D" obvious and undeniable. Her stomach turned despite herself and she looked in the rear-view mirror. She could still turn back—it wasn't too late yet. She could turn around and go home and forget this whole thing had ever happened. Pretend everything was still okay.

No, Mary told herself. *Can't turn back now.*

With a deep calming breath, she climbed out of the car and started for the house. She jogged along the row of evergreens, searching for any sign of her husband and that bitch in the blue dress.

What color are you wearing today, you little slut?

Inside the carport, she found two Tahoes, parked side by side, one black and one blue. The blue one bore a 60-day temporary tag. The words Central Plains National Bank were printed along the top of the tag. She was positive that the woman had been driving the black one back at the Flying J. But who was driving the blue one?

She moved quietly up to the house, watching and listening. It looked like all the windows on the ground level were open, and as she got closer she thought she heard something. A second later she stopped dead in her tracks, realizing what she was hearing.

A woman was moaning, loudly. And not from pain, but with pleasure.

Blood pounding in her ears, Mary tiptoed closer, trying to get a look through one of the windows. It was dark inside the house, and apart from the outlines of furniture and interior walls, she couldn't see much of anything else. She kept moving, trying to get a better view inside. Finally, at the window just past the end of the porch, she got one. She steeled herself and looked in.

The woman's back was to Mary. Her skirt was lifted, and she was astride the man who sat on the couch in the middle of the room. The urge to vomit crept up into Mary's throat. She stood there, paralyzed, watching the couple go at it.

"Stand up," the male said, his breath ragged.

Mary inched back around the window frame, then peered over the edge. The woman climbed off, flicking her long, blonde hair back, and gave Mary her first view of the man. Mary let out a clipped gasp and turned away from the window, hand covering her mouth.

It wasn't David.

Eleven

What the hell is going on?

Mary backed away from the window. Where was David? He had to be there; she'd seen his rig.

She moved around to the back toward the large barn she'd seen from the road. A shout of ecstasy drew her attention to an open door on the back of the house, propped open by an old, worn-out tire.

Muddy footprints led up a short set of stairs and into the house. Mary was wrestling with the realization of how dangerous it would be to try to get inside when something in the grass glinted in the sunlight, drawing her attention.

She bent down and picked up a large set of keys. They were David's keys. That stupid K-State keychain, with the faded lettering, staring her right in the face.

As Mary moved silently up the stairs and peered into the small mudroom, a stream of passionate shouts and cursing echoed through the house. Two pairs of shoes had been discarded just inside the door; neither pair was David's. She crossed the small mudroom, inching up to the door, and peered into the kitchen. What she saw turned her legs to Jello.

In the middle of the kitchen, David sat in a chair, his head hanging limply to one side. His clothes were tattered and dirty, his hands and feet bound to the chair by thick rope. Blood covered his face. His dark hair was matted to his skull, mostly damp from sweat or blood or both. Mary suddenly forgot about the two people in the front room and dashed to her husband.

"David?" she whispered.

David looked up at her, his face a mask of confusion and horror. "Mary, what the hell are you doing here?"

"I…" Mary trailed off, running her fingers over the rope binding his wrist to the chair. "Are you okay? What's going on?"

"I can explain later—but you have to get out of here. They'll kill us both if they find you here."

"Who are they?"

"Later," David hissed, eyes blazing. He gave the doorway a furtive glance, then lowered his voice even more.

"Mary, listen to me. The gun in my truck, you need to get it."

"I don't—"

"Grab that knife, there," he nodded to the counter. "Cut my hands free, then go and get it."

Mary hesitated. "But…"

"Mary, they'll be in here any minute!"

Stunned, Mary grabbed the knife and went to work. As

she sawed, the sounds from the other room seemed to be rising in intensity and frequency. David was right, they didn't have much time.

It seemed to take forever to cut through the thick rope, but finally it fell away and David pulled his first arm free, wiggling his fingers, trying to get the blood flowing again.

"Good, here," he took the knife from her. "I'll do the other one. Now, go and get the gun. Hurry."

"David, what the hell is going on?"

Her husband shook his head. "No time! Go."

Mary frowned. "David, what—"

"Later! Just get the gun. I may need it."

Mary stared at him for moment, unsure despite his insistence. She glanced over her shoulder toward the front room, then back to her husband.

He must have read the conflict on her face. "It's okay, Mary. It's going to be okay."

Twelve

The door creaked loudly as Mary pulled it open and climbed into the cab. She winced and looked back toward the house.

David's .38 special, the one his father had given him, was secured in a small holster fastened to the seat's frame. She pulled it free and carefully inspected the small pistol.

She'd never actually fired the gun—she hadn't ever wanted to—but David had gone over the basics with her. A glance at the cylinder told her the gun was loaded. She knew that much. Did she need to do anything else to make sure it was ready? A shiver ran threw her at the thought of him actually using it. David's instructions came back to her.

"This one doesn't have a safety. Just keep your finger off the trigger until you're ready to fire."

Gun in hand, Mary hopped down from the cab and ran back to the house. She jumped the steps to the mudroom. David might already be free now from the ropes, so they could—

Mary froze in her tracks.

A large man, his muscular back covered with tattoos, stood over David, wearing only his boxers. He looked over his shoulder at her as her feet slapped down on the wood floor. His hair was cut short, beard neatly trimmed, his eyes like deep pits of hate.

He straightened. "Now, where'd this puta come from?"

David leaned to the side. He was still tied by one arm. "Mary, run! Get—"

A wet smack echoed through the kitchen as the man backhanded David, cutting him off.

"David!" Mary leveled the pistol at the tattooed man, straining to hold it steady. "Get away from him!"

The man laughed. "Yo, Mira! Check this out!" He pointed at the pistol. "What you got there, missy?"

She gritted her teeth, struggling to pull the hammer back. "Get back! I'll shoot!"

The man laughed again. "You gonna shoot me with that little thing? No, no, no, I don't think so."

Behind him David let out a weak groan, fresh blood streamed out of his nose. "Get away," he said, his voice weak.

The woman appeared in the doorway, wearing an oversized t-shirt. "Alejandro, what are you talk—oh, shit." Her eyes went wide at the sight of Mary.

"Who is this puta?" Alejandro asked.

"It's his wife."

"Aww, now this is special," Alejandro said. "Don't think I've ever killed a married couple before. Excelente!"

"Shut up, Alejandro," Mira said, stepping into the kitchen. "Now, you go ahead and put that gun down, lady. Wouldn't want it to accidentally go—"

The woman lunged.

A thunderous crack echoed through the small kitchen and the woman spun backward, letting out a blood-curdling scream. She bounced off the kitchen door and fell back through the doorway.

The pistol bucked, sending Mary stumbling backwards, ears ringing. The man let out a wordless scream of fury and charged. Dazed, and only slightly aware of what she was doing, she tried to bring the pistol around.

It roared again.

This time Mary was prepared for the recoil and didn't stumble. The man howled in pain but didn't stop coming. He plowed into her, driving a shoulder into her chest, knocking the wind out of her. They landed hard, together, pain shooting through her spine. Stars danced in her vision as her head smacked against the floor.

"Mary!" She heard David shout from the chair. His voice, filled with horror and frustration, was a growl.

Alejandro was on her, his half-naked body pinning her to the floor. Mary tried to push him off but he was far too strong. Sweaty, meaty hands wrapped around her neck and began to squeeze.

"Usted puta de mierda!" he shouted, but his words seemed far away, distant.

Fire erupted inside her as he clamped down on her windpipe, cutting off her air. She opened her mouth, desperately trying to suck in air, but none came. She slapped at his arms, kicked her feet against the floor, trying for any kind of leverage.

He's going to kill me!

Blackness crept into her vision. Her hands clawed at her attacker, fingernails digging into his skin. It made no difference; his hands were like a vice, squeezing the life out of her.

She could feel consciousness begin to fade. The rage contorting Alejandro's face became her entire world. Teeth stained yellow, nostrils flaring, eyes that seemed to blaze with hatred and malice.

David, Mary thought, as her arms dropped to the floor. *I love…*

In the distance, somewhere in another world, a sharp crack echoed around her.

The vice-like fingers around her neck went slack and she gasped as air rushed into her oxygen-starved lungs. She arched off the floor then rolled to her side, frantically inhaling the wonderful air. Her throat burned, but she didn't care, every breath was a blessing. Everything around her was a blur. Black and purple flashes danced in her vision. In the distance, she thought she heard David's voice, but couldn't make out the words. After the thug was finished with her, David would be next.

She felt hands grabbing her again and terror washed over her, knowing the tattooed beast was coming back. Frantically, she pushed away, kicking and slapping blindly. He was coming for her, his hands were going to wrap around her neck again and this time they weren't going to let go. He was going to kill her. She backed into a wall and looked frantically for an escape route. The man was on her again. She turned away from him, not wanting to look at his face. She couldn't look at those eyes again. Eyes of pure evil.

Hands shook her.

"Mary! Stop."

David's voice. David was talking to her.

"It's okay, it's me!"

She forced herself to look up. Deep blue eyes, the eyes she'd fallen in love with, met hers. She looked down and saw he was holding the revolver. She must have dropped it during the struggle.

"Oh, David!" Mary cried, wrapping her arms around his neck. She shook against him, confusion, fear, relief, all gushing out of her like water from dam. "David! Oh, god!"

"It's okay, I'm here."

Mary sobbed into her husband's chest, glad to be alive, glad they were both alive. After what seemed like an eternity, she leaned back and wiped the tears from her face. David's lip was split in two places and the purple bruise forming around his eye looked horrible.

"Your face."

David shook his head. "I'll live."

Mary looked past him to the motionless heaps on the floor. Her would-be killer lay face down, a pool of blood slowly forming under him. The woman lay just beyond him, unmoving.

"Are they…?"

David looked over his shoulder and nodded. "I think so.

I hope so." His voice was grim. He turned back to look at Mary. "Are you okay?"

Mary touched her neck. The skin was tender to the touch and every breath ached. A headache was growing behind her eyes and a handful of spots still played across her vision—but she was alive.

Thirteen

"David," she said, frowning. "So what the hell was all this? Who are—were—these people?"

"What are you even doing out here, Mary? How did you find me?"

"No." Mary shook her head. "You first. You need to tell me what the hell is going on. Who was that woman? I saw you at the diner, saw you with her. Why did they beat you half to death and tie you to a chair in the middle of nowhere?"

"I made deliveries for her. Product."

It took a few seconds for Mary to process what he was saying. "Product? You mean… drugs?"

"I just delivered stuff for them. They told me where to pick it up and where to drop it off. Simple."

"Simple! David, we just killed two people! There is nothing simple about that. How could you let yourself get caught up with this?"

David shook his head. "I never meant to. I was only supposed to do one long haul and that was it. But, damn, the money was hard to resist. Hector from work got me the job, gave me Mira's number when Dan shit-canned me. I figured it would be an easy way to pay off everything after... after the surgery."

Mary touched her neck. She could still feel Alejandro's fingers wrapped tightly around her.

"You got fired. And you didn't tell me." The familiar pain arced down her back as David helped her stand up. The two of them walked slowly toward the back door, moving away from the horror in the kitchen.

"I was embarrassed." He shook his head.

"Oh, David." She took his hand, and gently felt the rope burns around his wrist. "So what happened today that made everything blow up?"

"I tried to tell them that I was done driving for them—I wanted out. Obviously, it's not that easy to walk away from a job like this."

Mary shivered, thinking about how close they had come to being killed. She turned to her husband, pushing the hair off his forehead, still matted with blood.

"David, I drove out here to find you because I was determined to catch you in the act. Of screwing your little blonde friend—or so I thought. And because I got your letter about the new car..."

"Thank god you did."

She nodded. "I know. The car—"

"The car was a gift for you. It was supposed to be a surprise for our anniversary, but—"

Mary shook her head. "I don't want us to have secrets any more, David. I trust you. And I need to know that you trust me."

"Hey," David said, his voice calm. "You saved my life. I trust you."

"And you saved mine." A sob caught in Mary's throat. "I'm sorry… about—"

"Shh. I said I forgive you, and I do." David touched her back, where the scars still throbbed. "No more secrets. We're in this for the long haul."

She felt herself smiling through tears. "We are."

He took her hand. "And it's going to be okay."

Q&A with Josh Hayes

That was quite the ride! What inspired this story? Any personal experiences with doing "long hauls" yourself?

The only experience I have with "long hauls" is when I was in the military. I guarded nuclear missiles and our sites were located off the installation. My work week consisted of staying out at one of those sites for four days at a time, which got more than a little tiresome.

The story came to me after a week of brainstorming, and I thought it would be interesting to explore the mind of a person who had already cheated. Going through those kinds of experiences, how would they interpret them?

You write science fiction as well as mysteries. Why those genres, and how are they different for you?

I love science fiction and fantasy! I love being transported to other worlds and experiencing something that is totally different from everyday life here on Earth. Usually, mystery appears as an element in my sci-fi, and aside from one other short story, "The Long Haul" was real attempt at contemporary fiction.

My favorite thing about the genres is the "I didn't see that coming" moment. *Seven* and *The Usual Suspects* are my go-to movies whenever I need inspiration. I love the twists (and double twists) that leave you speechless and amazed.

The most difficult part about writing a mystery is knowing what the mystery is and knowing where to draw the line between too much information and not enough.

What are you working on now?

Right now, I'm finishing up another short story for a themed science fiction anthology and going through final revisions on the third book in my *Second Star* series, *Shadows of Neverland.* It's been tricky getting all my characters to do what I need them to do.

Also, I've almost finished the pre-writing for a military sci-fi mystery about a detective investigating a failed mission in an effort to discover what went wrong. It's unique in that the majority of the book will be presented in third person limited, but as he's interviewing the survivors, the point of view will shift to first person, from the point of view of the person being interviewed. The catch is that some of the survivors are lying.

Please tell readers where they can catch up with you or find out about other books you have available.

You can find me on Facebook (Josh Hayes) and Twitter (@ joshhayeswriter) and I have a webpage: www.joshhayeswriter.com. I also have a podcast with fellow author Scott Moon, where we interview authors, review books and talk about the craft of writing: www.keystrokemedium.com.

All Secrets Lead to Lies

by Anne Kelleher

I

The red light on the answering machine blinked a silent reproach through the glass door as Margie Dowling turned the key. Her breath caught in her throat as her eyes fell on the names in gold block letters: Dowling, Dowling & Dowd.

There was only one Dowling now, and Dowd was long gone.

She pushed the door open, thinking of the last time she'd been here, almost seven weeks ago, when their investigative agency had been humming with activity. Lights were on, phones were ringing. There were open files on Rosemary the receptionist's desk, clients waiting in the reception area. She was in her office, combing through internet records; Larry was in his, arguing with the police about a dognapping.

Then the phone rang one last time, and their world changed forever. Larry called her into his office, closed the door, and put the doctor on speakerphone. They held hands and listened.

Cancer, the doctor said. No doubt. Pancreatic cancer. No doubt.

Larry was dead in three weeks.

Margie turned on the Tiffany dragonfly lamp atop Rosemary's desk. Larry had been so proud when they scored it at a tag sale. She blinked back tears. Larry was everywhere she looked– from the prize-winning orchids to the jewel-toned walls and Berber rugs. Photographs with members of local law enforcement, journalists, and celebrities smiled back at her from every angle. Even the new blinds bore Larry's stamp.

She couldn't let the memories stop her. There were cases to close or refer out, bills to pay, and a business to sell. The change from happy wife to sudden widow left her reeling. She needed to focus on something—anything—to help her get through each day. Getting the business ready to sell would do just that. She hoped.

She opened the blinds. Murky light from the dismal afternoon flooded the space. To her surprise, the plants looked well-watered. The mail, delivered through a slot in the front door when the office was closed, was neatly stacked on Rosemary's desk.

Someone had been in the office, she realized. Could it be the cleaning service, she wondered, although that wouldn't explain who had picked up today's mail. She'd told the service not to come after it was clear that Larry wouldn't recover.

And it wasn't Rosemary, because Rosemary had left on

an overdue vacation the week after the funeral, and still hadn't returned.

From down the hall that led to the offices came the distinct flush of the washroom toilet.

Margie froze. Someone was here. She pulled her small pistol from her purse and carefully unlocked the safety. "Hello?" she called tentatively. "Hello?"

The washroom door creaked open, and from the shadows at the end of the hall a bulky figure emerged.

"Ah, Margie, hello. It's me, Pastor Dave, from church? Um… sorry… I… you did know people from the church were coming by to water the plants? Today was my turn." He ambled forward, smiling from behind his round spectacles.

Margie relaxed, put the gun down, and held out her hand. "Uh, I… I did forget… but thank you, Pastor. I appreciate everyone's kindness." She tried not to flinch as his moist palm touched hers. There was something she didn't like about the man, no matter how unchristian that might be. He reached forward and enfolded her in a hug. From his clerical collar, she caught a whiff of his aftershave. It was the same as Larry's.

Her heart contracted, and her eyes filled with tears.

She withdrew a tissue from her pocket, maneuvering so that the edge of the reception desk was between them. "Thank you for taking care of the plants. Larry sure loved his orchids."

"We all loved Larry. Everyone wants to help any way we can. How soon will you get the office up and running?"

"Oh," she shook her head. "I'm selling the business."

"Gosh, that seems awfully quick." Pastor Dave stroked his comb-over. "Are you sure you want to do that?"

Margie shrugged. "I don't want to run it myself, Pastor. Larry was the rainmaker… I'm the computer geek. Now that Larry's gone…" Her voice trailed off as grief swept through her.

"I can understand that." Pastor Dave patted her arm. She suppressed the urge to recoil as he continued, "And I know you have work to do, so I'll—"

"I'm sorry, have I come at a bad time?" The voice at the door startled them both. A petite red-haired woman, dressed in a belted Burberry raincoat and holding a dripping umbrella, stood on the mat at the entrance.

Margie looked up with a sense of relief. "Oh, no, not at all—"

"Mrs. Holcombe." Pastor Dave was at the woman's side faster than Margie thought he could move. "I just want to say again how sorry I am for your tragic—"

"And you are, again?" Mrs. Holcombe interrupted him. Margie liked her just for that.

"Dave Brush." He pumped her hand. "I'm the pastor from Holy Spirit Lutheran? The one on the corner of Lexington and Concord?" He tittered, as if he'd made a joke. "I—I assisted Pastor Norris at your husband's…"

"Ah, yes. At my husband's funeral. Of course. I thought you looked familiar. Thank you, Pastor Brush. That was very kind of you." She glanced at Margie, who was wondering why she recognized the woman's pale face and haunted eyes. She looked more bereft than Margie.

The woman continued, "Mrs. Dowling? I think we've met briefly in the past but never been introduced. I'm Jocelyn Holcombe. I have a case I hope you'll take."

II

Margie waved a thankful good-bye to Pastor Dave, then gestured to the chair beside the receptionist's desk. She sank down in Rosemary's chair. She couldn't bring herself to go into the back offices, even though she knew she should if she were going to talk with a prospective client.

But then, she reminded herself, Mrs. Holcombe wasn't a prospective client because Margie wasn't taking her case.

"Thank you so much for taking time for me, Mrs. Dowling."

Margie tried to smile. "Well, the thing is, Mrs. Holcombe—"

"Call me Joss. Everyone does."

"Okay, and please call me Margie. But, you see, I'm not taking any more cases. My husband died a few weeks ago."

"Oh, my goodness." Joss sat straighter. "Oh, my dear, I didn't realize… how selfish of me… I…"

"No, how could you know, after all," Margie said. She opened Rosemary's desk drawer and pulled out a tablet. "Let me give you the names of a couple of others who could help you." She scrawled two, then handed Joss the paper.

To Margie's surprise, Joss glanced at it, then shook her head. "Any other ideas?"

Margie cocked her head. "You've already talked to them?"

"Both."

"Okay, let me think." In the greater Trenton area, there were dozens of private investigators. Margie tapped her pencil on the desk, then wrote three more names. "Try those."

Joss glanced down, then handed the paper back with an apologetic shrug. "I already have."

"They all said no, too?" Margie felt genuinely stumped. Who was this woman, and why did Margie think she should know who Joss was?

Then it clicked.

The Holcombe Home Invasion, as the press had dubbed it. It had occurred in a neighboring town, a couple weeks before Larry's diagnosis. Jocelyn and Jonathon Holcombe were both doctors. Dr. Jonathon Holcombe was especially well-known in his field of endocrinology. A noted researcher at Princeton University, his team had just announced a break-through in the hormones involved in the aging process. Some papers called it the "Fountain of Youth."

But in the middle of the night, the Holcombes' home was broken into by a couple of thugs. In the chaos, the house was set on fire, and Dr. Jonathon Holcombe was killed.

Dr. Jocelyn Holcombe, a black belt in judo, escaped with minor injuries after disabling one of the assailants. He'd died of smoke inhalation, and the other had died in a car crash while trying to escape. With both perpetrators dead, there was no one to prosecute. The case was closed with no motive but happenstance. It could've been any house, anywhere.

But fear lingered. Margie vaguely remembered a sudden spate of neighborhood watch flyers, calls for volunteers to serve as block captains, and community meetings across the greater Princeton area.

Beneath the blur of Joss's makeup, Margie could see the red line of a new scar. She felt a deep swell of sympathy for the other woman. As blindsided as Margie felt by Larry's death, at least she hadn't been attacked in her own home.

"Joss, forgive me, but I don't understand… what kind of case?"

Joss met Margie's eyes. "Everyone says we were just unlucky." She paused. "But I don't believe that. I heard those men talking to Jon. They came looking for money. And he seemed willing to give it to them."

"Why was he willing to do that?"

"I don't know—most of the conversation was in Spanish, and I don't speak Spanish. But we had a few minutes to talk, and Jon told me to go to the bank. They were going to make me drive, and I figured I could disable the one who was coming with me. I could've driven directly to the police station. But Jon insisted I get the money."

"Why? Why would he do that?"

"Exactly." Joss slapped the top of the desk with an open palm. "That's what I'm hoping you'll tell me."

"Why didn't you just go to the police, despite what your husband said?"

"Because it was clear from what I could overhear that Jon was involved in something... something not... not right." She broke off, face contorting, then took a deep breath, visibly composing herself. "They came looking for him... I heard one of them say, 'Now we come for you.'"

She gazed at Margie with the intensity of a high beam headlight. "Please help me understand the truth. Three men are dead. One's my husband. One is dead because of me. I need to understand why. And the police, the DA—they're not telling me what really happened. I just know it."

Margie took a deep breath. "You said you could tell from the way they were talking that your husband was involved in something 'not right.' Are you going to be okay finding out whatever that is?" She knit her fingers together. "Dr. Holcombe was very well-known. Well-respected.I remember reading all the articles about his new results… the Fountain of Youth…" She hesitated, wondering if she really wanted to get involved with this, and what an investigation might unearth.

"Yes, he was. But we all have a dark side, don't we? Isn't that how you and your husband made a living?"

She's brave, Margie thought, much braver than I am. She stared back into startling blue eyes that fortunately weren't at all like Larry's. But they were like Hunter's. At the thought of their old partner, her heart contracted again. They'd been such good friends and partners for so long. She hadn't heard from Hunter in over five years—not since right after the dramatic breakup of the partnership forced her to take sides. She had never understood why Larry didn't take Hunter's name off the door. She didn't even understand what the argument had been about. Maybe it was time she heard Hunter's side.

Margie made a sudden decision, surprising even herself. "I'll help you, Joss." She sighed and shook her head. "I have a feeling Larry wants me to. I dreamed last night that he told me to get my butt in here. I guess I can always pack this place up after your case is done."

III

For a long time after Jocelyn left, Margie sat staring at the retainer check. They'd discussed first steps. She wasn't going to be able to do this alone.

She should call Hunter, she thought. After it was all over, he'd called one night when Larry was at choir practice and told that her if she ever needed anything, she should let him know. It was a small omission she'd kept from Larry, figuring it would only upset him.

With a shaking hand, she punched in the number she still knew by heart. It rang three times, and then the familiar growl said, "Margie, that you?"

She sank a little, some of the tension leaving her body at the sound of his voice. "Hunter, how'd you know?"

"The miracle of caller ID. I read about Larry in the paper. I'm so very sorry, Margie. I should've come."

"After the way things ended…" She sighed. "I understand why you didn't."

"You doing okay?" He sounded somewhere between gruff and worried.

"I'm doing okay… it's the shock. One day he was fine, and the next day he was dying, and the day after that he was gone. At least that's how it seems."

"Maybe it's better, Margie. He didn't linger, he didn't suffer long. Things were good, right?"

She took a deep breath, hesitating. Were things good? Maybe as good as it was possible for them to be. The older Larry got, the unhappier he seemed. "Yeah… yeah, things were good. We were good, the business was good…." Margie shook herself. Whatever issues she had with Larry were gone with him. "I'm sorry, Hunter, that's not why I'm calling. How… how are you doing?"

"I'm doing all right. Hate the DMV. Other than that, not much has changed."

"You haven't found another pretty woman to settle down with?"

"Mm." He made a noise that somehow conjured Violet, his ex-wife. Violet could be a lot of fun… when she was drunk. "No, no more pretty women for me. The one I had and the one that got away were plenty. And no pretty woman wants an old bulldog like me. Did you call just to chat, Margie, or is there something you need?"

He knew her so well. She wondered fleetingly about the one who got away, but the time wasn't right to ask. "I guess there's something I really need."

"The doctor's in, kiddo. What can I do?"

"Does the name Jocelyn Holcombe mean anything?"

"The Holcombe Home Invasion… the one who survived. Why?"

"She came to see me this afternoon. She wants me to find out why it happened. She says her husband knew the perps. And that the police are covering it up."

"No shit." Hunter gave a long low whistle. "Margie, you sure you want to get involved in this right now?"

"Yeah, I think it would be good for me. I took a retainer from her."

"Give it back."

"I think Larry wants me to take this case."

"Oh, honey. What makes you think that?"

"Last night, I dreamed he woke me up and told me I'd better get to the office. It was so real, Hunter… he was teasing me about staying in bed on rainy days, like always. He even picked out my outfit. And then I woke up, and he was gone, of course. But it was raining, just like my dream, and the outfit he picked out was in the front of the dry-cleaning that came yesterday." She paused for breath. "So I took it as a sign."

"That you should go to the office?"

"Yeah, start picking up the pieces, try to move on…you know." She had to stop to swallow the lump in her throat.

"You know he wants you to be happy."

"So within ten minutes, Jocelyn Holcombe showed up. I tried to refer to her to five other agencies, Hunter. All of them already told her no."

"Of course they did, Margie. Anyone not in the throes of grief would."

"You really think I should turn her down, Hunter? You believe my dream was just a coincidence? That I just happened to be there when I haven't been in six—no, almost seven weeks?"

Margie could almost see his skeptical expression before he responded. "So what can I do?"

"You said you hate the DMV. Take a few days off. Come help me. For old times' sake." The words tumbled out of her mouth like stones. Until she said them, she had no idea how much she'd missed having Hunter around. He had always been a balance to Larry's mercurial nature.

"Oh, kiddo." The silence dragged on so long, she prepared herself for a 'no.' But instead, he surprised her. "Sure, I'll come. You can't do this without me. Not now."

IV

It was late by the time Margie left. She listened to the messages, sorted the mail, and called a temp agency for someone until Rosemary got back. Maybe by the time she closed out the Holcombe case, the entire office could be closed out, too.

And then what, she wondered. Maybe she'd take a cruise or go backpacking around the world. She was only forty-five, after all. She could find a Greek island, have an affair with a younger man, run away to Paris, and go to cooking school. Or art school.

The setting sun blinded her as she pulled into her street. At least the rain was over. As she turned into her driveway, she glanced up at the house, at the bedroom window that overlooked the street.

A white oval looked back at her.

And then it was gone.

A chill swept through her, gooseflesh rising up and down her arms.

No, she told herself. No, Larry wasn't haunting her.

Someone was in the house.

For the second time that day, she pulled out her gun. She put her phone in her pocket and cautiously opened the front door. From upstairs, she heard a crash and the sound of splintering glass. Without hesitation, she grabbed her phone, hit the 911 button, and ran up the steps, gun drawn.

"911, what's your emergency?"

"Someone's broken into my house," Margie replied in a fierce whisper.

She reached the top of the steps and paused, listening intently.

"What's your location?"

"1683 Morningside."

"Car's on its way, ma'am. What's your name?"

"Margie Dowling."

"Are you safe, Margie?"

Margie shoved the phone back into her pocket. She heard nothing but an ominous silence. The crash had come from the direction of her bedroom. The carpet muffled her steps as she edged down the hall, clutching the gun.

From far away, she heard the wail of a siren.

"Margie?" The 911 operator squawked in her pocket. "Can you answer me? Margie?"

The sirens were getting louder. Margie raised the gun and swung into her bedroom. A cold breeze blew the curtains, one out and one in the shattered window. The room was empty.

"Mrs. Dowling?" From the first floor, she could hear the policeman shout.

"I'm up here," she called. "Please, come… there was definitely someone here."

* * *

It was after eight by the time they were ready to leave. The detectives who came to the house took their time. They asked questions, took pictures, and dusted for fingerprints. They seemed marginally interested in the fact that Jocelyn Holcombe had come to see her.

It bothered Margie that despite their interest in her conversation with Jocelyn, they dismissed her concern that the two incidents were related. After all, the perpetrators in the Holcombe attack were dead.

She decided she wouldn't stay in the house, because there was no sign of forced entry, which implied that the intruder might have a key. The thought of staying here with the plywood-filled hole in the master bedroom window and being alone in the otherwise empty house unnerved her.

It was too late to call a locksmith, and she needed to consider a home alarm system. Or a dog, something Larry's allergies wouldn't have tolerated.

A dog, she thought, as she grabbed an overnight bag and began to pull a few things together. A dog might keep her from feeling too lonely. The plywood rattled against the window frame. The rain was starting again. Shards of glass glittered in the carpet. She was going to have to do a better job of cleaning up later.

The house phone rang as she was on her way out the door. She briefly considered not answering, then recognized the number. "Hunter," she said. "I'm on my way out. Can I call you in an hour?"

"Where're you going at 9:30?"

"Checking into the Holiday Inn. Someone broke into the house this afternoon."

"Margie." Hunter cleared his throat. "Did you say someone broke into your house? You're not going to a hotel. You're coming to me. I'm still in Hightstown. Same address. I'll expect you in an hour. No arguments." Then he hung up.

V

"Margie, this sounds dangerous. As your old friend and Larry's… I think you should take this warning seriously." Hunter poured Scotch into her glass. "I know you want to help Jocelyn Holcombe, but don't you think this is hitting too close to home?"

"So what're you suggesting? Say I changed my mind?"

Hunter shrugged. "Maybe. At least lie low a couple days." He paused. "What did the cops say? They think it's related?"

"They said it was most likely an interrupted robbery. They told me to get an alarm system. And a dog."

Hunter rolled his eyes. "Tell us something we don't know. I think you should hide out here a few days. Turn off your cell phone and go off the grid."

"I've been off the grid. Listen, I'm as spooked as you are. I don't intend to risk my life. But now this feels… personal, even if it's not."

For a moment, Hunter gazed at her with an unreadable expression. Then he raised his glass. "Feisty as ever, Mrs. Dowling. Here's to the temporary resurrection of Dowling, Dowling, and Dowd."

They clinked glasses, and Margie took a long swallow. The whiskey exploded in her belly with a comforting heat that gradually suffused her whole body. She closed her eyes, and for a moment, she could feel Larry's presence in the room. Then the feeling was gone. She let her breath out slowly. "Why did you and Larry fight?"

Hunter put his glass down and cocked his head. "He never told you?"

"He said you crossed boundaries you should never have crossed. I—uh—I asked him if he meant you made a pass at him, and he laughed. He said no, you didn't do that. But he never answered the question, either."

"Jesus, I thought you knew." Hunter took another sip. "I thought…well, I don't know what I thought, but I guess that's why I wasn't all that surprised that Jocelyn came to see you."

The hair stood up on the back of Margie's neck. "Why weren't you surprised?"

"Because that's what we argued about, Margie. Larry had gone to see Jonathon Holcombe. He wanted to sign up for some experimental drug trial. I was trying to talk him out of it."

"That's what he meant by crossing boundaries?"

Hunter shrugged. "I guess so."

"What kind of experimental drug?" Margie put the drink down, then immediately picked it up. This was something completely new to her. Larry had never mentioned seeing Jonathon Holcombe. And it didn't mean that his wife knew anything about it, of course.

Hunter finished his drink in one swallow, then poured more.

Margie's head was beginning to spin, her heart beginning to pound. Jonathon Holcombe was an endocrinologist, and a researcher. If he treated patients at all, it would be for things like diabetes. Larry, thin and fit, was an unlikely candidate for diabetes. "Hunter?" she prodded.

"I don't know what the drug was supposed to do, Margie. All I know was that I told him he should talk to you before he decided to be a human guinea pig." He met her eyes evenly. "I don't like secrets, Margie. They only lead to lies." Then he stood up. "Come on, kiddo. Let's get you settled. You look all done in."

VI

Margie followed Hunter to his surprisingly cozy guest room under the attic eaves. Painted a soothing shade between blue and gray, it had its own bathroom, a brass headboard, and a fluffy down comforter. He flipped on the light beside the bed. "Towels are in the bathroom. I think you'll find everything you need. If you want something, just holler. Here's the remote." He reached into the bedside drawer. "I have all the movie channels."

"Thanks, Hunter. This is really nice of you."

He paused at the doorway. "That's what friends are for, Margie. Right? Sleep well, and feel free to forage if you get hungry."

She listened to his footsteps fade down the steps then sank down on the bed. Hunter had already brought her bag up, and it rested on a luggage rack beneath a row of hooks. Rain tapped on the skylights over her head, and a light breeze ruffled the white curtains at the windows on either end of the room.

It didn't seem real that she was here, that the events of the last seven hours had happened, let alone the last seven weeks. From her purse, the buzzing of her phone interrupted her thoughts. Despite Hunter's advice to lie low, she answered. "Hello?"

"Margie? It's Joss." The other woman's voice crackled in her ear. The storm must be affecting their connection. "You mentioned going over my husband's records—the police have his computer, which has the most recent stuff on it. But the older files—the paper files—starting with two years ago, are in a storage facility in New Brunswick. If you wanted to meet me there tomorrow—maybe around ten—we could look for the schedule records. I know they're there. Somewhere."

"Sure," Margie answered, trying to focus. "Ten in New Brunswick—we could do that. Joss, I was just wondering… did you tell anyone that I was going to help you? You left around 3:30 this afternoon—did you mention it to anyone?"

"I went straight to my sister's. I've been staying here since… since. But they're all away. You're the first person I've spoken to all evening, Margie. What's going on?"

"When I got home tonight, someone had broken into my house... was still there, in fact. He crashed through a window getting out," Margie finished through Joss's gasps.

"Oh my God. Someone's trying to scare you off. I know someone's covering up something, Margie. There's a reason no one's listening to me."

Margie nodded even though she knew Joss couldn't see her. "Yeah, I get that. Text me that address in New Brunswick. I'll see you tomorrow at ten."

Margie showered and got into bed, her mind churning restlessly from one subject to another. A potential conspiracy. Her husband hiding a secret. Her house violated. And now this.

VII

On the way to New Brunswick the next morning, Hunter insisted they stop by the office.

Margie saw Hunter notice that his name was still on the door. As they stepped inside, she wrinkled her nose. The scent of Larry's aftershave lingered in the air, almost as if he'd just walked out of the room.

Even Hunter took a deep sniff. "Smells like Larry in here."

"I told you I felt him all around me," Margie replied. For the first time in weeks, she headed toward Larry's office, Hunter on her heels. She pushed open the door, reached around for the switch, and turned on the lights.

As illumination filled the room, she heard Hunter gasp behind her. "My God, Margie, what happened?"

Margie was too horrified to speak.

The coffee table drawers were turned upside down on the couch, the couch cushions thrown against the wing chair opposite. The supply closet, Larry's organizational dream space, was ransacked so thoroughly that paper clips and staples glittered at her feet. The small TV/VCR combination had been smashed. Every book had been pulled off the shelves, every drawer emptied from the desk.

Margie's hands flew to her mouth. "Oh my God." Hunter guided her to a chair in her own office as her knees buckled. "Hunter, who would do such a thing?"

"No idea. You want some water?"

"No, no, I'm… it's just… after last night…" She broke off, realizing suddenly that her own office was undisturbed.

"Of course we should call the police, Margie," Hunter said, leaning against the frame, arms crossed in his old familiar way, "But maybe we can thrash this out a bit first. You were here yesterday, right?"

"But I didn't come back here… into the offices," Margie said, knotting her hands. "I—I couldn't bring myself to look in Larry's office. I stayed up front, with—"

"So the ransacking could've happened any time between now and… when?"

"Between now and the last time Rosemary was in here. She stopped in every day to check the mail and messages. That's why I told her to take a vacation. She needed the break."

"You're the one who needs the break, kiddo. Other than the cleaners, who else has a key?"

Margie stared at Hunter blankly. "I can't think of anyone

other than the landlord." And then she remembered. "The Taking Care Committee at church has a key." She sat up straighter. "I'm not sure who actually has it—the pastor was here yesterday, in fact, when I walked in."

"Why?"

"He's part of the TCC. They help people going through crisis."

"What was he doing here?"

"Watering Larry's orchids. Everyone knows he loved them."

"Ah." Hunter raised one brow. "So you don't have any idea who's been in and out of here for weeks."

"I suppose."

"Damn." He ran his fingers through the military bristle on top of his head. "How about the back door?"

"What back door?"

"The one in my office? Or what used to be my office?" Hunter rolled his eyes. "That's what used to make me nuts about Larry—he was so exacting about some things and so devil-may-care about others."

"He probably forgot it was there," Margie said. "I did. Once your personal things were gone, he shut the door and never opened it again. I don't even think the cleaners go in there."

"Let's go look." He glanced at her over his shoulder. "This time I'll go first."

He led the way past Larry's door, past the washroom, to the office that used to be his. All the way at the end of the hall, it had the best view of the woods behind the parking lot and the hills beyond. It was obvious Rosemary had decided to use the space to store old files. Cartons were piled on the desk and on the floor in front of the door.

The cartons beside the door were pushed out in a wedge. On the dark red carpet, a few footprints were obvious in the dust.

"Someone's come in—and back out—through this door," Hunter said.

"It's ten after nine," Margie said. "If we call the police now, we'll never make our appointment with Joss."

"You want to wait until we finish with her?"

"We can meet her, see how many records there are, and then call the police on the way back."

Hunter shrugged. "Works for me. You want to take a look around Larry's office and see if there's anything missing?"

"All right."

Margie marched back down the hall. Now prepared for the sight, she paused in the doorway, snapping pictures with her phone. The surface of Larry's desk, the higher shelves filled with pictures and awards, even the surface of the coffee table and the credenza behind the desk were all undisturbed.

Margie scanned the room. Soon she realized what was missing entirely from beneath Larry's desk. The old computer tower, the one Larry kept even though they'd switched to laptops three years ago, was gone. The monitor, keyboard, mouse and laptop docking station were in plain sight on the desk; the printer was on the credenza. The wires dangled in a tangled mess.

"The computer's gone," she said, over her shoulder. "The old tower… the one he was keeping as an insurance policy. It was all hooked up to the rest of the equipment. And now it's not."

Hunter suddenly looked toward the reception area. "Hey, can I help you, sir?"

To Margie's surprise, she saw Pastor Dave peering around the front door. "Pastor Dave," she said, feeling annoyed. "I'm surprised you're here again."

"Oh—oh, Margie," Pastor Dave replied. "I didn't realize anyone was here. I didn't see any lights..."

"That's because we haven't turned any on," said Hunter. "Can we help you?"

"Oh, oh, sure," he answered, sounding just as flustered as yesterday. "I'm Pastor Dave... from Margie's church. I—uh—I was just going to leave the key. Since you don't need us any more, right? To come and water?" He edged toward the nearest table holding a single key on a small chain.

As he reached out, Margie noticed that his fingers were wrapped in gauze and he had scratches on his face. A jagged cut was held together with butterfly bandages near his scalp. He looked like he'd been in a bar fight.

Or jumped through plate glass.

Before she could say anything, however, Hunter took charge.

"Pastor," Hunter said, striding down the hall, "I'm Hunter Dowd, as in the Dowd on the door. Pleasedtameetcha, as they say where I'm from. I was wondering if you could help us out."

Pastor Dave glanced from Margie to Hunter and back. "Of—of course. How can I be of service?"

"You can provide us a list of everyone who's been in and out of here since you folks took over watering."

"A list?" Pastor Dave looked puzzled.

"Of the Taking Care Committee," Margie said. "Anyone who's been here. We'd like to talk to them."

"But… but… why?"

"Mr. Dowling's office has been ransacked, Pastor, and it looks as if his computer was stolen. Now, given that there're no signs of forced entry, it appears that the intruder had a key. But don't worry—if you don't get it together for us, the police will come asking for it."

For Hunter, that was a speech. Pastor Dave's lip quivered into a tight smile. "I'll—I'll get right on it," he said. "Right on it."

"You doing okay, Pastor?" Hunter asked. "You look a little cut up."

"Oh—home repairs. Not my strong suit. Mrs. Brush says I should stay off ladders. Fell through a glass window yesterday at the parsonage. Made quite the mess." With that, he practically fled.

"Something's up with him," said Hunter. "Or is he always like that?"

Margie nodded. "He's always like that… only not so cut up."

"You think it could've been him who was in your place? Then got away through the window?"

Margie opened her mouth, then shut it. She didn't think Larry would've given him a key to the house, but she hadn't known Larry had given the church a key to the office. And would a minister do such a thing? Even Pastor Dave, as off-putting as she found him? And what on earth would he want with Larry's old computer?

"He is peculiar… but that seems unlikely. You about ready, Hunter?"

"Just want to use the boys' room. Be right back." But instead of shutting the door behind himself, Hunter opened it almost immediately and stuck his head out. "We don't just have a thief, Margie. We have a thief who uses condoms and leaves them floating in the toilet." Then he paused. "Or doesn't, actually, because none of them have been used."

VIII

"Maybe it was the cleaners," said Margie when they were finally back on the highway. "I doubt it was Rosemary. I mean, I guess it's possible she got frisky in the office but… I doubt it."

Hunter had fished all five unused condoms out and put them in an evidence bag, despite her objections.

"When was the last time the cleaners were there?" he asked, easing over to the exit lane.

"Rosemary had them come once after the funeral." She broke off and exchanged a sardonic smirk with Hunter. "I guess that's exactly what they did."

He made a face. "Awful pun, kiddo, awful pun. But if you can make jokes that bad, I know you'll be okay. Look. Here we are."

Jocelyn didn't seem surprised to see Margie arrive with someone else; in fact, she seemed grateful. "It might take a while." She sounded apologetic as she led the way down a long corridor of climate-controlled storage units, then paused in the middle of the row of garage-style doors. "We moved all the paper files over here when we went digital."

Joss unlocked the padlock and rolled the door up. A ten-by-twenty foot space, filled with file boxes and arranged in long rows at least six feet high, greeted them.

"These are the files starting from two years ago. The rest are on the computers from the office that they won't let me have back."

"Holy cow," muttered Margie, hoping her dismay didn't show on her face.

"Interesting," said Hunter.

"The schedule calendars were boxed separately... we tried to keep the years with the files roughly together." Jocelyn pushed the flashlight function on her phone. "Let's see. Patient files are alphabetical, calendars by year." She walked up and down the rows, training her flashlight on the yellowing labels. Finally, she beckoned. "Okay... Mr. Dowd? Would you be able to grab that one for me? This one looks like it has the calendars for about four years." She waved her light around.

Margie looked at the label. It was clearly marked, "Office Calendars/JAP 9/2009-2/2014." When Hunter pulled the carton out, she opened it to see a pile of black calendars. "You mind if we take them, Joss?"

"Of course not. If you have any questions about anything, just let me know."

"I have a couple questions," Hunter said, "if you don't mind, Mrs. Holcombe." Margie noticed he hadn't been invited to call her Joss. When Joss nodded, he continued, "Could you tell me what makes you think your husband knew the men?"

"Those thugs?" Her voice was bitter. "I never said he knew them. I said he wasn't surprised by them. Not in the way I was. They spoke Spanish mostly, and I was in the next room. So it wasn't what I could hear them say, it more like… by his tone, I could tell he wasn't shocked. Why would he agree to give them money? And so much?"

"Maybe he hoped it would be a tip-off for the bank that something wasn't right. He must have known that they wouldn't give you that much cash," Hunter suggested.

"He told me to go to different branches until they did."

Hunter exchanged glances with Margie. Maybe years ago that strategy would have worked. But it did seem to indicate Jonathon Holcombe was serious about giving his assailants an exorbitant amount of money. "All right, Joss," she said. "If we have any questions, one of us will call."

As they approached the car, Hunter turned to Margie. "You mind driving? A couple things occurred to me. I have some calls I want to make."

"Sure," said Margie. "To who?"

"I want to see what I can find out about the perps. Let's see… Danny Divino and Orlando Velasquez. Excuse me a few minutes, will you?" He started to punch a number into his cell phone, then hesitated. "I think we should examine the files at my house. But let's stop by yours first, okay?"

By the time they reached Margie's neighborhood, Hunter's couple calls had turned into half a dozen, and each one yielded more and more notations in his unintelligible scrawl on the notepad on his lap.

She turned into her driveway as Hunter pocketed his phone. "Okay, so that was interesting. I found out a lot more than was ever in the papers." He took a deep breath. "I think there's a possibility Holcombe was involved in drug dealing. The one guy—Divino—was just one of those small-timers who've got so many strikes against them from the beginning that it's no wonder they end up in jail.

"However, the other one—Velasquez—he was a member of the Latin Kings. Pretty high up in the organization, too. He ran a piece of the Connecticut Pipeline from Bridgeport to Stamford when the real guy in charge—Juanito Ramos—went to prison. And when Ramos died… fast… pancreatic cancer… Velasquez was in line to take over."

Margie blinked, trying to keep up with all the information. "Ramos died of pancreatic cancer?"

Hunter looked down at his notes, then nodded. "Yeah. Beginning of the year."

"Like Larry," she said.

"A bit of a coincidence there." He patted her shoulder as she got out of the car.

"Come on," she said, "I'll show you upstairs."

Hunter walked up and down the hallway, peering into closets, the bathroom, and the room she used as a home office. "How about downstairs?"

"I walked through with the police. Downstairs wasn't touched."

"Hm." He stepped into the master bedroom. "Assuming it was the same person who took the computer from the office, I wonder why he decided to start here?" He glanced over his shoulder at Margie as she hesitated in the doorway.

She shook her head. For some reason, the condoms in the toilet flashed through her mind.

"Did Larry have a stalker?" Hunter asked. "Or an enemy?"

At that she laughed. "Not that we knew of. I guess it's possible."

"Think about it, okay?" replied Hunter. "You want to grab anything else while we're here? I'm just going to take a quick look around. If you don't mind."

"No, of course not. Go on." Their eyes met, and Margie was suddenly conscious of the fact that they were standing in her bedroom. For the briefest instant, something sparked between them, and Margie remembered that Hunter said there was one who got away.

"I'll just be a minute," she said.

"I'll just be downstairs," he said, at the same time.

As he maneuvered past her, she noticed the tips of his ears were red. She didn't have a chance to grab much more than a few items of clothing when Hunter called up to her. "Did you tell me that nothing was disturbed down here?"

"That's right." She peered over the banister, suddenly cold all over.

"You better come look, then. This looks just like his office at work."

She descended the steps in a state of disbelief and found Hunter in the doorway of the den. Someone had ransacked the drawers, the closets, and the bookshelves.

"Can you tell if they took anything?"

Margie gazed around in dismay, then shook her head. "It's too much of a mess. I mean, I can see what they didn't take… they didn't take the TV, the CD player, or Larry's framed Krueggerand…. They didn't take anything you'd think a robber might want."

"And you're sure you and Larry don't have any enemies? No one making threatening calls? No one just getting out of jail and maybe wanting to get back at you?"

In disbelief, she turned to look at Hunter. "I didn't even consider that. But… no, no one I can think of. Not offhand."

"That's where the police are going to go, you know. Although I think it's someone who has a key. Again, there's no sign of forced entry anywhere. I've checked—even in the basement. So not only is it someone who has a way in, it's someone who knows when you're home and when you're not."

IX

Margie left Hunter at the house with the locksmith and the alarm guy while she drove with the detectives to show them Larry's office at the agency.

But to her astonishment, while Larry's office was clearly still ransacked, the missing computer tower was back on the floor, placed more or less exactly where it used to be, wires haphazardly re-connected. "It's back," she said in disbelief. "This is bizarre… it wasn't here at 9:00 this morning. Look, I took these pictures with my phone."

The detectives glanced at each other. They were both middle-aged men, one in his fifties, one maybe a decade younger. They wore badly fitting jackets and shiny ties. But their faces were kind. They knew her, they'd known Larry. The last time she'd seen them was at his funeral.

"Mrs. Dowling," said the older one whose badge read Henry Wallace #312. "Is there any possibility that your husband was hiding something from you? Maybe involved in something he didn't want you to know about?"

"You mean like an affair?" She thought about the condoms in the toilet. But Larry couldn't have had anything to do with that.

"An affair, or a case. Maybe a business dealing? Some side investment?" asked the younger one, Jake Horowitz #546.

"Did he owe anyone money?" Wallace asked.

Margie shook her head. "I handle our finances. And we don't owe anyone anything, not beyond the mortgage company and a few credit cards."

The men exchanged glances. "All right, Mrs. Dowling," said Wallace. "We're going to dust for prints… this might take a while."

"There're footprints in the back office," Margie said. "Here. We took pictures of those, too."

"Could that be the same size as the imprint on the roof, Jake?" Wallace elbowed his partner.

"I guess it could be. Those still back there?"

"As far as I know," Margie said. "You need me to stay? I expect to be back with the locksmith after he's finished at the house."

Wallace glanced into the mess that was Larry's office. "We might still be here. Take your time."

X

Hunter had the office calendars spread all over the dining room table. The alarm company had left brochures, and the locksmith agreed to meet her at the office after stopping by his shop for more equipment.

"I want you to see this," Hunter said. "Dr. Holcombe was a pretty straight guy from everything I can see. When he wasn't seeing patients or teaching classes, he was playing golf, attending Rotary, or out with his wife. Except." He pointed to a crossed-out block of hours. "This starts in April of 2010 and continues all the way through to October of 2013. Every Tuesday. Six hours. Big yellow X. No explanation, no notation."

"I'll call Joss," said Margie.

* * *

Joss answered readily. "Of course. That's the time he spent at the prisons. All the specialists in the area take turns. It's part of a state program. If you agree to see patients who obviously don't have much access to specialists, you get a miniscule reimbursement and tons of brownie points. And a fairly homogenous population if you have research to do."

"Isn't it illegal to experiment on humans?" asked Margie, faintly repulsed.

"Not if they agree. The prisoners get incentives. It's a win-win for everyone."

"Are there records of who Dr. Holcombe saw?"

"At the prisons? Those are all state records… I can't access those."

Maybe *you* can't, Margie thought. "You wouldn't happen to remember any names, would you, Joss? Anyone who sticks in your mind?"

There was a long pause. Then Joss replied, "No, I'm sorry. I don't."

"Okay, no worries. It does seem like we've figured out where your husband could've met your assailants. We'll keep digging." Margie hung up.

* * *

Hunter said, "You know at least three names to search—Divino, Velasquez, and Little Juan Ramos. Juanito. The guy who just died."

"Of pancreatic cancer." She looked at Hunter. "Joss just said something that made me wonder if Holcombe was doing his own research on the prisoners. She said one reason a doctor would agree to join the program is that you get access to a large homogenous population. Who are incentivized to participate. You and Larry fought in October of 2010, right?"

"October seventeenth. A day that will live in infamy."

"What if Larry was part of this experiment… along with the prisoners? You said he was thinking of taking some experimental drug." She paused, her mind spinning faster than she could talk. "And what if this drug causes cancer? And that's why Holcombe stopped?"

Hunter sank down into a chair. "We don't know Larry ever took the drug, Margie. And two people… well, that's hardly a representative sample, is it? We don't know if Ramos even saw Dr. Holcombe for anything." He gave her what passed for a grin. "Why don't you go open up that pretty little computer of yours and see what you can find out about Juanito Ramos and the other two?"

XI

Once she found a way in, it was easy… almost too easy. The state cyber-security systems weren't particularly secure. Inside the prison hospital system, it didn't take Margie long to identify at least 75 prisoners or more who'd been seen by Dr. Holcombe.

By the end of Holcombe's first year, he'd seen every prisoner whose records she accessed at least once.

When she did a search for prisoners seen by Dr. Holcombe, she gasped at the length of the list. Over 3000 men had passed beneath Dr. Holcombe's watchful eye. "Why would they all be seen by an endocrinologist?" Margie mused, chewing her lip.

Hunter's voice came from behind her. "That was the locksmith calling back. He's going to have to finish up at the office tomorrow," Hunter said from the doorway. "Did you even hear the phone ring?"

"No." She shook her head and pushed her chair away from the table. "But from what I can find in these prison records, Dr. Holcombe was seeing everyone. Like, every prisoner there. If he was interested in trying out a drug… he must've been considering everyone."

"Or giving it to everyone," Hunter said. "Have you checked deaths? To see who died of what?"

Margie typed in a search. Nothing. She tried another. Nothing. "That's interesting," she muttered. She wrinkled her brow. "Let's go broader… prison deaths New Jersey." But no matter how Margie tried to search, nothing yielded results.

"What's wrong?" Hunter asked, watching intently.

"There's something odd here. I can find why an individual died. Like here, Ramos is listed as pancreatic cancer. And this guy… Douglas Iverson. And this guy… Raymond Tucker. So there's three. But if I try to search for "pancreatic cancer cause of death" or some similar search terms, I get nothing. If I try to search for the cause of death for any reason, in fact, I can't find it. Look… I'll try heart attacks… strokes… nothing."

"Glitch in the system?"

"Maybe. Maybe it's not set up to provide that kind of information, though I don't know why." She tapped a couple keys. "And the other thing I think is strange is that Divino, who did his time in 2014, was also given this drug . But that was after Holcombe left the program and took his drug trial with him. Presumably."

He patted her shoulder. "So someone was still experimenting? Come on, kiddo. Enough for tonight. Let's pack up and get out of here. The locks are all changed; no one's getting in. I'll buy you some dinner, and let's see where we are with all this."

"I want to try one more thing." She met his eyes. "I—uh—I think I found a way into Holcombe's own records… whatever he himself was storing in the cloud. I want to poke around a bit… see if I'm right. You mind?"

"Go ahead. I'll get started."

Margie slowly typed in Larry's social security number. She'd needed to use it so frequently in the last weeks, she didn't think she'd ever forget it.

The computer blinked. For a split second, Margie hoped Hunter was wrong, that Larry had never gone to see Jonathon Holcombe, had never taken an experimental drug.

Then, the screen flashed, and the name Lawrence D. appeared, citing his date of birth. The date of the original entry was October 16, 2010. The notes included the patient's weight, height, and blood pressure. Definitely her husband.

"Patient presents as a 45-year-old male, undergoing increasing emotional distress because of homosexual feelings. Patient believes these feelings are the result of hormone imbalance and would like to participate in the ongoing trial."

The last lines included the name of an unpronounceable drug and scribbles that must have been dosage instructions.

And Larry did take the drug, because there were follow-up visits, recorded in arcane notations she couldn't completely decipher. Larry had even been having his blood drawn regularly.

How had she not known? Her mind raced back through the last years. Larry hadn't acted any differently, at least not to her. Their sex life hadn't been the glue that kept them together, but she assumed most couples deteriorated to the same level after years of togetherness. She'd been proud in fact, on some level, that her relationship with Larry was more about friendship, shared values and respect than anything as ephemeral as lust. The idea that he was suddenly attracted to men didn't bother her so much as the fact he hadn't come to her… had decided to keep this all secret.

Oh, Larry, she thought. You didn't even give me a chance to help you, to figure out a way through this. A fresh wave of grief swept over her, and tears spilled down her cheeks. For all this pain that she had so blithely, blindly overlooked.

How he must have suffered, keeping such a secret from everyone. Especially her.

But it was the name of the referring physician that hit her like a punch in the gut. Joss Holcombe, M.D.

Margie sat back. "Hunter," she said. He looked up from

the box of Holcombe's records, but before he could speak, she continued, "I need to speak to Jocelyn Holcombe. Now."

"What did you find?"

"My client is the doctor who referred Larry to her husband."

XII

"I wasn't sure how much I should tell you yesterday," Joss said, when they were seated in her sister's kitchen over cups of cocoa. "It would be a very sensitive topic at any time, and given this…"

"I want you to explain why my husband came to see you, Joss. I know there's doctor-patient confidentiality, but he's dead, and I'd like to know why." Margie gazed at Joss, feeling anything but friendly.

Joss shrugged. "I can understand that." She took a deep breath. "Larry first came to me in the spring of 2010. He claimed he suddenly woke up one morning with homosexual feelings. He described the feeling as a 'switch having flipped.' I didn't quite know what to think, to be perfectly honest. I told him these were most likely latent feelings, long suppressed, finally making themselves conscious. He vehemently rejected that idea.

"So I put him through some tests to rule out anything physical, and when everything came back fine, I reassured him that there is a broad range of sexual expression that is considered "normal." I tried to steer him toward self-acceptance. I encouraged him to talk to you, Margie." She paused.

"Did you encourage him to try your husband's drug?" asked Hunter.

"First of all, it wasn't his drug. Jon was in on the initial development and testing, yes. But he left the program as soon as it was obvious there were reports of… side effects—side-effects he felt were too extreme to be tolerated. I believe I mentioned the drug to Larry, but not as a suggestion that he take it—only to make him aware that there was research involving brain chemistry, hormones, and sexuality." Joss shook her head.

"The drug wasn't supposed to change orientation. It was a side effect in about five to ten percent of the men who took it. And the change appeared permanent. That's what gave Larry the idea it might flip his switch, as he put it."

"This could explain why Divino and Velasquez might've been mad enough at your husband to come looking for him… if they were part of this experimental drug trial—something they did to earn brownie points—and discovered they were suddenly attracted only to men," Hunter said. "Machismo is everything in Latin culture. A man who loses his manhood… which how that would be perceived… would feel like he lost everything."

"I—I don't understand why Larry didn't tell me if he was having these feelings." Margie looked from Hunter to Joss and back. "I would've thought… given everything… he'd have known…"

"It wasn't just you, Margie," said Joss gently. "He mentioned to me that he'd had a very strict Christian upbringing. His father was a minister? He was active in church?"

Margie nodded. "We were both active in church… he loved singing in the choir…"

And spending time with Pastor Dave. The words rolled through Margie's mind before she could stop them. Was it possible that her dislike of the minister was based in an intuitive jealousy? It was one thing when Hunter, whom she'd known a long time, was the "other man" in the middle of both their business and personal lives. But without Hunter, maybe Larry craved something she couldn't give. She wrapped her hands around the warm mug, wishing with all of her heart that Larry could have come to her.

"How long did Larry take the drug?" asked Hunter.

"I'm not sure. Six months, maybe? It didn't seem to have any effect. So he stopped."

"Did Dr. Holcombe realize that it could cause cancer?"

"No. It was that side effect of the drug that Jon and I agreed made it completely unethical to give to anyone." Jocelyn paused. "Do you know how many have died?"

Margie shook her head. "Well, that's the funny thing. I can't find out. I can hack into the system and poke through individual records, but I can't make it tell me what I want to know. My guess, from what I was able to see… quite a few."

Joss looked from Margie to Hunter. "I guess that explains why Jon was willing to give those guys money. Guilt… or fear. He wasn't a bad man; he certainly wasn't trying to kill people. Or even change people." She turned to Margie. "But why the cover-up? And what do I do about it?"

"They're still giving out the drug, Joss… someone's still running the trial, obviously. But anything I find snooping around isn't evidence that can be used in court. And anyone invested in the criminal justice system is going to get only so close to the truth… and then, I imagine, will be told to back off."

For a long moment there was silence. Then Hunter said, "I might know a journalist or two who's itching for a Pulitzer. Let me see if maybe one of them would be interested in taking up the charge. Because to do something about this, you don't need a private investigator… you need a knight in shining armor."

XIII

"It's been a hell of a day for you, Margie. We need to get you some dinner. And a drink," said Hunter as Joss closed the front door behind them. "What do you say? I think you should stay at my place one more night… your stuff is still there, and you look all in. No need for you to drive home tonight."

"Okay." For a moment, Margie lost herself in the fog of all she had just been hit with. She turned to Hunter, attempting a smile. "Dinner sounds great, but do you mind if we stop at the office? The locksmith said he had one more lock to change… the one on the back door. I know it's obsessive, but it would help me feel more secure."

As they approached the front door of the office, Margie saw a light in one of the back offices. Larry's office. She gripped Hunter's arm and pointed silently to the long sliver of light that cut across the dark space.

"Let's go around the back," he whispered. "And let me go first." From a shoulder holster she hadn't realized he was wearing, he pulled out a gun.

The back door was open. Hunter pushed it wider, stepped inside and looked around, gun ready. Then he turned and beckoned to Margie. "Stay behind me."

They crept to the door. Larry's office was cattycorner, Margie's next door. From Larry's office, they could hear someone moving around, muttering to himself.

The scent of Larry's aftershave was strong in the air.

In two strides, Hunter was in the door of Larry's office, the gun high. "Hands up, you son of a bitch. Step away from the desk, and maybe you can tell us what you're doing here, before Mrs. Dowling calls the police."

Margie stepped around Hunter and gasped to see Pastor Dave cringing behind Larry's desk, arms raised, round circles of sweat staining his white shirt. On the surface of the desk, Larry's laptop was open.

"Pastor Dave?" she asked, incredulous. "What are you doing here?"

"Oh God! Please don't shoot. I'm so sorry, Margie. I didn't mean to cause all this trouble and make all this mess, truly I didn't. This was a—Larry made me promise on his death bed—that I would erase all the incriminating evidence from his computer, from his home."

"Incriminating evidence of what?" Hunter demanded. Margie touched his arm, and he lowered the gun, but only slightly.

"His… his affliction." Pastor Dave looked from one to the other. "At least, that's how he saw it."

Margie stared in disbelief. "You broke into my house? You?"

"Yes, yes, it was me… I needed passwords, and Larry said they were in the bedside table. But I didn't break in, Margie.

Larry gave me the key. He meant to give me the passwords, but… there was no time."

"You're the one who flushed those condoms?" asked Hunter. In response, Pastor Dave nodded.

"Oh my God," Margie said, sinking down onto the couch. "How could Larry have kept this from me? How could I not have known?"

"He didn't want you to know," Hunter and Pastor Dave said at once.

"He worked very hard so that you wouldn't know," Pastor Dave continued. "Believe me." He took a deep breath. "And believe me when I say I'll pay for the window and the TV and everything else, Margie. I really feel awful about this. I encouraged Larry to talk to you. This all is not what I… well, this is not my typical kind of Christian duty."

* * *

It was too late for dinner after all but not, fortunately, for a drink. They drove to the nearest bar, where Hunter ordered both of them beers and shots of whiskey. When she demurred, he insisted. "If anyone needs a drink, Margie, it's you. Here's looking at you, kid."

But the whiskey couldn't answer her questions. "I just don't understand, Hunter. If he knew I loved him, why couldn't he come to me?"

"You should ask your doctor friend that, kiddo," replied Hunter. "I know he loved you, he loved the life he had with you, and he loved the business we all built. I told him he had to work things out with you, not with some whack-a-doodle drug."

"But why did you leave? I can understand why you fought…why did you leave?"

"Because I told him I wasn't going to stand by and watch the woman I loved live a lie. All secrets lead to lies. And that just wasn't right."

"Hunter, what do you mean, the woman you loved?" Margie stared at Hunter, uncertain she had heard correctly.

"Oh, come on, Margie, don't say you didn't know something, at least on some level. We were quite a threesome, if only subliminally. My ex-wife showed me that when she left and said she wasn't going to be part of a triangle that didn't need a fourth. She was wrong about a lot of things, but she wasn't wrong about that. I had to back away. It wasn't healthy. Because even if it worked in some weird way, it wasn't what I wanted."

Margie blinked, uncertain how to respond. She couldn't deny the feeling that her world was a better place with Hunter in it, but now wasn't the time to deal with it. "Did Larry ever…?" Margie trailed off, afraid to ask the question.

Hunter laughed. "Approach me? Are you kidding? I was many things to Larry… but the object of his lust, never. And Larry noticed that he wasn't the Dowling I was most interested in." His lips turned up in the smallest of smiles, and then his expression turned serious. "But there is something else I wanted to talk to you about. You mentioned you wanted to sell the business; you couldn't manage it on your own. What if I bought the business, and we ran it together? Dowling & Dowd… not so much a resurrection as a reorganization?

Margie turned the beer bottle around in her hands. The condensation ran down the sides, her fingers slipping on the glass. She was tired. Now wasn't the time to make a major decision like this. And she could hardly process what Hunter was telling her.

She closed her eyes and took a breath. There was still follow-up to do on the Holcombe case, especially if there was going to be an investigation into the ongoing prison drug trials. Plus, there were other details to attend to before she could wrap up the business… or decide to keep it open.

She looked up at him. "I can't answer you tonight, Hunter, but I promise I will consider it. On one condition."

"What's that?"

"That you never keep a secret, ever. What was it you just said… all secrets lead to lies?"

Hunter clinked his bottle against hers gently. "As Ben Franklin said, two can keep a secret, if one of them is dead."

Q&A with Anne Kelleher

This is a very intricate story about two couples who both have secrets. How did you weave the threads together, and is this a typical example of your writing style?

"All Secrets Lead to Lies" is definitely the kind of story I like to tell. I'm always fascinated by the way people understand the same events differently depending on what they know—or believe they know.

Tell us about your background as a writer and what other stories have come before.

I sold my first novel—*Daughter of Prophecy*—to Warner Books in 1993. It was promptly orphaned when the acquiring editor left. It finally came out in 1995—since then I've published ten more traditionally and five more with a small press. Last year I discovered the magic of self-publishing. and published a collection of short stories and my first nonfiction title, *How to be a Happy Slob*. Most of my fiction falls under the broad category of speculative fiction; I've done everything from epic fantasy with a bit of science fiction thrown in to contemporary paranormal mysteries.

What's on your laptop now as a current project?

My current project is the third book of my erotic contemporary romance, *Wickham's Fat*e.

Where do you hang out online and how can fans find out about your other books?

You can find me online mostly on Facebook. Check out my author page at www.amazon.com/Anne-Kelleher/e/B001H-6SAXU or my personal website at www.AnneKelleher.net.

As Good as a Rest

by Lawrence Block

Andrew says the whole point of a vacation is to change your perspective of the world. A change is as good as a rest, he says, and vacations are about change, not rest. If we just wanted a rest, he says, we could stop the mail and disconnect the phone and stay home; that would add up to more of a traditional rest than traipsing all over Europe. Sitting in front of the television set with your feet up, he says, is generally considered to be more restful than climbing the forty-two thousand steps to the top of Notre Dame.

Of course, there aren't forty-two thousand steps, but it did seem like it at the time. We were with the Dattners-—by the time we got to Paris the four of us had already buddied up—and Harry kept wondering aloud why thc genius who'd built the cathedral hadn't thought to put in an elevator. And

Sue, who'd struck me earlier as unlikely to be afraid of anything, turned out to be petrified of heights. There are two staircases at Notre Dame, one going up and one coming down, and to get from one to the other you have to walk along this high ledge. It's really quite wide, even at its narrowest, and the view of the rooftops of Paris is magnificent, but all of this was wasted on Sue, who clung to the rear wall with her eyes clenched shut.

Andrew took her arm and walked her through it, while Harry and I looked out at the City of Light. "It's high open spaces that does it to her," he told me. "Yesterday, the Eiffel Tower, no problem, because the space was enclosed. But when it's open she starts getting afraid that she'll get sucked over the side or that she'll get this sudden impulse to jump, and, well, you see what it does to her."

While neither Andrew nor I have ever been troubled by heights, whether open or enclosed, the climb to the top of the cathedral wasn't the sort of thing we'd have done at home, especially since we'd already had a spectacular view of the city the day before from the Eiffel Tower. I'm not mad about walking up stairs, but it didn't occur to me to pass up the climb. For that matter, I'm not that mad about walking generally—Andrew says I won't go anywhere without a guaranteed parking space—but it seems to me that I walked from one end of Europe to the other, and didn't mind a bit.

When we weren't walking through streets or up staircases, we were parading through museums. That's hardly a departure for me, but for Andrew it is uncharacteristic behavior in the extreme. Boston's Museum of Fine Arts is one of the best in the country, and it's not twenty minutes from our house. We have a membership, and I go all the time, but it's almost impossible to get Andrew to go.

But in Paris he went to the Louvre, and the Rodin Museum, and that little museum in the sixteenth arrondissement with the most wonderful collection of Monets. And in London he led the way to the National Gallery and the National Portrait Gallery and the Victoria and Albert, and in Amsterdam he spent three hours in the Rijksmuseum and hurried us to the Van Gogh Museum first thing the next morning. By the time we got to Madrid, I was museumed out. I knew it was a sin to miss the Prado but I just couldn't face it, and I wound up walking around the city with Harry while my husband dragged Sue through galleries of El Grecos and Goyas and Velásquezes.

"Now that you've discovered museums," I told Andrew, "you may take a different view of the Museum of Fine Arts. There's a show of American landscape painters that'll still be running when we get back—I think you'll like it."

He assured me he was looking forward to it. But you know he never went. Museums are strictly a vacation pleasure for him. He doesn't even want to hear about them when he's at home.

For my part, you'd think I'd have learned by now not to buy clothes when we travel. Of course, it's impossible not to—there are some genuine bargains and some things you couldn't find at home—but I almost always wind up buying something that remains unworn in my closet forever after. It seems so right in some foreign capital, but once I get it home I realize it's not me at all, and so it lives out its days on a hanger, a source in turn of fond memories and faint guilt. It's not that I lose judgment when I travel, or become wildly impulsive. It's more that I become a slightly different person during the course of the trip and the clothes I buy for that person aren't always right for the person I am in Boston.

Oh, why am I nattering on like this? You don't have to look in my closet to see how travel changes a person. For heaven's sake, just look at the Dattners.

If we hadn't all been on vacation together, we would never have come to know Harry and Sue, let alone spend so much time with them. We would never have encountered them in the first place—day-to-day living would not have brought them to Boston, or us to Enid, Oklahoma. But even if they'd lived down the street from us, we would never have become close friends at home. To put it as simply as possible, they were not our kind of people.

The package tour we'd booked wasn't one of those escorted ventures in which your every minute is accounted for. It included our charter flights over and back, all our hotel accommodations, and our transportation from one city to the next. We "did" six countries in twenty-two days, but what we did in each, and where and with whom, was strictly up to us. We could have kept to ourselves altogether, and have often done so when traveling, but by the time we checked into our hotel in London the first day we'd made arrangements to join the Dattners that night for dinner, and before we knocked off our after-dinner brandies that night it had been tacitly agreed that we would be a foursome throughout the trip—unless, of course, it turned out that we tired of each other.

"They're a pair," Andrew said that first night, unknotting his tie and giving it a shake before hanging it over the doorknob. "That y'all-come-back accent of hers sounds like syrup flowing over corn cakes."

"She's a little flashy, too," I said. "But that sport jacket of his—"

"I know," Andrew said. "Somewhere, even as we speak, a horse is shivering, his blanket having been transformed into a jacket for Harry."

"And yet there's something about them, isn't there?"

"They're nice people," Andrew said. "Not our kind at all, but what does that matter? We're on a trip. We're ripe for a change..."

In Paris, after a night watching a floor show at what I'm sure was a rather disreputable little nightclub in Les Halles, I lay in bed while Andrew sat up smoking a last cigarette. "I'm glad we met the Dattners," he said. "This trip would be fun anyway, but they add to it. That joint tonight was a treat, and I'm sure we wouldn't have gone if it hadn't been for them. And do you know something? I don't think *they'd* have gone if it hadn't been for us."

"Where would we be without them?" I rolled onto my side. "I know where Sue would be without your helping hand. Up on top of Notre Dame, frozen with fear. Do you suppose that's how the gargoyles got there? Are they nothing but tourists turned to stone?"

"Then you'll never be a gargoyle. You were a long way from petrification whirling around the dance floor tonight."

"Harry's a good dancer. I didn't think he would be, but he's very light on his feet."

"The gun doesn't weigh him down, eh?"

I sat up. "I *thought* he was wearing a gun," I said. "How on earth does he get it past the airport scanners?"

"Undoubtedly packing it in his luggage and checking it through. He wouldn't need it on the plane—not unless he was planning to divert the flight to Havana."

"I don't think they go to Havana anymore. Why would he need it *off* the plane? I suppose tonight he'd feel safer armed. That place was a bit on the rough side."

"He was carrying it at the Tower of London, and in and out of a slew of museums. In fact, I think he carries it all the time except on planes. Most likely he feels naked without it."

"I wonder if he sleeps with it."

"I think he sleeps with her."

"Well, I know *that.*"

"To their mutual pleasure, I shouldn't wonder. Even as you and I."

"Ah," I said.

And, a bit later, he said, "You like them, don't you?"

"Well, of course I do. I don't want to pack them up and take them home to Boston with us, but—"

"You like *him.*"

"Harry? Oh, I see what you're getting at."

"Quite."

"And she's attractive, isn't she? You're attracted to her."

"At home I wouldn't look at her twice, but here—"

"Say no more. That's how I feel about him. That's exactly how I feel about him."

"Do you suppose we'll do anything about it?"

"I don't know. Do you suppose they're having this very conversation two floors below?"

"I wouldn't be surprised. If they *are* having this conversation, and if they had the same silent prelude to this conversation, they're probably feeling very good indeed."

“Mmmmm,” I said dreamily. “Even as you and I.”

* * *

I don’t know if the Dattners had that conversation that particular evening, but they certainly had it somewhere along the way. The little tensions and energy currents between the four of us began to build until it seemed almost as though the air were crackling with electricity. More often than not we’d find ourselves pairing off on our walks, Andrew with Sue, Harry with me. I remember one moment when he took my hand crossing the street—I remember the instant but not the street, or even the city—and a little shiver went right through me.

By the time we were in Madrid, with Andrew and Sue trekking through the Prado while Harry and I ate garlicky shrimp and sipped a sweetish white wine in a little café on the Plaza Mayor, it was clear what was going to happen. We were almost ready to talk about it.

“I hope they’re having a good time,” I told Harry. “I just couldn’t manage another museum.”

“I’m glad we’re out here instead,” he said, with a wave at the plaza. “But I would have gone to the Prado if you went.” And he reached out and covered my hand with his.

“Sue and Andy seem to be getting along pretty good,” he said.

Andy! Had anyone else ever called my husband Andy?

“And you and me, we get along all right, don’t we?”

“Yes,” I said, giving his hand a little squeeze. “Yes, we do.”

Andrew and I were up late that night, talking and

talking. The next day we flew to Rome. We were all tired our first night there and ate at the restaurant in our hotel rather than venture forth. The food was good, but I wonder if any of us really tasted it.

Andrew insisted that we all drink grappa with our coffee. It turned out to be a rather nasty brandy, clear in color and quite powerful. The men had a second round of it. Sue and I had enough work finishing our first.

Harry held his glass aloft and proposed a toast. "To good friends," he said. "To close friendship with good people." And after everyone had taken a sip he said, "You know, in a couple of days we all go back to the lives we used to lead. Sue and I go back to Oklahoma, you two go back to Boston, Mass. Andy, you go back to your investments business and I'll be doin' what I do. And we got each other's addresses and phone, and we say we'll keep in touch, and maybe we will. But if we do or we don't, either way one thing's sure. The minute we get off that plane at JFK, that's when the carriage turns into a pumpkin and the horses go back to bein' mice. You know what I mean?"

Everyone did.

"Anyway," he said, "what me an' Sue were thinkin', we thought there's a whole lot of Rome, a mess of good restaurants, and things to see and places to go. We thought it's silly to have four people all do the same things and go the same places and miss out on all the rest. We thought, you know, after breakfast tomorrow, we'd split up and spend the day separate." He took a breath. "Like Sue and Andy'd team up for the day and, Elaine, you an' me'd be together."

"The way we did in Madrid," somebody said.

"Except I mean for the whole day," Harry said. A light

film of perspiration gleamed on his forehead. I looked at his jacket and tried to decide if he was wearing his gun. I'd seen it on our afternoon in Madrid. His jacket had come open and I'd seen the gun, snug in his shoulder holster. "The whole day and then the evening, too. Dinner—and after."

There was a silence which I don't suppose could have lasted nearly as long as it seemed to. Then Andrew said he thought it was a good idea, and Sue agreed, and so did I.

Later, in our hotel room, Andrew assured me that we could back out. "I don't think they have any more experience with this than we do. You saw how nervous Harry was during his little speech. He'd probably be relieved to a certain degree if we did back out."

"Is that what you want to do?"

He thought for a moment. "For my part," he said, "I'd as soon go through with it."

"So would I. My only concern is if it made some difference between us afterward."

"I don't think it will. This is fantasy, you know. It's not the real world. We're not in Boston or Oklahoma. We're in Rome, and you know what they say. When in Rome, do as the Romans do."

"And is this what the Romans do?"

"It's probably what they do when they go to Stockholm," Andrew said.

* * *

In the morning, we joined the Dattners for breakfast. Afterward, without anything being said, we paired off as Harry had suggested the night before. He and I walked through a sun-drenched morning to the Spanish Steps, where bought a bag of crumbs and fed the pigeons. After that—

Oh, what does it matter what came next, what particular tourist things we found to do that day? Suffice it to say that we went to interesting places and saw rapturous sights, and everything we did and saw was heightened by anticipation of the evening ahead.

We ate lightly that night, and drank freely but not to excess. The trattoria where we dined wasn't far from our hotel and the night was clear and mild, so we walked back. Harry slipped an arm around my waist. I leaned a little against his shoulder. After walking a ways in silence, he said very softly, "Elaine, only if you want to."

"But I do," I heard myself say.

Then he took me in his arms and kissed me.

* * *

I ought to recall the night better than I do. We felt love and lust for each other, and sated both appetites. He was gentler than I might have guessed he'd be, and I more abandoned. I could probably remember precisely what happened if I put my mind to it, but I don't think I could make the memory seem real. Because it's as if it happened to someone else. It was vivid at the time, because at the time I truly was the person sharing her bed with Harry. But that person had no existence before or after that European vacation.

There was a moment when I looked up and saw one of Andrew's neckties hanging on the knob of the closet door. It struck me that I should have put the tie away, that it was out of place there. Then I told myself that the tie was where it ought to be, that it was Harry who didn't belong here. And finally I decided that both belonged, my husband's tie and my inappropriate Oklahoma lover. Now both belonged, but in the morning the necktie would remain and Harry would be gone.

As indeed he was. I awakened a little before dawn and was alone in the room. I went back to sleep, and when I next opened my eyes Andrew was in bed beside me. Had they met in the hallway? I wondered. Had they worked out the logistics of this passage in advance? I never asked. I still don't know.

* * *

Our last day in Rome, the Dattners went their way and we went ours. Andrew and I got to the Vatican, saw the Colosseum, and wandered here and there, stopping at sidewalk cafés for espresso. We hardly talked about the previous evening, beyond assuring each other that we had enjoyed it, that we were glad it had happened, and that our feelings for one another remained unchanged—deepened, if anything, by virtue of having shared this experience, if it could be said to have been shared.

We joined Harry and Sue for dinner. And in the morning we all rode out to the airport and boarded our flight to New York. I remember looking at the other passengers on the plane, few of whom I'd exchanged more than a couple of sentences with in the course of the past three weeks. There were almost certainly couples there with whom we had more in common than we had with the Dattners. Had any of them had comparable flings in the course of the trip?

At JFK we all collected our luggage and went through customs and passport control. Then we were off to catch our connecting flight to Boston while Harry and Sue had a four-hour wait for their flight to Tulsa. We said good-bye. The men shook hands while Sue and I embraced. Then Harry and I kissed, and Sue and Andrew kissed. That woman slept with my husband, I thought. And that man—I slept with him. I had the thought that, were I to continue thinking about it, I would start laughing.

Two hours later we were on the ground at Logan, and less than an hour after that we were in our own house.

That weekend Paul and Marilyn Welles came over for dinner and heard a play-by-play account of our three-week vacation—with the exception, of course, of that second-to-last night in Rome. Paul is a business associate of Andrew's and Marilyn is a woman not unlike me, and I wondered to myself what would happen if we four traded partners for an evening.

But it wouldn't happen and I certainly didn't want it to happen. I found Paul attractive and I know Andrew had always found Marilyn attractive. But such an incident among us wouldn't be appropriate, as it had somehow been appropriate with the Dattners.

I know Andrew was having much the same thoughts. We didn't discuss it afterward, but one knows…

I thought of all of this just last week. Andrew was in a bank in Skokie, Illinois, along with Paul Welles and two other men. One of the tellers managed to hit the silent alarm and the police arrived as they were on their way out. There was some shooting. Paul was wounded superficially, as was one of the policemen. Another of the policemen was killed.

Andrew is quite certain he didn't hit anybody. He fired his gun a couple of times, but he's sure he didn't kill the police officer. But when he got home we both kept thinking the same thing. It could have been Harry Dattner.

Not literally, because what would an Oklahoma state trooper be doing in Skokie, Illinois? But it might as easily have been the Skokie cop in Europe with us. And it might have been Andrew who shot him—or who'd been shot by him, for that matter.

I don't know that I'm explaining this properly. It's all so incredible. That I should have slept with a policeman while my husband was with a policeman's wife. That we had ever become friendly with them in the first place. I have to remind myself, and keep reminding myself, that it all happened overseas. It happened in Europe, and it happened to four other people. We were not ourselves, and Sue and Harry were not themselves. It happened, you see, in another universe altogether, and so, really, it's as if it never happened at all.

Q&A with Lawrence Block

You've written hundreds of stories, and are widely recognized as a master of the genre. After a lifetime of writing mysteries, what is it that triggers that itch to write for you?

Very little these days, I'm afraid. The ideas still show up, but there's less urge to do anything with them.

What's the story that got away—that you wish you had written, or had difficulty completing?

There have been more than a handful of books and stories abandoned over the years. I can't say I spend much time thinking about them, or regretting them. All part of the process.

What are your current projects?

As I write these lines, Subterranean Press has two novellas of mine in the pipeline, *Resume Speed* and *Keller's Fedora*. And Pegasus is about to publish *In Sunlight or in Shadow*, an anthology I've edited of stories inspired by paintings of Edward Hopper. A beautiful book, and the stories are outstanding.

If readers want to be in touch, how can they find you and find out about your books?

I'm hiding in plain sight. The website is lawrenceblock.com. And an email to lawbloc@gmail.com, headed NEWSLETTER, gets you on my mailing list.

* * *

Lawrence Block is the recipient of a Grand Master Award from the Mystery Writers of America and an internationally renowned bestselling author. His prolific career spans over one hundred books, including four bestselling series as well as dozens of short stories, articles, and books on writing. He has won four Edgar and Shamus Awards, two Falcon Awards from the Maltese Falcon Society of Japan, the Nero and Philip Marlowe Awards, a Lifetime Achievement Award from the Private Eye Writers of America, and the Cartier Diamond Dagger from the Crime Writers Association of the United Kingdom. In France, he has been awarded the title Grand Maitre du Roman Noir and has twice received the Société 813 trophy.

Thank you for reading ***Mostly Murder: Till Death***. We hope you enjoyed it! The plan is to publish a second volume with the theme of ***Revenge***.

The authors would so appreciate it if you would take the time to leave a brief review—and tell your friends. Word of mouth sells books.

Join us on Facebook at ***The Mystery Collective*** to hear about upcoming releases:

https://www.facebook.com/groups/872038472905473/

Acknowledgments

First of all, I want to thank all the amazing writers who contributed to this anthology. What a joy to be able to offer the tremendous stories in this book.

Thanks are also due to the individuals who collaborated in putting this volume together:

Ernie Lindsey, who had the original idea for this mystery anthology series, and was kind enough to let me take the helm when his own successful writing career required all of his attention.

Adam Hall, our wonderful artist, who managed to get just the right amount of creepy onto the cover.

Therin Knite, who expertly formatted the digital and print editions of this anthology.

Lawrence Block, who lent his famous author heft to a fledgling mystery series.

I am also grateful to the supportive indie author community, and to all those fans on Facebook who have encouraged us to create this new series.

And I thank my alpha beta, **Richard Leslie**.

Patrice Fitzgerald, Editor
Mostly Murder mystery anthologies

Made in the USA
San Bernardino, CA
14 April 2017